Night Music

Eight homicides in one night couldn't have come at a worse possible time for already-overworked Detectives Frank Vandegraf, Jilly Garvey and Dan Lee of the Personal Crimes Unit.

The night began with the audacious shooting of a shady and reviled investigator, and proceeded to get nonstop crazier. They can't rely on the over-strained resources of their department, and as the cases compound and unexpected connections emerge, they're on their own against the clock, fatigue, and mounting pressure from above. There's only their own experience and savvy to fall back on as they navigate the treacherous urban territory they know so well.

Open and Shut

The ultimate fate of a brilliant surgeon, convicted of the brutal murder of his wife, may be determined by two very different red-haired women. One is the mysterious lady in emeralds, who may be the key to proving him innocent, if only she can be located. The other is Detective Jilly Garvey, who doggedly worked to convict the surgeon but might now be his reluctant salvation. She and her partner, Detective Dan Lee, are driven to uncover the truth, following an elaborate and daunting trail of evidence through a maze of jet-set socialites, urban hipsters, shady investigators, low-life criminals…and still another murder…

"PERSONAL CRIMES" MYSTERY SERIES

Night Music

AND

Open and Shut

Two "Personal Crimes" Mysteries

TONY GLEESON

WILDSIDE PRESS

To Ed McBain, who inspired,
And Mary Burgess, who encouraged and taught…

Published by Wildside Press LLC.
www.wildsidepress.com

Contents

Night Music

1.

For a character with such a checkered past, there was surprisingly little you could say with authority about Al Land.

He was hardly a taciturn man—by all accounts he was loud, arrogant, and a braggart—but still, only a few real facts were known about him.

His real name was Albert Landreaux, and in the spirit of his original home of New Orleans, he enjoyed acting as a meeting point for all kinds of people from all manner of backgrounds and walks of life. Only a chosen few intimates knew him well. Very few, for that matter, knew him beyond the context of whatever had brought them into a room with him to begin with.

Al had served in the Army and then had a short stint as a cop in his new home town. He would have said that he then decided to take his wisdom and experience to a more profitable arena. Several members of the force would have said that it was suggested he leave because he was an undisciplined lout and a general all-around problem.

For whatever reason, he had bid the department farewell, obtained a private investigator's license and founded his own security agency. The general stock in trade of the real-life PI—divorces and skip-traces—were hardly beneath him, but he also worked for high-profile clients of all varieties: corporate security, industrial espionage, personal bodyguard, security consultant, and a range of dubious services for the fringes of the legal profession. Al was a conspicuous spender and favored expensive three-piece suits and all the accoutrements thereof.

Very little was publicly known about most of this.

He had been fortunate in finding his soul mate in his wife and business partner Anita, a tight-lipped, firm-jawed woman with dishwater blonde hair and a nasty attitude. Few people could tell you the color of her eyes since she apparently always wore heavy dark-tinted glasses. They ran their small agency and their lives together in a free-wheeling, tough and irreverent manner, and kept their own counsel.

Needless to say they had nurtured their fair share of grudges, resentments and enmities. All very privately.

So what happened that night, some thought, was perhaps inevitable.

Somewhere around ten o'clock on the night of Thursday the twelfth, Al and Anita were sitting in Al's favorite bar, *Saint Expedito*, near the waterfront.

Saint Expedito is the patron saint that New Orleans musicians pray to, to get paid on time, and the bar's owner, Mitch LaRoche, had brought his Cajun music and atmosphere to this city from the hometown he shared with Al.

This particular evening, Al and Anita were the only patrons in the establishment, sitting at a table near the bar quietly discussing the day's business. Al was turned three-quarters towards the front door where, as per habit, he had a view of the entryway. Anita got up to use the ladies' room in the back. Mitch, who had been swabbing up back there shortly before, left his station at the bar to go move his mop and bucket. She had no sooner entered the restroom when there came two loud shots from the front. Mitch turned to look and was whacked in the head by the ladies' room door as it flew open.

As a result, what he saw was patchy: the back of a man in a dark hoodie running towards the door. Al was slumped backwards over the heavy oak chair. Anita had bolted the loo, yelling in her hoarse voice. She ran to Al, ascertained almost immediately that he was dead, shot through the head and heart, and bolted out of the bar after the assailant. There were shouts, the grinding sound of car ignitions, the squeals of a couple of sets of tires.

Mitch called the police.

* * * *

Detective Frank Vandegraf was not very happy at having drawn this case. For one thing, he hated going anywhere near the waterfront. For another, he had known Al Land and saw his violent death as an unsurprising occurrence with a large cast of possible suspects.

This looked to be one of those cases with nowhere to go and an impossible number of ways to get there.

It was now about two-thirty. He stood, notebook and pencil in hand, looking over the scene while a handful of uniforms and crime-lab investigators coolly went about their business, deftly avoiding jostling one another in the narrow saloon. The entrance to the bar was wrapped with skeins of neon-yellow police tape.

Al, Frank noted with approval, had not moved since his untimely demise and still reclined backwards over the captain's chair, lifeless eyes gazing toward the rafters of the ceiling, rusty-colored puddings of congealed blood spotting his expensive white shirt and black leather windbreaker.

Sitting nearby were Mitch and Anita, each with a bottle of beer. Anita, in her tinted glasses, was dragging on a well-worried cigarette, understandably distraught but surprisingly composed. Smoking was illegal now in these establishments, Frank thought, but who really was going to care.

He had to admire her toughness. Quite a broad, he thought sarcastically. You weren't supposed to use that expression anymore, were you? He was constantly being reminded that his attitude was prehistoric.

Anita's voice was deep and tobacco-raspy. "So Mitch opens up the restroom and he's moving the pail outa the way and no sooner am I in the stall and pulling down these pants and sitting down than I hear the shots. Damn, these tight jeans, if it had been a few seconds sooner I would have been able to get right out. But I've got to pull these things back up and…"

"I got the picture, Anita," Frank interrupted quietly. He did not particularly care for profane women. Sometimes he really did feel like these just weren't his times any more.

"Yeah, so I was right out the door and there was Al lying back in his seat and this guy running out the door, all I can see is he's wearing a dark hoodie, black or maybe blue…"

"She swatted me right good with the door too," Mitch grinned grimly, rubbing the side of his head. "Raht good" was how it came out in his Louisiana drawl. "She was outa there like a shot."

"I took a quick look at Al and yelled to Mitch to call for an ambulance. His gun was gone. The scumbag took his gun. Can you believe it!"

"So you say you went after him."

"Damn right. He had a dirty old piece of junk of a Chevy Blazer right outside and he jumped in and peeled out. Luckily our car was parked right down the street. I took off after him."

"Not a smart thing to do, Anita," Frank shook his head, never looking up from his notebook.

"I wasn't exactly thinking straight," she said. She drew savagely on her cigarette and stubbed it out in the ashtray. "I chased the creep all over but I finally lost him."

"What did you figure you were going to do if you caught up with him?"

"Bring him in. I've been a bounty hunter, for God's sake. I've brought 'em in. Barring that, plug the SOB."

There was an awkward silence. Frank looked up at her. She shrugged.

"Well, I *said* I wasn't thinking straight."

"So you carry a gun, too?"

"Sure. Al and I both do."

"I'm going to need to see that, Anita."

She reached under her jacket and pulled out a small revolver, carefully placing it on the table.

"I had it out on the seat in case I needed it. Hasn't been fired tonight," she muttered. "If that's what you're worried about."

"Is this your only gun?"

"It sure is. Wanta search me?" She raised her hands in the air.

Frank sighed still again. "No, that will not be necessary, thank you. What kind of gun did Al carry? Any chance he was shot with his own weapon?"

"A .9 mm Glock. No way. No way in hell would Al have let a guy like this get close enough to pull his gun. The perp must have shot him first and then taken it."

That made sense. Anyway, there were no casings anywhere in the bar. Probably a revolver.

"Al was a wary sort," Frank mused. "Why would he let the guy get close enough to shoot him at close range? Could it have been someone he knew?"

"Sheesh…could have been anybody!" Anita shook her head. "Al *knew* a lot of people and a lot of people *knew* him." She made the word sound positively nasty.

Frank sighed. Quite the love match all right, these two. He would charitably chalk her demeanor up to her own peculiar form of grief. "Anybody who *knew* him that particularly didn't like him at the moment?"

"If you've got an hour to spare right now," Anita replied, "I'll start an enemies list."

She had no idea who the assailant was and couldn't give any better a description than Mitch had offered. A medium-height fairly lean guy in a dark hoodie—and maybe jeans. The only person who had seen the shooter from the front was Al, and he was of no help just now.

They talked a bit about Al's recent well-publicized legal problems. He had been accused of threatening a potential witness in a pending case involving his current client, a company called DKM. Anita dismissed the accusations as unfounded. Some more names were mentioned. There were no individuals she seemed able or willing to single out.

Al, it would seem, was an equal opportunity offender.

Frank ran through it one more time. In a brief wink of an eye, the killer had come into the bar, fired two shots at close range into Al, taken his gun, and run out the door.

"If it had just been a minute earlier," Anita rasped. She had just seen her husband shot dead in cold blood and taken part in an ill-advised high-speed chase through town, but she was composed and lucid. She was tough, all right. You had to respect that. "I would have nailed the lowlife. I had just, well, just sat down, if you follow me."

"Yeah," Frank nodded, holding up a hand, "I gotcha, you said that. No need to paint me a picture."

Anita was nonetheless beginning still another description of her travails in the small room, when Frank's cell phone rang. He still carried one of the older models, the kind that folded up and that couldn't play films or talk back to him. One of these days he'd enter the new century and pay some exorbitant amount for a big-screen phone, but for the moment he was a happy dinosaur.

He gratefully excused himself, stepping away to answer. He curtly answered a couple of times then snapped the phone shut, with a head shake.

"All right," he announced to them both, "I think I've got everything I need for the moment. I'll most likely be contacting you again. You've each got my card. Please let me know if you can think of anything else."

"Sounds like you're a popular guy tonight," Anita said wearily, not looking up at him while searching for another cigarette.

"Some more bodies in a parking lot," Frank replied over his shoulder. "Some kind of brawl or something. Nice night."

He looked at the crime scene gang and added, to nobody in particular, "See you in a while."

2.

Detective Jilly Garvey wasn't delighted with her own situation either at the moment.

She had already been warned that there would be a wait for anybody from the coroner's office or the Scientific Investigation Division. Apparently it was one monster of a night for the city's already-strained thin blue line.

She surveyed the dark side street, about two blocks from the main thoroughfare, lined with quiet inexpensive apartments. Two uniformed officers were giving her the tour of the late-model Acura sedan, parked curbside, and its ill-fated inhabitants. Keeled over to her right side in the driver's seat was a young woman with blonde hair and unblemished light brown skin.

She had been very pretty, Jilly thought. Her eyes were large and brown, fixed open in a final stare of surprise and shock. She had been shot once in the head at reasonably close range, perhaps five or six feet, through the driver's side window. Her bag laid open on the car seat, with wallet and other items spilled out over the seat and floor. Jilly was able to find and read an ID easily enough without disturbing anything else.

Her name was Marina Belize. In the passenger's seat, slumped into the corner made by the door and the seat back, was a thin darker-complexioned man in a black shirt. He, too, had been shot from the driver-side window—possibly one shot through the back of his head and throat. There was not yet any identification as to who he was. The officers did not want to further disrupt the scene to look for his wallet until the coroner's van had arrived. Both had been shot, they agreed, in what looked like a drive-by.

Sirens were sounding off in the distance. No doubt some of them at least were headed here. Jilly smirked. A little night music. Her nights were seldom without it.

Just exactly when, she asked herself, did this kind of thing stop getting to me and start becoming just another part of the job? When did the chaos and noise become something I think of as a sound track?

One of the uniforms interrupted her reverie. "Detective Garvey? Your partner would like a word."

A few doors away, Dan Lee was trying to calm down a very agitated woman in a long black coat. Dan was trying to keep her from approaching the car. The woman was crying, cursing, yelling, and trying vigorously to get past Dan.

As Jilly approached, Dan looked up almost plaintively, clearly uncomfortable, as he tried to keep a hand on the woman's shoulder.

The youngest member of her squad, Lee still wasn't very comfortable in this kind of situation and seemed to be hoping Jilly would step in.

"This is Johnny," he said. "Didn't catch her last name. She's the deceased's sister."

The woman was perhaps mid-thirties, with long, jet-black hair. She was jabbering nonstop in a confused jumble of English and another language—it didn't quite sound like Spanish, possibly Portuguese.

Jilly moved to put her arm around the woman's shoulder, which seemed to slightly calm her, and Jilly nodded to Dan to step back.

The sound of an orchestra suddenly punctuated the scene and halted her in mid-motion.

"That cell phone of yours," Dan shook his head. "What is it with the classical music, anyway?"

"It's *Eine Kleine Nachtsmusik*—A Little Night Music. Personal joke…" Jilly said, as she reached into her pocket and brought her phone to her ear. Mozart stopped. The woman's babbling continued, but was softer now.

"Hello?" She listened a moment and handed the phone to Dan. "We've got another call. My guess is you'd rather go handle it."

Dan had an unmistakable look of relief as he took the phone, his eye still on the unsettled woman.

He spoke tersely and handed the phone back to her. "Stabbing over on Webley. Give me a call when you're done here."

Without further ado, he fled the scene.

Jilly turned her attention back to the distraught woman. She was getting more agitated again, and let loose with a string of unmistakably serious non-English cuss words.

"He's the one who got her killed, that...that..."

There was another string of foreign oaths, spat viciously. Now Jilly was sure the woman wasn't speaking Spanish. She tried again to slip past Jilly to reach the car.

Jilly was a fairly tall woman—taller than the younger woman—and that came in handy in situations like this. She placed her hands on the woman's shoulders and held her firmly, looking her in the eye, which made her halt.

She tried to speak tough but quietly. "Okay, look, believe me, you really do *not* want to go over there. You don't."

The young woman seemed to take that to heart and hesitated. Jilly continued. "I need you to calm down. I know this is hard but I really have to ask you some things."

The woman stopped, began to shudder and sob. She put her face in her hands and began violently shaking. The crying erupted. Jilly let her go.

"Listen," she said after a minute or so. "My name's Detective Jill Garvey. You can call me Jilly. I need to talk to you but we can wait a little bit. Take your time and tell me whenever you're ready."

It took a long time. She slowly wound down. Jilly waited patiently.

"Can you talk now?" The woman nodded, looking down and wiping her face with the back of her hand.

"So your name is Johnny, is that right?"

It's Jah-nay. You spell it Jane, but in Brazil you say Jah-nay."

"And the woman in the car back there is your sister?"

"*Sim*—I mean, yes. Marina. Her name is Marina Belize."

"And you think she was shot because of the man in the car with her?"

"He must be the reason. He's no good." She spat out an unfamiliar epithet.

More Portuguese, Jilly assumed. It sounded highly impolite if not downright graphic. She wished she understood Portuguese just to appreciate some of this colorful profanity.

"So who is he?"

"His name is Ricky Wright. I don't know why she hangs around with him. He's trash."

"Why do you think he got her shot?"

"It's one of those other girls he's with. He thinks they don't know about each other. One of them must've gotten wise and come after him and her."

Jilly pulled out her notebook and started to make some notes.

"So that's Ricky in the car with her?"

"Gotta be. Tall skinny guy, messy mop of brown hair, thick eyebrows, always wears black?"

"Sounds about right," Jilly nodded. "So how did you and she and he happen to all be around here tonight?"

"Marina and I met at the club around the corner. *Las Candilejas*. We both love to dance, but we don't get to do it much. My husband Eddie's working tonight. We walked in and there was Ricky, dancing with a legal secretary he had just picked up. Marina had already found out about some dancer he was seeing and was gonna have it out with him.

"Now she sees him with this other girl—so she figures, this is the dancer, right?—and confronts him. He's being all smiley and nice and says he wants to talk with her privately, in her car. He's trying to be real charming, you know? Marina's not real happy about it but she finally agrees and they go outside. The secretary is getting all bent out of shape and I'm telling her to butt out of it, this was between the two of them. We said a few more things back and forth, then she pushes past me and goes out the door all mad."

"How do you know she was a legal secretary?"

"One of her friends at the bar tells me. Three of them, they were all legal secretaries at this law firm. The two girls still in the bar, they were cool enough, trying to make peace with me so I wouldn't go out after their friend, maybe. I wanted to follow Marina and Ricky out to make sure she was okay but they told me it'd be better to let them work it out. They said they didn't think their friend would go after them, she wasn't like that, she was probably right outside the club getting hold of herself and she'd come back in.

"Now I wish I *had* gone after them. I started telling them what a bum and a liar Ricky was and we all got to talking for a few minutes. They were real nice, sympathetic. They even offered to buy me a drink."

"Ricky Wright, huh," Jilly mused. "Hardly sounds like she met Mr. Right."

"Yeah, and Marina's a smart girl! Works in a bank, she's got a good career. She's pretty and she's sharp. She could do so much better than that fool!" Jane was speaking in the present tense, as if Marina was still alive.

Jilly didn't correct her. "So then what happened?"

"These two gals and I, we did have a quick drink together, and we got caught up in just complaining about guys, you know? I suddenly realized Marina wasn't coming back. Their friend didn't come back either. We paid our bills and went out on the street. That's when I heard the sirens."

"This secretary, the one dancing with Ricky—what was her name?"

"Lemme think…they called her Cat. Catherine, maybe?"

"What'd she look like?"

"Nothing special. Brownish hair, blonde streaks, kinda long and straight. Not all that attractive. But a nice figure, I guess. Dressed nice. Short black dress."

"Any chance either of the other girls are still around?"

"They were gonna try to find Cat and go home. I don't know. I haven't seen any of them around here."

It was suddenly momentarily very quiet on the street. Then, the crackle of a patrol car radio. Sirens in the distance, some of them at least, probably heading here, hopefully bringing the crime scene investigators.

More night music. It was never quiet for long, Jilly thought. The music always turned up again.

She continued to talk with Jane—her last name was Nascimento—for a few more minutes and then told her the best thing she could do was to go home and try to rest. She gave her a card with her contact information and called over one of the uniforms to drive her home. She walked over and scrutinized the car a while longer, then decided she'd try the club real quick before moving on to the next show of the evening.

The secretaries were nowhere to be found among the few people scattered outside the club catching air or trying to talk.

Las Candilejas was still roiling, oblivious to the excitement less than two blocks away. The salsa music roared in her ears as she entered. It was a fairly small place, a lot of chrome and dark wood, not much in the way of lighting, and a small claustrophobic dance floor.

She shouted questions as best she could above the din, and found the bartender who had served the girls, a young, friendly, good-looking dark-haired guy. She showed her badge, motioned him to the side and tried to make herself heard over the night music. Toward the rear of the bar the noise was at least muffled a bit.

He remembered the secretaries; he didn't know them on a first-name basis but they were fairly regular.

"They like to dance. And they seem to like us romantic Latin guys, you know?" He said that rather ironically, rolling his big dark eyes and smiling with a kind of charming self-effacement. "What are you supposed to do?"

Despite herself, Jilly smiled back.

"Did you notice the guy who picked one of them up?"

"Ohhh yeah. You gotta mean Ricky. Yeah, we *all* know him. I won't tell you some of the names they call him around here. He's so stupid he thinks they're compliments."

"So he's a regular?"

"He's in here enough that we all know him. Thinks he's a real stud. Brags he's got three, four girls on a string."

"Do you know any of his supposed girlfriends?"

"There's a nice girl, I think she's Brazilian, she comes in here now and then. Kind of too good for him, you ask me. Smart, classy, looks like she's got a good career. But Ricky's got a certain charm. He's a bad boy, you know?"

"Did you see her here tonight?"

"Actually, yeah. She and a friend, her cousin maybe, I dunno. Real cute girls, both of them. She saw Ricky chatting up this other girl, getting like too friendly with her, and she tore into him. He was trying to sweet-talk her down. Trouble is, maybe a week ago she found out about Luisa, the red-head dancer from Tooey's down the street. Not like it was any great secret around here. I think maybe Ricky finally got enough dimes dropped on him."

"Oh, he got a dime dropped on him," Jilly mused. "I'm going to need to talk to you again. You here most nights?"

"Thursday through Sunday. And the managers always know where to find me. What's going on?"

"Drive-by shooting around the corner. I think it was your nice little Brazilian girl."

"Ohhh no! No way!"

"Ricky too, it looks like. What else do you know about the redheaded dancer?"

He shrugged. "Nothin'. Just heard her name. You could check out Tooey's."

"Did any of the secretaries pay with a credit card tonight?"

"No, they were cash."

"Any way I might find any of them?"

"Actually..." he walked to the register and sprang it, then returned with a folded cocktail napkin. "One of them sorta slipped her name and number to me."

He smiled, half-pleased, half-embarrassed.

Jilly jotted down the information in her notebook. Her name was Samantha Covington.

He watched her as she wrote it all down. "So they're both—like, dead?"

"Afraid so."

"*Dios mio*." His expression turned grave. He crossed himself and murmured a prayer in Spanish. All in all, Jilly thought, he was taking it quite well. Conceivably this was not the first patron he had known to wind up dead.

Fifteen minutes later she stepped out of *Las Candilejas*. It was a welcome change—cooler and quieter.

A little more Mozart. Her phone again.

"What, nobody else is up tonight? Yeah, Yeah, Okay." Jilly took the info. "I'll be there as soon as I can," she sighed, broke the connection, and dialed Dan.

"Hey partner, how's it going over there? We caught another DB. Yeah, another. Corner of Parker and San Mateo. Meet me there when you can?"

3.

The officer was young, probably not long from being set loose by her training officer, and was doing her best to be brisk and businesslike. Frank couldn't help thinking that she was afraid that an old Neanderthal like himself wouldn't be taking her seriously. He didn't think he was like that, despite the kidding he took from some of his younger colleagues about being a dinosaur, but there certainly were guys in the department who were.

They were looking at a fair amount of blood on the ground. The parking lot fronted a 24-hour Ready Rite drug and convenience store that might have seen better days. About a dozen witnesses and looky-loos had gathered, being kept a distance away from the scene; the coroner and crime-scene personnel had already begun arriving and setting up shop around the bodies. Two other officers were interviewing individuals off to the side.

"This one," Officer Pardo was saying as she pointed her flashlight at the crumpled guy sprawled on the pavement, "got hit full-on. No witness accounts of the vehicle involved, but it seems to have hit him pretty hard and kept going, run right over him. Maybe it careened off that old Chevy Blazer over there, maybe one or two of the other cars. The driver didn't stop even after that."

The man had been crushed beneath the wheels of the vehicle and he lay spread across the concrete. Even though the night was chilly, he wore only a grey tee shirt over his grimy jeans and work boots.

"He had a wallet and ID. Name's Rudy Caliente. Thirty-nine years old. He was also packing—a cheap five-shot .38. Nobody's quite sure yet if he was involved in the other killings over there."

She motioned to a second and third body perhaps thirty feet away and began to lead Frank towards them.

"Severin Foster," she announced, indicating a short dark young man in sweatshirt and jeans, lying on the pavement on his side, arms in a defensive position above what was left of his skull.

"Called 'Sonny' by two of the witnesses. Neighborhood kid. Nineteen years old. Beaten to death with a large blunt metal object, most likely that metal pipe over there or whatever it is."

She pointed to an object on the ground a few feet away from them.

"Looks like a piece of rebar," Frank interjected.

The lot was home for all manner of trash and castaway objects. Driving around here presented a challenge.

"It's not unusual for these guys to hang out here, work on their cars, even late at night. Nobody's willing to say what happened or how many people were involved; some kind of confrontation that degenerated into a brawl."

Or maybe, thought Frank, this was premeditated? Somebody showed up here with the definite idea of taking a few people out? It didn't seem all that likely, but time would tell.

He stepped over to the metal rod, rusty brown, with recent smears of dried blood. This had been lying in the street for a long time. If you're on a death mission, he considered, would you rely on using whatever instrument of opportunity might be lying around handy on the ground?

"Third victim," Officer Pardo was continuing, "Nicholas Lowell. Thirty-two years old. Car salesman."

The unfortunate Mr. Lowell was laying more or less prone, arms and legs spread, where he had fallen out of his expensive looking maroon SUV. His legs still hung from the cab, the drivers-side door halfway open, having closed back on his legs after he fell. He had apparently been trying to get out of the car, an unsuccessful act made all the more difficult by the fact he had been shot in the left side of the face, apparently at extremely close range.

Another flashy leather jacket, Frank noted, not unlike Al Land's. The collar of a light beige shirt. Khakis—maybe Dockers—and black loafers.

"We have not yet ascertained which, if any, of the vehicles in the lot belonged to Caliente and Foster, sir. Nobody will admit to having actually seen what occurred. They all claim to have been inside the store or elsewhere at the time."

"Sure. Of course they were. Would it be too much to ask if there were any security cameras working?"

Pardo got a sour-lemon expression and shook her head.

"One outside camera on this whole lot. Out of order for a couple of weeks."

"Thank you, Officer Pardo," Frank grunted, hands in his coat pockets, surveying the scene around him.

He began to pace around. Slowly he made his way back to the prone figure of Rudy Caliente, who resembled a mannequin made out of hamburger stuffed into a gray tee shirt.

Strange coincidence. A dead guy with a .38, who possibly could have been walking back to a white Blazer when he was hit. The driver creamed him and then smacked into the truck.

Frank knelt down next to the body, took a pen out of his shirt pocket and carefully slid it into the trigger guard of the pistol lying slightly underneath the body. He edged the gun out from underneath and peered at it.

He walked over to the beat up Blazer, pulling on a pair of the latex gloves he always carried in his pocket, and opened the drivers-side door. There was a bunch of detritus strewn across the passenger's seat: empty beer cans, a brown-bagged pint vodka bottle without a cap that had apparently spilled, a bag from a burger joint, scraps of onions and blobs of ketchup. A small cardboard box of .38 shells, top open, a few of them spilled out onto the seat. A cell phone on the console.

And a dark blue hooded sweatshirt on the floor, with even darker stains that looked a lot like blood.

He looked in the glove box. A lot of miscellaneous junk. And a photocopied registration.

Rudolph Caliente. 3426 Hatchings Avenue. Bingo.

Slightly underneath the front seat, he spotted the slight gleam of something made of shiny black leather with a gold metal trim.

Frank carefully edged it out with his pen—a large billfold-style wallet, stylish and new looking. The gold snap had come loose and items were spilling out. A few credit cards, and a driver's license which pictured an Asian woman, attractive despite a severe expression, with a sort of page-boy haircut not quite to her shoulders.

Probably snapped before she was ready: the typical highly-flattering portrait from DMV Studios. Her name was Tia Miyakawa. Her address was also 3426 Hastings. Wife? Girlfriend? He noticed her birthdate was today.

Or rather, it *had* been today until midnight. Now it was yesterday.

Further underneath the seat was something a little more worrisome. There was a hunting knife in a scabbard. The snap was not fastened. It stuck as he tried to slide it out—it was caked in brown blood.

In fact, Frank now noticed, there were blood stains over the passenger's seat. The knife and sheath had been tossed there and had fallen to the floor. Probably the knife had slid and bounced around when Caliente drove away from somewhere.

Frank stepped out of the Blazer and yelled, "Officer Pardo?" She came briskly walking back to him.

"Were any shell casings found around the car salesman?"

"No, sir."

Frank considered the possibility that Rudy had shot Al Land, stabbed someone else somewhere else, then shot Nicholas Lowell. Did he also bludgeon Sonny Foster to death? The increasingly logical solution only presented more questions, starting with: Why shoot Al Land?—and ending with: So who killed Rudy, and why?

Frank continued to stroll around the scene. No shells—.38 revolver may be right. He walked around Lowell's SUV. It was a nice, almost new, well-kept car, recently detailed. That would figure if the guy sold cars for a living.

There was a fairly deep dent in the front that stood out from the pristine quality of the rest of the car—had to have been very recent, maybe that very evening. Flecks of paint from the other car still remained.

He paused to inspect something else that stood out even more—a bullet hole in the passenger-side door.

Lowell had been shot from the driver's side. Somebody had taken a shot at him from the other side as well.

Also Rudy? Somebody else?

Next to Lowell's face-down body was a cell phone, a carbon-grey, wafer-thin, expensive-looking one with a large screen. The wireless Bluetooth earphone was still stuck in his ear, reminding Frank of a character in some science fiction movie he had seen. He had apparently been in the act of making a call when he was shot.

Frank knelt down and carefully picked up the phone. The person Lowell had been calling was familiar: he had it on his contacts list. The name was still on the screen.

"Well I'll be…" Frank muttered.

* * * *

The young woman lay sprawled in the alleyway on her left side, her right arm stretched out as if still trying to hold off her assailant. Her fur-trimmed suede jacket and her off-white blouse and dark skirt were saturated with large darkened blots. She had been stabbed repeatedly. A big caramel-colored leather bag was a few feet away, articles spilling all over the pavement around it.

The patrol officer and Detective Lee gazed down at the body.

"Looks like a robbery," the officer was saying. "And she fought back. No ID on her yet."

"Who called this in?" Dan asked the officer.

"Somebody on the street, I guess, happened upon her. I was told they wouldn't leave a name. That's not unusual."

"No it's not. Nobody wants to get involved."

The alley ran from Webley, a major thoroughfare, to Wesson, a smaller parallel street.

She had gotten about halfway down the alley when she was overtaken by her attacker. She could have been coming from either direction but Dan decided it made more sense she was coming from Webley.

Among the items strewn around the ground were an unopened pack of cigarettes, a pack of breath mints…and a box of prophylactics. One door up from the alley on Webley was the 24-7 Market.

"Good chance she was in the quickie mart around the corner," Dan muttered. "I'm gonna go talk to them."

A twenty-something slacker kid was leaning against the snow-cone machine behind the counter. He instantly knew who Dan was and why he was there. He registered what would have to pass for enthusiasm.

"She was in here," he told Dan. "Geez, that's awful."

"So, you were just gonna sit here, weren't gonna come tell us?"

"No, man, nothin' like that. I'm, y'know, not supposed to leave the store. I can get fired for that! I knew you'd find me."

Dan rolled his eyes, pulled out his notebook. "So what can you tell me about her?"

"Well, she was in a hurry. Bought a pack of smokes and a couple other things. Personal things?" He snickered. "Guess she had a hot date. Kinda dressed up. She was kinda hot. For, you know, an older lady."

Dan marveled that a prodigy like this guy hadn't yet meteorically risen above a minimum-wage counter job. Maybe he was CEO material.

"Was she alone?"

"Yeah. I think somebody dropped her off out front. I'm not sure though."

"Did you see her leave? Was anybody waiting for her?"

"Nah, don't think so. There was some noise outside as she finished paying…she ran out the door. I did kinda, y'know, check her out as she was leaving. Kinda interesting. For her age, I mean."

"Yeah. You said that. Did you see where she went or anything else?"

"She turned right, towards the alley. That's about it."

"Hear anything after that?"

"There's always stuff out there. Cars, people yellin', fights, all sorts of stuff, y'know? I heard somebody peeling out, some brakes, some shouting but I didn't think much of it."

"So you didn't think anything had happened until?..."

"Some lady runs in, yelling she needs to use the phone. She must've called you guys. I'm not supposed to let anyone use the phone, you know? But she was so nuts and said it was an emergency. So she calls, hollers into the phone, and then runs out again all scared, I didn't see where she ran. And then, oh, man, the sirens. The cops started showin' up. Coupla black-and-whites with the lights, man." He spun a finger in a circle. His eyes momentarily crossed.

"This good Samaritan woman—what'd she look like?"

"Man, I don't remember. She was just yellin' and crazy."

Great, Dan thought.

"So then you left the store to see what was going on?"

"Well—I just, sorta, stuck my head out for a minute, yeah. Asked somebody what was goin' on, they said some chick had gotten stabbed in the alley. Geez, that's awful."

Dan shook his head. "Any idea who she was?"

"Well, she paid with a credit card. That oughta help, huh?"

The kid opened the register and fished around under the change tray. He pulled out the charge slip and handed it to Dan.

"Yeah," Dan said, looking at the slip. "That oughta help."

* * * *

Parker and San Mateo was a remote corner a few blocks off the main drag, neither well-lit nor well-traveled. It was what was called a "transitional" neighborhood, mostly transitioning downward.

Dan pulled up and had no trouble parking two doors away. Jilly and a lone uniformed officer were the only living souls present. A third figure lay supine on the pavement, her head slightly resting against the stucco wall of the corner building, but she could no longer be counted among the living.

She was a middle-aged woman with greying hair and a long, shabby dark overcoat. Dan came closer and bent down to inspect her. She had been shot through the throat and had bled profusely. Probably hit the carotid artery.

Jilly was prying at the wall itself with a small penknife. There was a hole at approximately breastbone height—the right size and shape to have been a bullet hole. The uniform was looking on. Jilly looked up and nodded acknowledgment to Dan.

"Not much more to this one," she said. "Pretty cut and dried. Drive-by shooting. Not sure who she is. No ID. Felix here says he's seen her around."

Felix, the veteran officer, looked up at Dan and shrugged. "Once or twice. Someone from the neighborhood. Street person. Not sure if she's got a home or not. That's all I know."

"There's some glass on the street out there, and what looks like some fresh rubber burns," Jilly said, pointing.

They had hastily erected some yellow tape around the curbside area with a few trash cans they had dragged from down the street.

"Maybe the fool perp shot right through their car window before peeling out."

"That would be pretty stupid," Dan said.

"Well, it doesn't make much sense that someone would drive up and execute a neighborhood street lady, either. But that looks like what we got here. Coroner catching up yet?"

"They're at the quickie mart," Dan said, yawning. "Maybe they'll even get here before sunup and we can get out of here."

"We've got a bullet here," Jilly grunted, suppressing the urge to yawn along with him. "Aside from that, we haven't got much."

* * * *

"I'm sorry, Detective, but there is absolutely no way I can spare anybody right now."

Captain Howard Crowley, a jowly and morose individual to begin with, had the look of a man with the weight of the world on his shoulders. The news of eight nocturnal homicides had brought him to the office in the middle of the night and he was not a happy man.

Frank, sitting across the desk from him, was out of any further pleas, arguments, or cajoleries after perhaps ten minutes of doing his exhausted best. The look on the captain's face told him: case closed.

"I don't have to tell you about the caseloads we've all gotten dropped on us recently," Crowley said. "And you probably know that this being an election year, we were already getting the pressure from above to clear crimes—and I'm sure you already understand that that pressure is going to get lots stronger on us with this sudden spate of new homicides—especially when the media get to work on them.

"This couldn't have come at a worse moment. We are stretched beyond thin right now. We've got several sickouts from this flu that's been going around. Two detectives are on vacation. It's just bad luck. Next week I can hopefully get somebody back and assign them to help you out. In the meantime, I have to leave it all in your capable hands."

Frank did not at the moment feel all that capable. His own table had not exactly been clear when the fun had started this past evening.

"Can I at least get some priority on the ballistics or the lab work?" he asked.

Another deep sigh from the man in charge.

"I've just had another fight with Morgan in ballistics over this. He found himself in the middle of a turf war, he says he's got two of his own best people out sick, and he's had it. He's adamant that everybody has to wait their turn. I'm sorry, Frank, I can't help you there. The medical examiner, blood work, fingerprints, maybe, but I think, right now, you'd do better trying to persuade them yourself."

It was pretty bad, Frank reflected, when his people skills were considered the better choice. He resigned himself to what was coming.

"Now, if there's any silver lining on this," Crowley continued, "it's that I can pretty safely say that this time, I can authorize all the overtime necessary, so your paycheck will be getting a significant boost this week. Lee and Garvey picked up four homicides tonight as well and when they come in, I'll be telling them the same things I've just told you. I'm going to need you all to step up on this. We need to see these cleared."

What was not mentioned, but which Frank tacitly understood, was that multiple homicides like this would bring a new wave of pressure down on the captain from above, and that would of course be passed down to him and his colleagues.

Crowley stood up to signify the end of the conversation. "That's about all, Detective, thank you."

* * * *

The sun was already coming up when Jilly and Dan returned to the Personal Crimes unit. Jilly could remember when the unit had been called Special Crimes, and before that the more prosaic, but accurate, Robbery-Homicide.

Throughout those years they had dealt with the same types of crime, almost entirely felonies: homicides, severe assaults, and robberies.

The Department, apparently, had felt a change of name would convey more *gravitas*, but their task had remained basically the same.

A thin crew of three or four were the only others in the squad room. Frank looked to be just leaving, dark circles under his weary eyes.

"Frank, you look like warmed over road kill."

Frank was reminded of the actual human road kill he had so recently witnessed.

"Caught four homicides tonight. Four." He wearily held up four fingers.

"Well, what a coincidence," said Jilly. "So did we. Where exactly is everybody else tonight? Are we it?"

She looked around the deserted squad room.

Frank shrugged. "Eight deaths in one night! A little of your 'night music' tonight, Jilly."

"A little," she grunted. "*Eine Kleine Nachtmusik.*"

"There you go again," Dan said.

"More like *Eine Kleine Achtmusik*," Frank said.

"Huh?" asked Dan.

"*Nachtmusik* means Night Music," Jilly murmured. "In German."

"I know that," said Dan.

"*Acht* means eight in German. Frank's making a joke."

Dan just stared.

"Dan's got no sense of humor," Frank said. "You know that, Jilly. By the way, just a heads-up. Crowley himself is here."

He jerked a thumb back to the commander's office.

"He's going to give you the same speech he just gave me. There's no help right now. As you just said, Jilly, we are it."

"As if we didn't already have plenty to deal with," Dan said wearily.

"And now, the good news," Frank said with mock enthusiasm. "This is going to be authorized overtime, whatever we need. For once it won't be an issue."

"Lovely," grumbled Jilly. "Well, we can all use the money, can't we?"

Frank thought of recent fights, not always successful, to win even a few hours of overtime to reduce his case load. Be careful, he considered, what you ask for.

"I'm gonna go catch a few hours of sleep and get back on the horse. Probably see you two later this morning."

After Frank had departed, Dan and Jilly sat down to work out a plan of action and to divide up their tasks, postponing the inevitable heart-to-heart with their captain.

"Makes sense for me to follow up on the alley stabbing," Dan said.

Jilly nodded. "For the moment I'll try to cover the unidentified woman. Not much to be done on that one—maybe some canvassing. But I'm more interested in Marina Belize and Ricky Wright. I think I at least need to start there. There's the possibility of a warm trail that might cool down rapidly."

Dan nodded. He had a similar feeling about the particulars of his own case. "You want to take lead on Belize and Wright, then? No problem."

Dan was the junior detective in the squad, having just made his promotion from patrol only a year earlier. In many ways he felt he was still proving himself, but he also had the self-confidence to take it in his stride. He had learned that his partner had excellent instincts and organizational skills. Whatever plan she worked out, he could trust it.

"I'll connect up with you later today on Marina and her boyfriend."

"Some boyfriend," Jilly snorted, resting her head in her hands. The exhaustion was catching up. "More like a bad luck charm. How about we follow Frank's lead and clock out for a few hours, then meet back here at, say, nine?"

"How about more like four?" yawned Dan.

Jilly shot him a look. "Just kidding, just kidding. Nine it is."

For him, that probably meant sleeping in the break room, but it would hardly be the first time.

They heard the voice barking across the funereal quiet of the squad room from Crowley's office. "Garvey! Lee! A moment?"

4.

"So what can you tell me about Mr. Lowell?" Frank was asking. They were sitting in the showroom of the dealership Nicholas Lowell had overseen. "Single? Married?"

"No, he was single. Divorced. Geez, I still can't believe this happened to Nick."

The associate manager was named Doug Dresser—perhaps in his early thirties, obviously fighting the onset of portliness. The surname, Frank noted wryly, was apt. He clearly spent a lot of money on his clothes, though even Frank, hardly a fashion maven, could see it wasn't necessarily spent wisely or with great taste.

"His ex-wife still in the picture?"

"Naw, they divorced years ago. She re-married, has two small kids by her new husband. They don't—I mean, didn't—have much to do with each other anymore."

"So was he seeing anybody regular?"

"Nick went out with a lot of ladies, met a number of them right here when they were looking at cars, you know? But he had just met some girl. I don't know anything about her except he really seemed to like her a lot. I do know he had made plans to take her out last night. I think it was some special occasion."

"Like her birthday perhaps?"

"Yeah, possibly. I remember because we were discussing something in his office and he excused himself to call and make reservations for two at a restaurant."

"For last night," Frank affirmed.

"Yep."

"You don't happen to know where?"

"Some seafood restaurant he liked. Maybe *Langostino*. He liked the lobster there. I can't be sure."

5.

"Did he use the company phone?"

"No, his mobile. He uses it all the time. Nick is a real gadget guy. Always with the latest tech stuff I mean, he was. My God, I can't believe he's gone!"

"Did Mr. Lowell ever go out with married women to your knowledge?"

Dresser raised his eyebrows and smiled wanly. "I don't think he ever asked or ever cared, to tell you the truth."

"Lived large, Mr. Lowell did?"

"Yeah," Dresser smiled more broadly. "He made decent money here and he led the good life."

Dresser seemed to think better of his statement and looked more serious. "I still can't believe he's gone."

"Yes, sir, I believe you said that," Frank muttered, making notes.

* * * *

Jilly entered the Goff Boulevard branch of Western Empire Security Bank to find it heavily grief-laden. Marina Belize had been a well-liked and popular manager and the word had passed through the employees and customers like wildfire. Handwritten expressions of heartfelt sympathy, little sprays of flowers, and other tokens of bereavement had been left on her desk and other places around the office.

The senior bank manager and other employees were of little help, as Jilly had suspected. Marina lived alone and by all accounts was friendly, intelligent, and helpful. Nobody could suggest a single enemy she might have had. Nobody was at all familiar with Ricky Wright by name or description. Furthermore, nobody seemed able to volunteer a single fact about Marina's family or friends outside of work. Apparently Marina did a good job of keeping her professional life separated from her personal life.

Marina had purchased a condo in a fairly nice part of town. Jilly couldn't catch a clue there either. There was no building superintendent and many of the neighbors were at work. There was an elderly couple on Marina's floor who had only encountered her casually, but said she had always been cheerful, polite and helpful.

She never played loud music—"Even though she was, I think, Latin of some kind," the wife volunteered...then looked embarrassed at having said that aloud.

Jilly decided to return that evening. Maybe there would be someone who could shed some light on an increasingly murky puzzle.

* * * *

Samantha Covington had answered her cell phone immediately; she was bewildered by Jilly's phone call but gave her the address of Byrd, Farmer, Blakey and Silver, the law firm where she worked.

The young receptionist's moony eyes opened still wider at Jilly's badge and she picked up the phone, hit a button, and said, "Sam, there's a policewoman here to see you?" with her voice rising into a question at the end.

Jilly took a deep breath, and kept her voice reasonably even. "Detective, actually."

Samantha Covington was in perhaps her late twenties, with short dark hair and expensive designer glasses. She quickly led Jilly back to a vacant conference room.

"Were you in *Las Candilejas* Thursday night?"

"Sure. I've only been there a couple of times. We had to work a little late and we were, you know, unwinding a little. "

"And you were there with friends?" Jilly consulted her notebook. "Especially someone named Catherine?"

"Kathleen, you must mean. Kathleen Mueller. Kat, we call her. There was Kat, me, and Gail. Why?"

"Your friend was with a man named Ricky Wright?"

"Oh yeah, I know who that must have been. He was just dancing with her, trying to make time, you know. There was a little problem. Is that what this is about?"

"Problem?"

"Seems that some other girl decided he was her boyfriend or something and started getting real possessive over him with Kat. Latina girl. Nasty temper. Really got in her face. Kat wasn't happy about that and started giving back some attitude. The guy tried to take the other girl aside to talk to her, and asked her to go outside."

"And you were nearby while all this was going on?"

"Gail and I were at the bar, talking to the bartender. I heard it start to get ugly."

"It must have been pretty loud in there. You could hear them arguing over the music?"

"Well, yeah—come to think of it, it must have been a pause between songs, you know? You know how it suddenly gets quiet, and you hear people talking loud over the music? It was like that."

"So what happened?"

"Kat was trying to get the guy to stay with her, not to leave, and the other girl's got a friend who comes over and tells Kat to stay out of it."

"Her sister, actually. It was her sister."

"Really? She didn't say anything about that. Well…Kat just lost it, called her a witch or something like that, and shouldered past her and left. I started to go after her to see what was going on. The friend stopped me and asked me if I was with Kat. I told her, yeah, we worked together and what business was it of hers?"

"Then what?"

"She was actually okay, she seemed concerned. I was touched by how she seemed to be worried. We ended up talking and she was telling us about what a jerk this guy is and how she wished her friend—her sister, you said?—would just get wise. We actually had a drink together and started talking about all the losers we had all known. It was funny, we got kind of caught up in it and started warming up to each other."

"Did Kat or the other girl come back into the bar?"

Sam thought for a moment. "Actually…no. We all of a sudden realized we should go find them. We finished our drinks and paid our bills and went outside to look for them."

"And did you find them?"

"Well, Kat was right outside the door, she looked a little sick."

"Any idea what she had done after she left the bar? Did she follow the other girl?"

"I don't think so. I think she started feeling sick as soon as she was outside. We scooped her up and headed back to Gail's car down the street."

"And the other girl?"

"No idea. She had walked away, I guess. The guy might have still been trying to talk to her, cool her down. That was the last we saw of her."

"You said she—Kat I mean—looked sick? How do you mean?"

"Like she was going to throw up. I think she had a few too many drinks and she was upset. We drove her home."

"You saw her right to her door?"

"Well, yeah!"

"I'm going to need to talk to Gail and Kat."

"No problem," said Sam. "I'll go get them for you. What's this all about?"

"Ongoing investigation," Jilly said.

The stories told by Kat and then Gail were consistent with what Samantha had told her.

Kat looked exactly as thumbnails had described her except perhaps a little nicer looking, but strangely demure, not brassy. Her demeanor outside of the festive atmosphere of a dance club was quiet, thoughtful, and self-conscious. She seemed embarrassed by the occurrences of the other night that had led up to the tragedy. Jilly judged that she was not likely the type of woman who would carry a pistol nor be capable of a crime of passion fueled by a man she had just met. What had originally appeared to be a promising lead—jealousy, an argument, the heat of the moment—suddenly looked anything but promising.

Jilly couldn't see any of these three plausibly being involved in the shooting, and none of them seemed to be able to shine any further light on what had happened. It was also evident that they had not known about the shooting before she told them, and then, she judged, they were genuinely shocked.

She had tried to maintain discretion, but before her interviews were finished, the word had spread around the office that a police detective was investigating some lurid crime or other.

Suddenly, numerous staffers had discovered crucially important tasks that required them to walk past the conference rooms or interact with one of the women outside of the interviews. Their furtive peeks into the conference room had quickly become annoying.

The three women themselves didn't act too concerned with the excitement and, in fact, seemed thrilled to be in the midst of a real-life crime drama. That just reaffirmed Jilly's gut feeling that she was not on a particularly helpful trail at the moment.

She was disappointed, but somehow also relieved, when she finally wrapped up the conversations and exchanged contact numbers in case she had further questions or the women had further information.

* * * *

"Morgan, please," Frank tried to persist, rubbing his eyes as he held the phone. "All I'm asking is to move a couple of these up the line a little. If I can get some results maybe I can clear one or two...."

"My heart bleeds, positively bleeds for you, Detective. The answer is still no."

Lovely man, Morgan. Even the captain, hardly a lightweight when it came to confrontations, hesitated before stepping into this lion's den to ask for special consideration.

"You want sob stories? I got plenty of them. My two best people are out sick. My backlog is piled high here. You know we also do the county and some other municipalities contract out to us as well, right? Every week or two I get some desperate plea from you guys or somebody else about just this one case, just this one time. All these just-this-one-timers. I got the scars from all the fights, Detective, do you want to come over and see them? For the last time, you get in line and you wait your turn! Do I make myself clear?"

"Can you at least give me an idea of how long we are talking?"

"It takes what it takes. Maybe a week, maybe two. Maybe more."

"I'll check back with you in a few days," Frank said.

"Just remember, the more I'm on the phone with you guys, the longer it's going to take me to get my *real* work done!" Morgan barked. "Are we done here?"

"Yeah. We're done here."

As bad as his conversation had gone with Morgan over expediting ballistics, his earlier conversation with the medical examiner had been worse. By comparison Morgan was a total sweetheart.

Ballistics, as Morgan unhesitatingly pointed out, honored contracts with multiple agencies, but the ME's regional responsibilities extended even further and their plate was stacked even higher. On top of that, the county coroner was an elected office, and this was a re-election year, which added exponentially to the agenda—and the stress factor.

Frank was hardly a shrinking violet but he had backed off from the fire-breathing individual on the other end of the phone who seemed ready to make it downright personal during that brief but memorable exchange.

He had encountered more equitable sorts in his quest to expedite blood work and prints from the lab. But ultimately they were turning him down as adamantly, just in a nicer manner. Things were hard all over, and the bottom line was that none of the information he desperately needed would be forthcoming in the immediate future. He was on his own.

When the technology wasn't forthcoming, maybe a dinosaur like Frank, plodding and old school, was exactly what was needed.

Frank, still at his desk and phone, took another deep breath, perusing the list of names he had jotted down during his interview with Anita.

No question, Al Land was not the most popular man in town. There were a lot of people who bore Al grudges or ill will of some sort. Frank was going to have to work smart, pare the list down to the most plausible leads and start with those. Maybe he'd get lucky. Otherwise he'd have to return and work his way down the list thoroughly and exactingly. He didn't relish that.

He was lucky enough to catch Anita on the second ring and asked her if he could follow up on that first conversation. Neither of them exchanged any false pleasantries but got right to it. It didn't surprise Frank that Anita was measured, without any sign of grief. She was like that.

"Anita, tell me about some of the people you were talking about. Who would strike you as having it in for Al the most?"

She gave it some thought for a long moment. "Well, he did have that run-in with Billy Wilde. He and Al had a few words late last year."

Frank needed no introduction to Billy Wilde. Officially he owned several garbage disposal companies that contracted with the local municipalities.

Unofficially Wilde was well known to people like Frank for other reasons: gambling and a lovely variety of other illicit operations. There were several racketeering indictments in process against him, and Frank's own department was investigating rumors of a homicide with little to go on. Wilde spent much of his life in court. He kept a battery of attorneys fully employed and seemed untouchable.

"Yeah, I remember when you told me that. What was the beef between them?"

"Billy suspected his wife was less than faithful and hired us to look into it. Al found absolutely nothing. Billy's kinda paranoid that way. Then he came back and had us follow his girlfriend as well, thinking she was double timing him too."

"Hard to find a faithful spouse any more. Or a girlfriend for that matter."

"Turns out Al couldn't find either of the gals doing a blessed thing wrong. His wife shopped and lunched with her friends. His girlfriend just shopped. Billy wouldn't believe it. One day in a bar, they had it out and Billy refused to pay Al the remainder of his fee until he came back with some results that he liked better."

"Most guys would have been relieved to learn there actually was no, er, co-respondent, in that kind of case," Frank said. "Go figure."

"Yeah, well, Billy hates to be proven wrong about anything. It was a bit of a tense conversation. But I've been thinking about it and I can't see Billy doing something like this. He's nasty but more thoughtful, if you know what I mean. He and Al were still posturing about the payment. It hadn't reached a stage past that *posturing* stuff.

"And Billy would've sent Al a warning first, like a visit from one of his associates. At the very worst, if he had gone drastic on us, he would have done something cleaner. One day Al would have just not been here anymore, with nobody having seen anything. This was sloppy."

"I'll look into it anyway. Who else rises to the top?"

"Like scum on a pond, you mean? Scudder, maybe."

Frank checked his notes. "Duane Scudder. As in Scudder Investigations."

"The same. He and Al were on the force together briefly. Scudder cashed out on his retirement a few years after Al left, and opened his own agency. He and Al were known to step on one another's toes now and then in the pursuit of clients."

"Hardly reason to shoot someone."

"Not likely, I'll grant you. But Scudder's got a bad temper. Al told me he hurt a few people when he was a cop but his connections in the department were always reliable enough to get him past it. But in private business it was a different story when a client's money was on the line. Duane's messed up a few deals, and Al was always there to step in and scoop up the clients while they were still upset. The two of them were not on speaking terms."

"Could you see Scudder doing something like this, though?"

"Duane? Uh-uh. What I'm thinking is, he's got a lot of young tough guys working for him, not the brightest bulbs in the box by any means, the kind who wouldn't be above looking to make a name with him if they heard him bad-mouthing someone, you know?"

"Like a young guy in a hoodie and a beat up Blazer? Would he have that kind of guy?"

He could almost see her shrug on the other end. "Possibly. Just a thought."

"Incidentally…what about that shooting that was in the paper last year involving Al?" Frank asked. "Any likelihood of a reprisal?"

"Ha! That? I seriously doubt it. Didn't even think it was worth mentioning. We helped a skip-tracer find a guy who had jumped bail. The bondsman stood to lose a good hunk of money. The guy turned out to be armed with some pea shooter starter pistol, he took a blind shot and hit Al in the leg, then got all scared, dropped the gun and gave up. The guy was still apologizing when they got him back to lockup. He's been in prison ever since."

"But maybe a relative or friend…"

"Doesn't feel right to me, but knock yourself out."

Frank was jotting down additional thoughts in his notes when Anita added, "But now that I think of it, the one that would stand out to me is the DKM gang."

Another name that needed no introduction to Frank. "Do tell."

"He made *lots* of enemies on that one. I wouldn't know where to begin. A lot of indignant little twerps jumped on the bandwagon when the word HARASSMENT first started coming up."

"But I'm thinking, we're talking stuff like whistle blowers and media crusader types, Anita. Not the kind to pull out a gun and shoot somebody."

"De-*tec*-tive, my husband was killed by an amateur. You know that and I know that. The DKM thing is crawling with people out of their element, ticked off to the max, pushed to their limits, frustrated and willing to believe that Al was Satan himself. I would NOT dismiss the possibility. You asked me."

"Okay, okay." Short pause. "Anita, I also have to ask you this...."

"I bet I know what's coming. Was Al fooling around, was there a jealous husband or boyfriend or something? As the cliché goes, he was no choirboy, but no, there had not been anyone...in some time."

"Uh...forgive me, but, you seem awfully sure of that, Anita. Couldn't there...."

"Detective, Al and I were straight with each other. That's one thing we were, was honest with one another. Believe me when I tell you this: he would have told me if something along that line was going on. I would take that to the bank."

Why did conversations with this woman elicit such deep sighs? "Okay, Anita. Anybody else or should that do it for now?"

"That's all I got. Go find the schmuck that did this."

* * * *

When Jilly returned to Marina Belize's condo later that evening, she wasn't sure what to expect, but hoped at least to encounter more people who could tell her something about the enigmatic Marina.

Something wasn't fitting. According to her sister Jane, Marina loved to dance and was full of life. She had a boyfriend who looked to be a bad boy for sure. Yet according to Marina's co-workers and, so far, her neighbors, she was decidedly quiet in her private life. How to reconcile these two sides?

She was surprised to find the door to Marina's condo open when she came down the hall. She peeked inside. There were two young men inside, dragging large cardboard cartons across the carpeted floor. Kneeling on the ground filling one with small articles was a woman, who turned around to look at Jilly.

Jane Nascimento.

"Detective!"

"Hello, Jane. Packing up Marina's things?"

Jane looked somehow guilty. The two men, who could conceivably also be Brazilian, walked over to stand beside her and glower at Jilly silently.

"I…I thought I might as well get started on it. There's nobody else to do this. I need something to keep me busy, you know?"

"I can understand that," Jilly said, eyeing the two men. They weren't particularly threatening but they did look apprehensive. Jane caught the looks of the men and quickly stood up.

"This is my husband, Eddie." She gestured to the taller of the two, a lean guy in a shirt with a soccer team logo. He nodded at Jilly. "And his brother, Martin." Jilly nodded back at both. They continued to stand and stare mutely.

"You know," said Jilly evenly, "there might be something that could help us find her killer in here. I'm thinking you shouldn't be moving this stuff so quickly."

As if, she thought, they wanted to clear it out before she could get to it.

"Oh, I didn't think of that. Of course. But do you really think there could be any kind of clue in this stuff?"

"Jane, I don't have any idea just yet. I have to consider everything. And I'd think you'd want me to be doing that. Why are you here doing this right now?"

The postures of the two young men turned subtly more aggressive, or so it seemed to Jilly. Instinctively she balanced her weight on both feet and moved her hand closer to her bag and the gun within, remaining outwardly casual. Best to be ready for anything in this situation.

Eddie, never taking his eyes off Jilly, muttered something in Portuguese to Jane. She shook her head and made a gesture towards him as if to wave him off. Something seemed to defuse, although everyone was still clearly apprehensive. Jane turned back to face Jilly.

"I'm not sure, but I think you're someone I can trust, a little bit," she said.

"I'd like to think so. But it will depend on what you tell me. No promises, Jane. But I'm the most trustworthy investigator you're going to get in this case, I guarantee you that."

Jane considered that and finally, with a sag of her shoulders, said, "Let's all sit down over there," motioning to a sofa and chairs. And then only to Jilly: "It's a long story."

* * * *

The story began with the most formidable criminal element in Brazil's most celebrated city.

There is a powerful and feared cartel in Rio de Janeiro called the *Comando Vermelho*, or Red Command. It began as a dissident political group in the early 1980s but gradually shed its ideological base and evolved into an out-and-out criminal organization dealing in drug and arms trafficking.

At some point, a splinter faction broke off from it, seeking its own power and means, and began to engage in a particularly vicious battle with its parent organization (who dismissively called it the "Little Command") over control of certain neighborhoods in the city. Not only were members of both groups in constant peril for their lives in this merciless struggle, but so were their families and friends. There was no such thing as a civilian in this war. Anyone could and would be made a brutal casualty—and an example—if the opportunity arose.

So Paulinho Silva, one of the major leaders of the Little Command, had decided it wise to send his family out of the country ten years earlier. His wife had not escaped—Red Command "soldiers" had located her— but their daughters had safely reached the United States and changed their surnames to Belize. Paulinho hoped that his enemies would never find them. The sisters might never learn the ultimate fate of their father.

For ten years now, they had lived quietly and without incident in this same American city. Jane had met and married a loving, reliable, and hard-working Brazilian man here. Marina had completed her education and found a good job at which she excelled. They both tried to keep reasonably low profiles, lead quiet lives and not make waves—but they both loved to dance, and the one thing in which they indulged themselves was an occasional trip to a familiar dance club to let off some steam.

And Marina's eye could not always overlook a flashy handsome young man in such a club, and she had found herself in a dubious but exciting love relationship.

They had come to believe they were secure in their new identities, safely off the radar of the vengeful criminals of Rio.

But of course when Marina was killed, that was precisely where Jane's thoughts went. And the only person that might have sold her out, as far as she could figure, was Ricky Wright.

* * * *

When the story had been told, Jilly said, "You think, then, that there's evidence here in Marina's place of who she really is—who you both really are?"

Jane nodded, tears forming in her eyes.

"We weren't supposed to keep photos of Mama and Papa, letters, keepsakes, anything about them at all—but I think Marina might have. Who knows if the *Comando* has people here in this city, or even just 'friends'? If anything were to be found here, anything at all...."

Jilly nodded. The two men stared at her from their seats, arms crossed, still clearly suspicious.

"You were right to tell me this," Jilly finally said, gently. "Perhaps this had nothing to do with the Comando. But if it did, we can and will protect you."

"I was convinced—we were convinced—that Papa was dead and the war was over, maybe they were all dead and gone. That we were safe."

"And maybe you are right, Jane. I'm going to look into this. But for the moment, I'm going to need you to leave all of Marina's things here."

She took out her cell phone and keyed in a familiar number. "I'm going to get a team over here to seal this off and keep an eye on the place. I'll also get you a police guard while we figure this out. As soon as the officers are here to accompany you, you should all leave."

Jilly further instructed them to continue to keep their low profile and watch out for each other but to otherwise act normally—and let her know of any new developments—while she tried to ascertain if a danger actually existed from the horrific cartel six thousand miles away.

6.

Al Land's most notorious recent client was Alfonse D'Yquem—elusive, seclusive, and not just rich but filthy rich. He was the brains and sheer power behind the digital mega-giant Prophet DKM. At nineteen, he had founded the company along with two partners, computer wizards like himself but both several years his senior. Within two years he had bought out one and outmaneuvered the other.

He was responsible for a number of brilliant technical innovations, and combining his expertise with an aptitude and taste for cutthroat business practices, he grew his enterprise at impressive speed but always somehow out of the public eye. Mergers and acquisitions, one after another, constantly enhanced DKM as it evolved into a shadowy empire that spanned first the country, then the continent, and finally the globe, quietly dominating a considerable corner of the digital industry.

Al had worked on contract and retainer for D'Yquem and his companies for several years, partially because he was local to the corporate headquarters and partly because of his reputation as a rough-edged, unprincipled operator who was most comfortable in the shadows.

This was precisely the kind of guy, Frank mused, that a spectral and ruthless nabob like D'Yquem would find useful. At the time of his demise, Al was under multiple subpoenas stemming from allegations that he had attempted to intimidate not only plaintiffs and witnesses in a lawsuit against D'Yquem, but also several journalists reporting on the case. It was a high-profile ongoing story that the media, stung by threats to their own, had been riding ceaselessly, to the great distaste of Al and his employer.

Frank figured it would be next to impossible to reach D'Yquem directly, and he was right. He did have a phone conversation with an unctuous, officious little irritant from company twelve, battalion six of the DKM legal department. He was told the earliest he could possibly speak with anyone was the next morning, and that he should ask for Jan DeVries in the security department.

A few more phone calls convinced Frank that Anita had been correct in giving a low priority to the bail-jumper who had taken a shot at Al. His name was—no kidding—Johnny Doe. He was currently serving a sentence in a state prison a hundred miles away and would be doing so for the foreseeable future.

As far as Frank could ascertain, Doe had no living relatives and no close friends locally. He was a transient from Arkansas who had arrived in town and immediately gotten himself into stupid trouble. Frank wasn't totally ready to write him off, but felt he could safely be shelved in favor of more promising leads.

The one that came to mind was Duane Scudder.

* * * *

Scudder Investigations occupied most of the third floor of a building that had seen better days. Frank had debated the relative merits of calling ahead or showing up cold and had decided on the latter.

As luck would have it, the receptionist informed him that Mr. Scudder was indeed in his office, and if he wouldn't mind waiting, she'd check on his availability. There was, remarkably, only a short wait before Duane Scudder blew through the door into the waiting room, a huge smile on his face, and extended his hand in greeting to Frank, who rose from the overstuffed sofa.

"Always delighted to help out law enforcement," Scudder gushed in a deep voice. Frank wondered if the guy consciously worked on resembling an actor playing a PI on a television show—flashy dress, salon tan, styled hair, what was once termed a Pepsodent grin. He was diligently trying to maintain his youth against the onset of years. "Come on into my office and tell me what I can do for you, Detective, uh…"

"Vandegraf. Frank Vandegraf." He followed Scudder back through the door into a small but nicely-appointed office and sat himself down in front of a large, surprisingly empty desk. Scudder deposited himself behind it and waited expectantly.

"Al Land," Frank began. Scudder nodded vigorously.

"A shame, a real shame. Just terrible."

Crocodile tears. This was beginning to look fairly promising, Frank mused to himself. He kept his eyes on Scudder, looking for any tells.

"You knew him well?"

"Of course. We were on the force together for a while. After we had both gone private, we crossed paths quite often. It was inevitable. This isn't all that big a city."

"Did you get along?"

Scudder shook his head and looked down at his desk, a half-grin twisting his mouth. "Not really. No."

Frank waited a few beats. Finally Scudder continued.

"Al was a pain in the neck, Detective. I won't lie to you about that. He was a weasel. Unprincipled. A bottom feeder—let's just say he'd stoop to activities I wouldn't. He'd steal clients. Look for unethical advantages and shortcuts. He would undercut anyone he felt was his competition, and that was sometimes me."

"So you didn't get along."

Scudder met his gaze evenly. "Of course not, and you must have known that. Are you thinking I had something to do with his murder?"

"Honestly? No. But maybe somebody you know might know something?"

Scudder leaned across the desk, his arms crossed, keeping his eyes locked on Frank. His words were measured. The Hollywood façade was gone.

"What exactly do you mean?"

"How many employees do you have, Mr. Scudder?"

"Scudder Investigations employs nine people. Our receptionist Janet, whom you met; two administrative assistants, a clerical intern, and five field operatives, who perform a large range of duties out of the office. We also have an outside accountant and an attorney on retainer. Not a huge operation but we do cover a lot of ground."

"You had some public disagreements with Al Land."

"Yes, I did."

"And how about your staff members? Did any of them ever cross paths with him?"

"Not that I know of. Would you care to ask any of them yourself?"

"In due time, yes. Let's you and I talk some more first."

Scudder conspicuously checked his watch. "I've got fifteen minutes before I need to be somewhere. Go ahead. But maybe I can save you some time. Al died on Thursday, correct?"

"That's right."

"I happened to be out of town, traveling to three cities, for the past week, and just returned on the red eye this morning. It's an easy enough matter to show you plane tickets, hotel and restaurant credit receipts."

"Well, that is convenient," Frank said, allowing himself the slightest of smiles.

"I travel a lot. I give seminars on security. You might enjoy one some time. Let me know, I'll comp you."

Frank rubbed the back of his neck, reflecting that Scudder didn't feel right for this anyway, neither to carry it out nor to consciously order it done. It was a rash and stupid act, and this was anything but a rash and stupid man.

His hired help, on the other hand…

"Okay. Let's talk about your field operatives," Frank said.

Two of Scudder's field agents were female—so much for Anita's "a lot of young tough guys"—and the whereabouts of two others, including Scudder's second in command, could be verified for all of that Thursday night, since both had been on assignment.

That left only Scudder's most recent hire, Gerald Lombard, whom he had taken on right out of community college. Lombard happened to be off that day.

Scudder, at Frank's urging, described him. "Hard working guy. Associate's degree in criminology, really gung-ho about it. He was happy to get a job in the investigation field. I gotta say, not the sharpest employee in the office, but he makes up for it in enthusiasm. Eager to help out around here, puts in a lot of hours, never complains." He buzzed the receptionist to bring in Lombard's file. "We naturally checked him out. Clean record, no problems with the law, not even juvie stuff. I took him out in the field a few times and he did well. Handled himself well."

"By that you mean he handled himself well in physical confrontations, that sort of thing?"

"I mean he couldn't be intimidated. He stood his ground. He wasn't the type that went looking for a fight, but he made it quite clear that he wasn't going to back down from one either."

"Were there physical fights involving him?"

"No, nothing ever came to that. And Gerry wasn't pushy. He's actually a pretty easy going guy."

"Does he carry a weapon?"

"All my operatives are encouraged to train and qualify in side-arms and to have up-to-date carry permits, yes. Gerry is a decent shot, if a bit inexperienced, but I have to say he seems a bit reluctant with a sidearm."

"Does he carry it with him out of work?"

"Often the work here is pretty routine, chasing down information, and in those cases a few of our ops prefer to lock up their weapons in the office when they're off work. He's almost always one of them. Ah…

thanks, Janet." The receptionist had entered and placed a manila file in front of him on the desk. He passed it over to Frank.

"I can't see Gerry being involved in this in any way," Scudder said as Frank browsed the few brief pages and looked at Lombard's photo and vital statistics. He had dark hair. About the right height and weight.

"Just routine. This his current address, 9600 Dorritt?" Frank jotted down the information in his notebook.

"That would be it."

"Would you happen to know what kind of car Mr. Lombard drives?"

"I'm not sure. I've seen him pull up in the parking lot. Maybe a Jeep Cherokee or a Bronco or something like that. Light, maybe white or beige. Some kind of a utility vehicle, which as you know are pretty common right now."

Some investigator, thought Frank. He didn't seem to be all that observant when it came to his employees. "Later model? Older?"

"Oh, it's a few years old. A little beat up."

"Possibly a Blazer?"

Scudder shrugged. "Certainly that type of vehicle."

"So you are saying that Gerald's weapon is here on the premises? Can that be confirmed?"

"Certainly." It was said somewhat grudgingly. Scudder picked up his phone and keyed in a few numbers, spoke briefly, replaced the receiver. "This doesn't sound so routine any more, Detective."

Frank shrugged. "Just covering all the possible bases, Mr. Scudder."

Scudder's phone buzzed and he picked up, uttered a few more words and again hung up. "Yes, Gerry's weapon is in the safe. You're not saying you need to see it?"

The words sounded accommodating but Scudder's expression was anything but. Frank realized he would likely need a warrant to get that gun. He shook his head.

"Not just yet. But I might be back." He stood up from his chair. "Thanks for your help."

Scudder also rose and extended his hand to shake, but remained behind his desk. "Any time. Always happy to help out the police." The Pepsodent grin was gone.

"No need to walk with me, I can find my way out," Frank smiled wryly and turned to the door.

* * * *

It was a short drive to Western Waste Removal, Billy Wilde's flagship company. Frank decided he'd take a chance on a cold call, hoping to find Billy there, just to see if his luck continued to hold out. Wilde was infamous for his extremely low profile and this facility, in line with that reputation, consisted of a small low building and a lot filled with garbage trucks. The garbage itself was carted off site to a dumping area, but the place still did not exactly smell like a rose garden. Drivers and others in blue jumpsuits bustled everywhere.

Wilde was indeed in his office, and when notified by his secretary told her to admit Frank. His executive office looked more like a large storage room: desks, tables and chairs piled high with papers and folders, and a line of jammed old file cabinets along one wall.

"I think I know you," Wilde said in a hoarse voice. He was heavyset, impatient, with a definite underlying air of menace—not a man to mess with. He made no effort to shake Frank's hand but directed him to a chair.

"Possibly," Frank replied, shifting a pile of forms to another chair and sitting. "I certainly know you."

"Cop, yes?"

"Detective. Frank Vandegraf."

"So what do you want?" Wilde asked.

Again, right to the point, which was fine with Frank. "You knew Al Land."

"Ah. Yeah, sure I did. I figured that might be it, why you're here. I heard about him the other night."

"Seems like everybody did. Tell me about you and him."

Wilde shrugged, casually shuffled some of his own papers around on his desk as he spoke. "Not much to tell. He did some work for me. We weren't like friends or anything. Don't know much about the guy, to tell the truth. Taciturn sort."

"I hear you had an argument a while back?"

"Who told you that? That wife of his? Aargh. Now she's a piece of work, that one. I wouldn't exactly call it an argument, uh…what's your name again?"

"Detective Vandegraf." This guy was not going to call him Frank, not by any stretch.

"Okay, Detective. I'm sure I know you! I do, don't I? This thing with Al, it was more like a disagreement. A misunderstanding over services rendered and fees. We were working it out. He and I, we're businessmen. We understood how to deal with misunderstanding, if you get me?"

"He didn't get you the results you wanted?" Frank asked.

"I at first thought he hadn't been sufficiently thorough. Turns out I may well have been wrong, but for a long time we were discussing that issue. Nothing more."

"Just covering all the bases," Frank replied, pulling out his notebook while still keeping an eye on Wilde's facial expressions. "Let's talk a little about that, and about your whereabouts Thursday night, if you don't mind."

"You don't seriously think I had anything to do with Al's death?" Wilde asked, clearly surprised—to Frank it seemed genuine. He began to laugh, shook his head as if in disbelief. "Oh no, this is a joke! You said you know me, right?"

Frank just stared. Wilde stared back. After a long silence, he said, "If you think I did this, then maybe you don't know me. Not like you think you do, okay? That's all I have to say. Now if you'll forgive me, I got work to do, a company—a few companies—to run."

He looked down and began to sort through the forms before him. The interview was done.

Frank stood up and pocketed his notebook. He had gotten what he needed here. "I might be back for more questions."

"If you do," muttered Wilde without looking up, "be prepared to bring me in. With my lawyer. We're done here."

Returning to his car, dodging garbage trucks in the lot, Frank reflected: maybe he could have ordered this. I can't dismiss it out of hand. But something just doesn't feel right about it.

Something hadn't felt right about anything today.

He did, however, suddenly have the urge, when he had a moment, to look into the current health and whereabouts of Wilde's wife...and girlfriend. Just out of curiosity.

* * * *

Frank's last stop of the day, he fervently hoped as he observed darkness beginning to fall, was to 9600 Dorritt—Gerald Lombard's address, a two-story apartment house that looked to house perhaps eight units, with access to the upper apartments via scattered stairways to an outer balcony that ringed the building. There was a fenced pool in the rear with the metal gate ajar. He found the name on the row of buttons at the front door and rang. A voice came through the fuzzy intercom.

"Yeah, who is it?"

"Police," Frank spoke into the grille. "Detective Vandegraf. Can I have a few words?"

There was no answer. A moment later the intercom clicked off.

He heard a door open on the second floor, towards the rear, on the balcony. Steps running.

Lombard was moving!

Frank wheeled around, looking for access to the rear. He heard footsteps going down concrete stairs, back in the outdoor pool area.

Oh no. He hated this.

He surprised himself with the quickness with which he took off, hitting the metal gate to the pool area and pushing it open with a smash. Lombard was on the next to last step of the staircase from the second floor, glancing over his shoulder at him.

Frank made quick calculations. He could still intercept Lombard as he ran from the other side around the deserted pool and the chairs.

They met at a corner of the pool, with only a few moments before the younger man would be able to outdistance him. Frank gasped an epithet and shoved him in.

"Would you like to explain to me why you took off like that?" Frank asked him a few minutes later.

Lombard was soaking wet, sitting on a deck chair, his arms cuffed behind him, looking alternately defiant and miserable. A number of tenants had come out to investigate the commotion and Frank would periodically flash his badge and tell them to go back indoors. No doubt many of them were peering curiously through the blinds of their windows at them now.

"How'd you find me?" was the only reply Lombard would give.

Frank looked him over, tried to imagine him in a dark hoodie. It would work.

"Went to the source. Your boss."

Genuine shock. "Duane? What does he know about this?"

"So you're saying you were alone in this, right?"

"What? Wait. What are you talking about? Alone in *what*?"

"Suppose you tell me, Gerald? What did you do that made you panic and run when a cop came to your door? Don't you work with cops and law enforcement types all the time?"

"I was only trying to help. I didn't mean any harm. Nobody got hurt."

Frank stopped at that. "What do you mean, nobody got hurt? You *killed* him, for Pete's sake!"

Lombard froze and stared at Frank, not comprehending.

"What—what are you talking about? Nobody got killed!"

Frank wondered how often in the course of the day he unconsciously rubbed the back of his neck, like he caught himself doing right now. "What are *you* talking about?"

"Amanda! I was just trying to help Amanda out of a jam!"

"Who's Amanda?"

"Amanda Darcy. She works with me at Duane's agency, she's the intern there. Isn't that why you're here?"

"Uhhh...no. No, Amanda is not why I am here, Gerald. Let's take you upstairs and inside and dry you off and we'll talk about this. But the cuffs stay on until I decide if I like your story."

"If it's all the same with you, can we stay out here?"

Lombard looked downright alarmed at the prospect of returning to his apartment.

"So…there's something, maybe some kind of contraband, up in your place, is that what I'm hearing? Something Amanda wanted you to hold on to for her?"

"Ohhh man," Lombard moaned, mostly to himself. "I am so screwed. My job is *gone*. Am I gonna get time for this? We thought it'd all be okay. I was just trying to help…"

Frank couldn't wait to see what it was. Drugs, he figured. Narcotics. Cocaine. Guns? How did this fit in with the shooting of Al Land, and what was he involved in? This might be bigger than he had possibly imagined! How big a headache was this going to turn out to be?

* * * *

When it was all sorted out, Frank felt badly, but he had little choice but to call for uniformed backup to come pick up Lombard and confiscate the contents of the apartment.

"Now let me get this straight," he said to Lombard as they waited for the uniforms to arrive. He gestured all around, at the endless stacks of cardboard boxes that jammed the living room to a height of maybe seven feet, with only narrow corridors left between them. "Cigarettes? Really?"

Lombard, sitting on the arm of a ratty chair, still cuffed, hung his head and was barely audible. "Her cousin Randy brought them in from across the state line. The taxes are less there so he can sell them cheaper and make a fortune."

"I hate to tell you this, Gerald, but there are NO tax stamps on these. These are stolen. His profit is better than you think, like a hundred percent. So he was going to cut you in on this?"

"It was just a favor," Lombard murmured. "For Amanda. She said she couldn't keep them anywhere in her place, they had no other place for them. It was only for a few days…"

"Amanda must be pretty cute, I'd guess?"

The downcast young man actually smiled. "She's beautiful, actually."

"And you and she…?" Frank waved his finger back and forth, here and there.

Lombard nodded.

"Anybody else at work know about this?"

He shook his head. "We kept it all a secret, our being together. And the cigarettes, of course. She couldn't trust anybody, but she said she could trust me."

"And—just a wild guess—just before these cigarettes were coming into the picture, that was when she decided she wanted to be your girl-friend, right?"

"I know it sounds bad, but it's real."

"Was she worth risking your whole future for, son?"

Lombard could only sadly nod. "And we'll still be together when this is all done. We'll start a new life somewhere…"

Well…Scudder had said that Gerald was not his brightest employee, after all. Understatement indeed. This was a dim bulb if there ever were one. "So when did these cigarettes start arriving here?"

"They dropped them off late Thursday. I helped them unload. It was after dark. We brought them in from the back alley. Took us hours, 'til past midnight."

Frank felt with some certainty that, when Amanda Darcy and her "cousin" got picked up, they'd corroborate that story, knowingly or oth-erwise. Or if by some fluke of luck they had already made their success-ful getaway, there would be a paper trail for a rented truck or *something* that bore out his story about Thursday night. He just knew it.

Gerald Lombard was a fool, and he was about to become not only unemployed but likely incarcerated. But he was not a killer. At least he was not the killer that Frank was looking for.

Hang the luck.

Frank turned back to Lombard. "Another question, Gerald. What kind of vehicle do you drive?"

"A Cherokee, ten years old. Pale green. It's parked out front. Why?"

"Just wondering. One last question. Did you ever hear your boss talk about a guy named Al Land?"

Gerald looked up, taken aback momentarily. "Uh…sure. Duane al-ways talks about him. He hates the guy, man. Why?"

"That's what I was afraid of," Frank said, to nobody in particular. The intercom buzzed and he went to answer it.

7.

Frank started the new day with a call back to DKM, asking to be put through to Jan DeVries, who turned out to be Assistant to the Head of Security and was, surprisingly, reasonably co-operative.

"We're sorry to hear of Mr. Land's death," DeVries began smoothly. "What can I do to help you?"

"Tell me about Land's services for you, what he was involved in."

"There were allegations being publicly made about irregularities in the company's business practices. The allegations were totally groundless and violated the non-disclosure agreements signed by several of our personnel and independent contractors."

"Whistle blowers, in other words," Frank interjected.

"Well, there were those who used that expression, but in fact they were agitators pure and simple. As I said, their accusations were groundless."

"Okay, and how did Al Land figure into this?"

"There were accusations and counter-accusations flying, the media involved, lawsuits initiated, that type of thing. Matters threatened to become unmanageable. It was all very irresponsible. We suspected some kind of industrial espionage, personnel plants within DKM to derail ongoing projects, concerns along those lines. Mr. Land had performed various functions on our behalf for some time. We were familiar with him, approved of his approach, and knew he was utterly reliable. We asked him to step in and investigate the backgrounds of the complainants, make confidential inquiries, and other similar undertakings."

"Some would say he was brought in for intimidation of the whistle blowers."

DeVries made a puffing sound in dismissal. "Nobody was being *intimidated*. Mr. Land was investigating the covert associations of the troublemakers. We are a leading, perhaps the preeminent, multinational company in our field, Detective. We deal in sensitive, confidential leading-edge digital development. You can certainly understand that there are unprincipled factions out there that would profit from doing harm to us. There are also people who spuriously claim our proprietary entities should be theirs. A company like DKM has to defend itself constantly. But first and foremost, we're also a responsible corporation. We do not involve ourselves in the kinds of unethical and frankly unwise practices of which we were being accused. It was all totally without merit and potentially toxic."

"Toxic. Interesting word. Just what was the nature of the lawsuits that these individuals were bringing against the company?"

"They ranged over a large spectrum. Total shotgun approach. Alleged illegal business practices such as extortion and espionage. Human resource issues such as abusive treatment, bullying, sexism, unjust termination. Some contractors alleged theft of intellectual property. I can go on and on. You'd have to speak with our legal department but I believe at last count there were something like sixteen separate ongoing cases at various stages."

"Who did Land report to at DKM? Who did he get his orders from?"

"I was his usual liaison. I acted as interface with our legal department, Human Resources, and others."

"I assume his business with the company generally went smoothly? No notable differences of opinion or rough spots?"

"Mr. Land was a consummate professional. He understood our concerns and was familiar with the landscape. We were all on the same page. That's why we consistently employed his services."

"Who were the people he personally dealt with—the 'troublemakers' as you call them?"

"There were perhaps a dozen individuals he was doing backgrounds on. Perhaps another dozen collateral individuals related to the issues. And, of course, the baseless harassment suits."

"I'm going to need a list of all the people he had contact with, especially the ones bringing suit against him. Just out of curiosity, are any of them still with the company?"

"None of them are active. We severed any free-lance contractor agreements with involved parties. Some of the employees brought legal injunctions against us and couldn't be terminated, so they are on administrative leave pending the outcomes. I'll have my assistant email you a list of everyone Mr. Land was backgrounding."

Backgrounding. Frank shook his head. He had little tolerance for the creative nonsense of corporate speak. "Off hand, does anyone in particular strike you that might have had it in for Al Land?"

"Hard to say. There were a few ringleaders beginning to emerge in the media flurry. Cassandra Washington comes to mind: she was perhaps the highest profile. Lester Lanier. Those two made the most outrageous allegations in the press about Mr. Land's supposed threats."

Frank posed a few more questions and asked if the list could be faxed to the department rather than emailed. That provoked a slight sniff from DeVries but he said they could indeed do that.

A few more calls established that Lester Lanier had been missing from town for over two weeks. A relative simply said that he was on extended vacation somewhere in the Caribbean. The definite if unspoken impression was that Lester was frightened of something or someone.

Cassandra Washington, on the other hand, was easy to reach. Frank arranged a meeting—but not at her home, she insisted. It would have to be on what she termed "neutral ground." She too was scared of the tentacles of DKM, it would seem.

This might be cutting-edge tech industry, he considered, but at least some of their techniques were still familiar to a Neanderthal like himself.

Upon hanging up, Frank contemplated whether this line of inquiry was going to be worth it. Given the options of fight or flight when threatened, all these people seemed to be more of the tendency to flight.

He wanted to be thorough, despite the insane morass of enmities surrounding Al Land. But he increasingly liked the other theory in the back of his brain, the one that was gradually being reinforced by tidbits he turned up.

Frank stared at his car keys on the desk next to his phone. It was time to get back out on the street. But first, he took a moment to flip through his ever-growing notes. He had gotten thoroughly caught up in them when his phone rang. "This is Mallory, down at the desk. There's someone here to see you. I'm sending her up, okay?"

Now what?

A lady of perhaps fifty, jaw firmly set, came up the stairs to the squad room and looked around. The various personnel milling around paid her scant attention. She called out in a loud and hoarse voice, "Where's Vandegraf?"

"That would be me, Ma'am," Frank called out, walking over to greet her. "How can I help you?"

He had seated her at his desk and learned she was Mrs. Catherine Foster, widowed mother of Severin "Sonny" Foster, victim at the Ready Rite parking lot. Frank made the mistake of referring to him as Sonny. She snapped at him, "His name is Severin. That other name is something that street trash called him. So what are you doing to find the person who killed my Severin?"

"We're doing what we can, Mrs. Foster," Frank replied, willing himself to be patient and respectful. This was a mother who had lost her son.

She eyed him without warmth or trust, her jaw remaining hard-set. "I'd like to believe that. But I have my doubts, Detective. Young kid, you probably have him pegged as a street hoodlum, from a bad neighborhood, am I right? You probably think that's all any of them are, don't you? Why do I think nothing is ever going to be done?"

"We treat every case equally, Ma'am," Frank said carefully.

"So why haven't you found somebody yet, can you tell me that?"

"Ma'am, you are probably not aware of this, but we had eight homicides that night. Eight. I am personally investigating four of them. You have to understand, we're drawn a little thin right now. I'm doing everything I can…"

"Like what?" she interrupted, anger growing in her voice. She was starting to tremble. Her voice began to shake with emotion. "I'm just betting whoever those other murders are, they're people you put a higher value on than my boy! Tell me, why would it not surprise me if those other killers are found *long* before anybody finds who killed my Severin? That is, if you *ever* do find who did!"

"I understand your concerns, Mrs. Foster. And I am very sorry for your loss. Believe me, that is not how we work around here. Everybody counts. Everybody."

"I've had to raise that boy all by myself ever since his father passed away. Six years. Do you know what it's like to raise a teenager as a single mother? To be breadwinner *and* a parent? It's like being both father and mother! I've done what I could!"

Frank saw a tear begin to form in the lady's eye.

"No, truthfully, I do not know what it is like, Ma'am," he said. He didn't know what else he could say. "But I will find the person who took him away from you."

She looked at him intensely for a long time. "Promise me," she said in almost a growl.

"Yes, I promise you."

"We'll see about that," she said more quietly. There were still a few tears and she wiped them away with the back of her hand. Frank looked around for tissues. There was a small box on a nearby desk that he grabbed and placed in front of her.

"Let me ask you some questions while you're here about your son's friends, the people he associates with, that type of thing. Can we do that?" She nodded.

It was a good half hour later that he escorted her downstairs and once again promised he would find the murderer of Severin Foster.

The trouble was, of course, he knew he couldn't be sure he could keep that promise. But he felt he had to make it. To be honest, he did feel a bit guilty. He had intended, without realizing it, to put the teenager's death on the back burner. Certainly the sheer complexity of Al Land's case had been distracting him, he had to admit. There was something about the case of Nicholas Lowell that was compelling as well.

But there were four cases here and, yes, they all counted. That had not just been something he had said to get Mrs. Foster off his back. Sonny Foster—and Rudy Caliente—required his attention as well.

Another trip to his desk for his car keys. Another few minutes to refresh his memory on his recent notes. And then quickly, while he still could, he was out the door and off to his car.

* * * *

3426 Hatchings was a two-story apartment building on a quiet street about a block off a major thoroughfare. Frank was not surprised when he rang the buzzer under the name "Caliente/Miyakawa" and got no answer.

He did get an immediate reply over the intercom when he buzzed the super.

"Yeah, who is it?" blared a woman's voice.

"Police. Detective Vandegraf."

"You got more questions, huh?" the voice replied. "Okay." There was a buzz and Frank opened the barred door. Immediately down the hall, beyond the stairway, a door opened. A heavyset woman in an old sweatshirt and jeans stepped out, cigarette dangling from her mouth.

"Oh, a new guy. You here about Miz Miyakawa too, I assume?"

Frank was momentarily taken aback. "Somebody's been here about her?"

Now the woman looked surprised. "Uh…*yeah*-uh." She said it with sarcasm as if the answer were obvious to anyone but a fool. "Young guy. Mighta been Chinese?"

"Was his name Lee by any chance?" Frank asked, rubbing the back of his neck.

"That would be the one."

Frank muttered something, hopefully inaudible, under his breath.

She didn't seem to hear it and continued. "How awful what happened to her. She was a very nice young lady." She gave a world-weary shake of the head and a far-off look and took another puff from her butt before returning her gaze to Frank.

Frank was feeling a bit foolish all of a sudden. He found himself rubbing the back of his neck. "Uh, what happened to her. You mean…"

"The murder, I mean. That's why you guys are here."

Tia Miyakawa was dead also? One of the other murders from the other night?

The woman gave Frank a skeptical look, raised an eyebrow. "So, now, you must be looking for her husband, right?"

"Rudy Caliente, you mean. That's her husband?"

"I guess so. I mean, I don't ask questions. None of my business. They've lived here for a couple of years now. Anyway, he wasn't here when the other detective came by and he hasn't returned yet."

She peered at him expectantly.

"And I'm afraid," Frank said, "Mr. Caliente will not be forthcoming at all. May I come in and talk to you?"

* * * *

Tooey's, though not much more than a small hole-in-the-wall lounge, possibly was single-handedly responsible for the local importation of most of South Africa's chromium. Every surface in the place gleamed with a silvery mirror chrome finish.

Jilly decided to leave her sunglasses on.

Dan Lee, who had gallantly volunteered to accompany her on this particular leg of the investigation, seemed extremely distracted, though it was most likely not from the flashy chrome.

Despite it being fairly early in the day, there were three or four taut, pneumatic young women gyrating on an elevated catwalk to excruciatingly loud music, including one with long, thick bright red hair and a skimpy red outfit. Probably Luisa, guessed Jilly, not quite sure why she had come to that conclusion.

This type of place depressed her immensely. Five guys of varying ages sat around the chrome bar that abutted the dancers' area, looking alternately jaded and desperate.

Nobody smiled.

The bartender affirmed Jilly's suspicions and called Luisa over after the song ended. She sauntered over, taking a few moments to work one or two of the customers with a smile and a pat on the back.

"You wanta know about Ricky? He's not in any kind of trouble, is he?" Luisa had huge, deerlike brown eyes and (Jilly noted) glossy, suspiciously over-full lips that never seemed to be able to completely close. "He's such a sweet guy, but the record business can be pretty nasty, can't it?"

"Music business?" Jilly asked.

"Yeah. Ricky works for Casablanca Records. He's helping me get a record deal. He's such a nice, generous guy." She nodded excitedly.

Jilly looked over at Dan, who was looking back at her, and then down at her hands.

"Luisa, Ricky wasn't in the record business." When she looked up, Luisa was blankly staring at her, not reacting. The look was not so much deer-like as deer in the headlights, maybe. Stuffed deer would be closer, perhaps, Jilly decided.

"And I'm afraid something has happened to him."

She waited for dawn to break in the ingenuous sky of the dancer's face. It took a while.

The conversation went quickly and without much promise. Luisa seemed to know less about her supposed boyfriend/ benefactor than Dan and Jilly did.

As they were leaving, Jilly muttered to Dan, "Geez, gives the rest of us redheads a bad name."

"Intellectually, maybe," mused Dan, looking back wistfully. He grinned at Jilly mischievously.

"Does she strike you as a cold-blooded killer?"

Dan shook his head. "It'd take her an hour to figure out which end of the gun to point."

"By the way, nice of you to volunteer to join up with me on this one, partner. Where next? Shall we split up again?"

Dan smiled at the jibe, even seemed to blush a bit.

"It was my pleasure to help out, partner. Yeah, I've got to follow up on Tia Miyakawa. Catch up with you later, Jilly."

* * * *

After some time and effort, Frank tracked down Officer Pardo on car patrol and asked if she had a few minutes. The uniform patrol force had also been stretched thin and for the moment she was working without a partner. She had had a busy morning but suddenly there was a welcome lull for a lunch opportunity, so they sat at a fast food stand and talked over greasy cheeseburgers and fries.

"Sonny Foster," Frank began, popping an underdone French fry into his mouth. "I spoke with his mother today. She mentioned that he hung out with a few neighborhood kids. She didn't know any names."

"Yes, sir, there are a few who hang out there. Mostly teenagers, almost all boys, after school, weekends. The store tries to discourage them but if they purchase a drink or something now and then and don't bother other customers or interfere with parking or the flow, the manager doesn't complain much. He doesn't let them change their oil or work on their cars in the lot but he does let them hang around and talk cars and sports or whatever. You've seen the store. It's the kind of place where the store personnel don't want to be involved any more than they have to."

"You can drop the 'sir,' Officer, feel free to call me Frank. Anybody stand out, problem kids? Any fights, arguments, that type of thing?"

She seemed to relax at least a little, and he noticed her speech grew a bit less formal.

"Not really. A truancy violation now and then during school time. We've had to disperse them once or twice when they got a little rowdy. Once in a while there's an argument that gets loud. Broke up a fight or two. Fist fights, old school. Minor stuff. There's never been any major incidents, no arrests, nobody giving us a hard time. No incidents with weapons or drugs or anything like that. I couldn't even tell you any names, to be honest. Nobody seems to be gang affiliated.

"They're basically good kids, I'd say. Gearheads, not punks or gang-bangers. There's some peeling out in the lot, laying rubber. They do get out of hand like teenagers do. Now and then there's the typical young-male posturing and arguing, and as I said, now and then a scrap. It's all inconsequential."

"So it's not like somebody was out for Sonny, no notable grudges?"

Pardo shook her head. "Nothing stands out, nothing at all. I'll keep my eyes and ears open and let you know if anything comes up."

"Anybody ever get ticketed? For moving violations, parking, stuff like that?"

"Yeah, likely. Not by me. I can ask the other unis if you'd like."

"Can't hurt, thanks. Especially that green car. Let me know if anybody ticketed a green car of any kind. That would be very helpful. Now, how about the other deaths? Know anything about any of them?"

"I never saw either of the others before. None of the regular patrol officers seem to have either. I don't think any of them frequented the Ready Rite."

"Thanks, much appreciated. I'm going over to talk to the Ready Rite manager next. Anything you might come up with could be of help here."

"I'll do what I can, sir."

"And I told you," Frank said, balling up the wrapper from his consumed burger as he stood up, "Cut that 'sir' stuff, okay, Pardo?"

* * * *

"Yeah, I was the manager that night. I already told you guys everything I knew when it all happened."

His name was Sammy and he was maybe thirty, dark-haired and heavy set, on the nervous side, eyes constantly shifting. They stood awkwardly across from one another over the cluttered counter. Frank flipped through his notebook for a moment before continuing.

"I understand. Bear with me here, if you would. Did you know any of the individuals who were killed that evening?"

"I'd seen the kid a few times. He hung around outside with his friends. Never spoke with him, didn't know his name or anything."

"What can you tell me about the kids he hung out with?"

"Oh man, nothing, really. I've been manager here about five months now, y'know? The guy I replaced pulled me aside when I came on and gave me some advice. Part of it was not to confront any of the teenagers out front. He said to call the cops if customers complained or something really radical was going down, you know? Otherwise, he said, I was better off just leaving it alone, minding my own business."

"So you don't know anybody's name, or anything about any of them?"

"Zero," Sammy said with a blank stare. "Already told you guys all this. Like everyone else, I heard the noises. It was all confused, just a bunch of bangs and stuff, people running out to see. Didn't learn anything 'til the cops came in and started asking questions. None of the names meant anything to me."

"And curiously," Frank interjected, eyebrows raised, "absolutely nobody else was outside either. Everyone was in the store and saw and heard nothing. That's pretty remarkable, don't you think, Sammy?"

Sammy just shrugged.

"Do you happen to recall anyone who you saw run outside when the action started?"

Sammy extended his lower lip as if he were actually engaged in thought but quickly shook his head.

Another heavy, resigned sigh. Frank wondered if he should patent his sigh.

"So none of you knew this kid, Sonny Foster, and nobody knew any of the people he associated with, even though they were out here, like, four or five nights a week, driving their cars around, coming in the store to buy stuff?"

"Well, yeah, they did come in to buy stuff," Sammy said.

"But you don't remember anything about them. Any of them. Never talked with them, shot the breeze with them."

"Shot the breeze?" Sammy asked, eyes blank. "What's that mean?"

Frank sighed again. "Like, talked with them."

"Maybe. Don't remember."

Another thought occurred to Frank. "Any of them ever try to buy beer? Or cigarettes?"

"Yeah, probably."

"And you'd have to proof them, right? Look at their ID?"

"Oh yeah. That's a biggie around here. You get fired if you don't proof someone for that, or if you actually sell to them if they're under-age."

"So…maybe someone had an ID, maybe a fake one?"

"Hey, I never sold anything to anyone with a fake ID. Or without ID. No way." Now there was alarm in those previously blank eyes.

"No, that's not what I'm getting at, Sammy. I'm wondering if maybe you saw an ID with a name you might remember?"

The light went out again behind the eyes. There was a long pause before Sammy replied, "Uh…naw, I don't remember."

Frank sighed again. It had been worth a try.

The interview terminated shortly thereafter. Frank departed the Ready Rite knowing no more than he had when he came. In fact, he thought to himself, was it possible he might now know even less? Guys like Sammy just had that effect.

8.

Frank tried to put together the bizarre pieces shaping up in this in-sane jigsaw puzzle as he drove. Nick Lowell's phone had indeed shown a call, somewhat earlier that ill-fated day, to *Langostino*. A phone call confirmed that Lowell had made a reservation for two there that night.

He was heading there right now and he had mixed feelings about where he was going.

It was in his least favorite part of the city, the waterfront.

A block around the corner from *Saint Expedito*.

Langostino was nicely furnished, casual but definitely upscale, with lots of greyish *faux*-weathered wood paneling, heavy oaken tables and chairs. Vintage tinted photos of scenes from long-ago harbors and fisheries were nicely hung on the walls, sort of a Steinbeckian air, or so Frank thought, remembering photos he had seen in a book once.

It was low-lit and quiet. No doubt it would be quite crowded later in the evening.

The manager remembered Nick Lowell and his date from both a photo and the name. "Certainly, Mr. Lowell has come here many times. I took his reservation myself. We reserved our best table for him and his guest. He requested our dessert chef prepare a special little brandied chocolate raspberry torte for her—it was her birthday."

"Did he come here with a lot of guests?"

"Mr. Lowell had different companions, yes. He seems to enjoy the bachelor life. Is there a problem, Detective?"

"You might say that. I don't think Mr. Lowell will be enjoying much of any kind of life from here on out. He died late Thursday night."

"My God, no!"

"I'm afraid so. So I do need to find out some information from you."

"Why…why of course," the manager sputtered. He was a neat little man with careful manners. "May I ask what happened to him?"

"That, I am afraid, is what I am trying to figure out. I know he came here and brought a young lady. What I need to know is what happened after that."

"We all know Mr. Lowell fairly well here. I think he wanted to impress the young lady so we made a little fuss over them. She seemed to like that."

"Did she enjoy being sung 'Happy Birthday' by the wait staff?"

The little man sniffed distastefully. "We don't quite do it that way, Detective. The waiter brought her the torte and I quietly came to the table to extend our best wishes. This isn't a diner."

"So tell me about her. What did she look like?"

"A young Asian woman, dark hair about shoulder-length. Very attractive. A particularly nice smile as I recall. She was wearing a simple but elegant ivory blouse and a mid-length taupe skirt, if memory serves—minimal jewelry."

Memory seemed to be serving, Frank had to admit—quite a course. "Anything else you remember about the evening?"

"He gave her a present while they were having coffee and cordials. A bracelet, it looked like."

"So when they left—did they seem cordial after the cordials?"

The manager allowed himself a small smile at the corners of his mouth. "I try not to intrude upon the privacy of the guests, but, yes, they seemed quite happy and friendly with one another."

"I assume you have valet parking?"

"In this vicinity? We have to. Parking is at a premium, as you must have noticed. This is an old part of town. We have a parking lot but it's tiny."

"Any idea who might have parked Lowell's car?"

"Actually, it was probably either Wayne or Sean. They're both on duty now."

* * * *

Sean, a lean young man whose hair and service jacket were both dark and very short, was trotting back to the valet stand as Frank approached. He remembered Lowell immediately from the photo and the description of the car.

"Of course I remember him. Man, he's a great tipper. We all keep our eyes peeled for that one. Flash guy, pretty cool. Always has a styling car. Usually has a styling lady with him too."

"So you parked his maroon SUV last night?"

"Oh yeah. That was the one. It was a busy night. I had to take it about a block-and-a-half away and park it. But that's why you pay us. We know how to find the good spots, where the car won't be touched up and you don't have to walk."

"Tell me exactly where you parked it, if you can remember? Was it anywhere near *Saint Expedito*?"

Sean smiled. "Yeah! In fact I parked it just about in front of *Saint Expedito*! How'd you know?"

Frank rubbed the back of his neck. "Let's just say I'm psychic."

"Uh…this got anything to do with the stuff going down at *Saint Expedito* the other night?"

Frank stared at the young man briefly. "And what stuff would that be?"

"The crazy bitch with the gun."

Frank momentarily buried his face in his hand. "Maybe you better tell me exactly what you mean."

"I'm running over to get Mr. Lowell's car. I'm about maybe twenty feet away when I see it's boxed in by some jerk's double-parked beat up old SUV, and I'm trying to figure out what I'm gonna do when this guy tears out of the bar and jumps in the beater and peels out. A few seconds later this lady comes running out, stands stock in the middle of the street, takes this stance like cops on TV"—he assumed a two-hand, locked-elbow, spread-legged pose—"and pumps a round at the guy from about a half-block away. Then she runs up to this car parked right in front of Mr. Lowell's. She backs right into Mr. Lowell's car, WHAM, and leaves a dent in his fender, then peels out after the guy. I had to go explain that one to Mr. Lowell and he wasn't too happy. But he was cool, said it wasn't my fault."

So much for using the valet to keep your car from being touched up, Frank thought. "She took a shot at him. You're sure?"

"Oh yeah, for sure. No mistake there."

"What can you tell me about this, uh, crazy bitch with the gun?"

"I don't know. Dark clothing. Jacket came down below her waist. Looked like she might be blonde but I'm not sure."

"See her car?"

"Yeah, it was a silver Lexus."

"And that, you're sure of?"

"Oh yeah...I notice cars like that."

"So she took off down the street after the guy in the truck. Notice anything else about the guy's beater?"

"Dirty white old piece of junk, might have been a Blazer."

"Anything else you remember at all?"

Sean gave that a moment. "I'm afraid not, Detective."

"Here's my card. If you think of anything else at all, it would be a great help if you called me."

The valet took the card and pocketed it. "Is Mr. Lowell all right?"

Frank looked at the earnest young man and put his hand on his shoulder. "Not exactly, I'm afraid."

* * * *

"Jilly, you know I'd help you out if I could, but we're jammed. I can't move anything up."

After several unsuccessful conversations going up the ladder at the crime lab, Jilly had finally arrived at the very top.

Lauren Ochoa, who oversaw the entire operation, had a friendly history with Jilly going back to their earliest days in the department, and might have even owed her a favor or two, but this time she was stymied. At least Lauren was being cordial despite the obvious strain and weariness in her voice.

"Look, you know about the big blowups with the brass. We're still recovering from that. It's all just really bad timing. If this had been before that…"

Jilly nodded behind her phone, leaning back in her chair. She had gotten wind of the major to-do of the previous week involving the higher-ups. A perfect storm of short-staffing, backlogs and political pressures. The worst possible time to come up with four more major crimes—eight, she corrected herself, remembering Frank's cases.

She caught herself in her mental drift.

"Check back with me in a couple of days," Lauren was saying. "Maybe I can slip something in with the blood work or the prints or something. But not today. I'm sorry."

Not many supervisors would be caught saying they were sorry, Jilly reflected as she hung up. Lauren was a special one indeed.

She opened her notebook and perused her notes from earlier in the day, still another canvass along the neighborhood around Parker and San Mateo in search of the true identity of Mary—for some reason, she and Dan had started to refer to her as Mary X, as if they were uncomfortable with the indignity of her not having a real name or simply being "the bag lady" or "the street lady."

They both hated terminologies like "Jane Doe" for anonymous victims. Early on in their partnership, Jilly had discovered that Dan shared her distaste for such depersonalizations. She might have become inured to the harsh realities of her nightly world but she refused to forget that every single tragedy was still ultimately a human one. They were people, almost always with loved ones and friends, and somehow she knew that the day she forgot that was the day she would begin to lose her own humanity.

She had carried around a photo of the unidentified dead woman, taken at the morgue. It was stark but it was all they had. She knocked on doors, stopped individuals on the street and in the stores, inquired of bus and cab drivers. Nobody could identify her. Mary X remained an enigma. She knew she would return tomorrow at some opportune moment and try again. Dan had volunteered to do the same.

Turning her attention back to the searches she had been pursuing, she closed the open windows on her computer screen and sighed. As far as she could ascertain, the Little Command didn't seem to exist anymore. Paulinho Silva was presumed dead since nothing had been heard from him for almost nine years. There was no new information on the group or the man, or on any of his former lieutenants. They had all descended into obscurity—a common enough fate for criminal figures with misguided pretensions to power. The scene and the cast of characters in the Rio underworld appeared to have moved on with the times.

As far as Jilly could tell from earlier phone conversations with experts in global organized crime, the Red Command was a local, almost insular, concern concentrating in Rio. It had tenuous organizational connections in Colombia and one or two other South American nations but did not extend into the United States in any significant way, nor did it seem to have alliances with other organizations that might.

It seemed farfetched to think that after so many years and so much water under the bridge, the cartel would have either ordered or contracted the murder of a relative of a long-deceased rival. Of course it was not totally off the table just yet. A personal vendetta could have burned within some criminal heart. The Colombians might have connections here in the city, and there might be a link to the Red Command, but the idea struck Jilly as awfully flimsy.

She considered the Ricky Wright angle. Not much had come up on him either. A minor player, or more likely a wannabe. No serious brushes with the law—nothing violent, no weapons, no felonies. He was only known on the street to the extent that he was regularly seen in clubs and similar hangouts. There were no apparent aspirations to an extra-legal career of any kind. He seemed to concentrate on making time with girlfriends and concocting various fantasies about his music business career.

Jilly kept running a scenario through her head with minor variations: Ricky finds out about Marina's secret. He tries to ingratiate himself with some "connected" character who might in turn have music connections, or maybe even just access to some intriguing young woman, by passing on the info. It gets back to someone who okays an opportunistic killing. And, perhaps not coincidentally, Ricky gets taken out as well, cleaning up loose ends.

There was something about it she just did not like. Instinctively she felt it didn't make sense. In her forays back to the bar, she had encountered a good number of people who casually knew Ricky, but nobody had ever seen him in the company of gangsters or the like. He did aspire to be a music industry player, and perhaps that was the connection, as meager as it seemed.

She had to continue to consider this avenue, long shot though it might be. And she had to keep a guard on Jane and her husband until she could be sure—or as long as the strained Department would let her keep one on her.

Ricky was a true riddle. He hung out with lots of people but there didn't seem to be a single close friend who actually knew him. No family had yet turned up. She'd have to keep asking, keep looking.

For a lot of reasons, Jilly hoped this would turn out to be a false trail.

It was just too complicated and there were too many bad possibilities if it did turn out to be true.

She got on the phone to Dan. "Hey partner, when you're done with your current follow-up on your stabbing, how would you feel about looking into some angles on our friend Ricky Wright?"

* * * *

The foreman on the loading dock at Builders Depot was a burly hirsute guy named, appropriately enough, Harry. He was in the middle of orchestrating several ongoing tasks but when he saw the proffered detective's shield, he put down his clipboard with an air of resignation and turned his attention to Frank.

"I'll tell you what I told the other guy, Rudy ain't been here today."

Frank put his hands on his hips and stared. "And what other guy would that be?"

"The other detective. Younger Asian guy?"

"Detective Lee."

"Yeah, that's the one. I already told him. Rudy never came to work today. Probably still sleeping it off. Don't you guys talk to each other?"

"Humor me for a minute," Frank said. "How long has Rudy worked here?"

"Maybe three years. Used to be the foreman on the dock here. Good worker…"

Harry trailed off as if he was going to continue the thought but thought better of it.

"You were going to say a good worker except….?"

"…Yeah. Good man, when he's…well, sober."

"So Rudy's got a bit of a problem with the drinking?"

"Now and then. More lately. So what'd he do anyway, if it isn't out of line asking?"

Frank sidestepped the question. "Was he at work Thursday?"

"Until I sent him home. He was tipsy, to say the least. Before lunch."

"Is that usual for Rudy?"

"Lately he's been bent outa shape about something. I think it's his wife. Something at home. Whatever, I told him he wasn't good for anything, told him to clock out and go home, get some sleep. He said something about there being nothing at home for him anymore. Probably went and had a few more. So then he went and got himself in some kinda trouble, it sounds like?"

"Himself and a few other people. Violent guy?"

"When he's sober, naw, he's a pussycat. Probably lets people walk over him too much in fact. When he drinks he gets a little touchy. Still not violent, exactly, just a little sensitive? It's like he's got a line, and as long as he doesn't cross it...."

Harry seemed reticent to volunteer too much more information. "Hey, look, Detective, I'm sorry, but as you can see, there's a lot going on here right now, and I've already talked to that other detective..."

"I don't think Detective Lee mentioned that Rudy is dead," Frank said. That stopped Harry in his tracks. "And may have taken a couple of people with him. So how about I take just a little more of your time?"

* * * *

When Dan Lee had first made detective, he could have been assigned as a partner to several experienced colleagues, and he well appreciated that he had lucked out being paired with Jill Garvey.

One of the other possibilities could have been Detective Marlon Morrison, and as he sat talking with the man now, he reflected on his good fortune. Morrison was a weathered veteran but there was something about him that definitely rubbed Dan the wrong way.

"Ricky Wright. Sure, I've heard the name."

"Anything specifically come to mind with him?"

Morrison shrugged. "Not really. Minor street hustler type of guy. There's dozens of 'em."

"Any chance he could have been involved with anybody more serious? Drug dealers, that type of thing?"

Morrison scrunched in his chair, looking bored and impatient. He waved a hand. "Nothing comes to mind."

"So how do you know him? Ever arrest him?"

"I think I questioned him...robbery last year. Yeah, that's it. Holdup of a club. Couple guys got shot. No deaths. Wright was one of the people there. I think he was with the DJ. He seemed a little off but I couldn't establish any involvement on his part. Never came to arrest or charges or anything of that nature. I still think he might have had something to do with it."

Dan's interest was piqued. "Why's that?"

"Well, we figured there was an insider, so to speak, someone who knew when and where there was cash? Wright was one of the guys who seemed to know the club owners and workers. Nothing substantial."

"Ever find the perps?"

"Nope."

Big surprise, Dan thought. Morrison had a reputation for putting in the minimal effort. He was likely coasting to his anticipated retirement. Still, he had been around a long time and if anybody in the squad room would know something it would likely be him.

"Any chance that this involved anyone from out of town or out of country? Drug cartels, syndicates, anything like that? Some kind of grudge maybe?"

"Doubt it. Couple, three punks decided to knock over a club. We looked at regular patrons, business associates of the owners, that kind of thing. Thought maybe there'd be some word out after the fact, but no luck."

"What kind of business associates did this club involve?"

"The usual. There's always somebody unsavory back there. Lower level types. This wasn't like a mobbed-up establishment. There's not actually a lot of that, and even when there is one, you'd have to be crazy to try to rob a connected joint."

"So there's no way you can see that Ricky Wright would have had some connection to anything, uh, above his station?"

"Above his station. Nice way to put it, Lee, you got a way with words. Not that I could see. He's just a dime a dozen hustler. Not the brightest one either."

"But you do think he might have had something to do with the robbery."

Morrison shrugged again. "Maybe yes, maybe no. Couldn't prove anything."

"So where was this club and who were the owners?" Dan asked, reaching for his notebook. He quietly felt relieved that this conversation was coming to a conclusion.

* * * *

The club was called Selena, after its highest profile owner, Selena Chance. Dan doubted she was a majority owner by any means, but she was a perfect choice for the face of the establishment. She was in her late thirties, personable and highly attractive, a local performer and minor celebrity, and her patrons in general were fans, delighted to interact with her.

It was fairly late by the time Dan was able to get to the club and the music, dancing and partying were in full swing. He had to wait while she tended to her proprietorial duties, making the rounds welcoming and chatting with her customers and dealing with matters at hand.

She finally greeted him and indicated a staircase to a small, nicely appointed office-lounge. There were low couches, a mirrored bar, and a small desk. Photos of Selena with various notables lined the walls. When she closed the doors, the room was reasonably insulated from the noise of the club. Only a vague muffled thump of bass could be heard intermittently. She motioned for Dan to have a seat and offered him a drink, which he passed up with a wave of a hand.

"So how may I help you?" she said with a disarming smile, gracefully seating herself across from him. Dan got right to business.

"Are you familiar with Ricky Wright?"

"Sure, I knew him. I heard what happened. Terrible thing."

"What was his connection to this club?"

"He didn't really have one, not officially. He hung out here now and then. He knew my DJs. I think he liked to associate with anybody who had anything to do with the music business."

"So he was in the music business himself?"

Selena raised her eyebrows. "I think he *wanted* to be, do you know what I mean? Ricky really wanted to be a part of that scene. He liked to tell people he was involved in recording deals, things like that."

"But you don't think he was actually in the business."

Selena shook her head with a knowing smile. "Ricky was a wannabe. He picked up girls with stories like that, tried to impress certain guys. Most of them saw through his stories. Now and then he'd score with a young woman not quite so wise to things, shall we say."

"It doesn't sound like you thought much of him."

"Oh, Ricky was a sweet enough guy, Detective, uh…what was your name again?"

"Lee. Detective Lee."

"Of course, forgive me. Ricky could be very charming and very amusing. He was likable enough, and he was kind of handsome, in his way. But he could also be tiresome, if you get my meaning. A lot of people got bored with him. Or fed up."

"Sounds like maybe you were one of them. How exactly do you mean fed up?"

"Well, Ricky tended to overstep his bounds. He would be overly familiar with people and sometimes they were the wrong people." She hesitated a moment as if considering what she was about to say. "He would hit on women indiscriminately, even if they were far out of his league, do you know?"

The implication was clear that Selena was one of them. But this was an intriguing new possibility.

"So Ricky may have made overtures to the wrong young woman, perhaps somebody's girlfriend or wife?"

"Oh, he got set straight on that score a few times, yes."

"Could he ever have pushed the boundary too far, earned a grudge from the wrong person?"

Selena laughed. "It's not out of the question, I suppose. But Ricky was the type to charm his way out of a confrontation, or in any case back off. He wasn't the bravest guy. Once or twice he did get things explained to him a bit more physically. He got the message and moved on."

Still, Dan considered, something worth returning to, maybe.

"So Ricky wanted to be a major player. Were there patrons here that he might have especially admired or tried to emulate?"

"Probably quite a few. We have a rather high profile clientele. A number of music and entertainment industry figures. Ricky would try to play up to many of them."

"Was there anybody in particular you can think of that he especially wanted to impress?"

"The guy he made the biggest play for was Neil Cassara—Tech-Now Entertainment?" She raised her eyebrows, expecting recognition.

Dan drew a blank.

"Ricky would have loved to get a foot in that door," she continued. "He made himself a bit of a nuisance. We had to step in and suggest he stop bothering Neil." She shook her head. "That was the one time I had to have a talk with Ricky and set him straight. After that he left Neil alone. Kind of like a restraining order."

She smiled sweetly at her own joke and Dan couldn't help smiling as well.

"But I don't want to give the impression Ricky was a problem. This is a club; people drink, dance, let off steam. We allow a certain leeway within reasonable limits. Usually he behaved and enjoyed himself here, observed those limits, and everything stayed cool."

"I understand there was an incident here last year?"

"The robbery, yeah." She rolled her eyes. "Unfortunate. It was late afternoon, not too many people in the place. No bouncers stationed at the door yet. Some guys came in, followed the manager into the back office—the bigger one—pulled guns and demanded the take. It happened to be just before the regular cash pickup. We have a service that comes by in an armored car at regular but irregular periods."

"So it's not precisely predictable," Dan interjected.

"Exactly."

"But they seemed to know when this was going to happen?"

"The police certainly thought so. It was curious."

"How many robbers? Were they masked?"

"Three. At least, three went into the office. No masks, nothing. Our accountant was back there tallying the money when they entered. They had him put the money into some bags they pulled out. The manager and the accountant cooperated, nobody was going to get hurt, it seemed. It all took about five minutes—that is, until they came back out."

"Then what happened?"

"One of our security guys, Trask, figured out what was happening. He hit the alarm and drew his own gun at the bottom of the stairs. There were some shots exchanged, people running for cover and screaming. Nobody, it would seem, was a great shot. Trask and another employee got hit. Nothing serious. They both got taken to the ER and recovered. The gunmen got away in the excitement. The wall caught a couple of bullets, a mirror got shattered. Cops *finally* showed up"—Dan caught the dig—"that was that."

"There was some thought there was an insider, someone who maybe kept their eyes and ears open and knew about the cash?"

"That was explored, without much success. You're not thinking Ricky had anything to do with that?" Selena seemed genuinely surprised at the prospect.

"Is it possible?"

She bit her lower lip and thought for a moment, then shook her head. "I don't see it. I just don't." She left it at that.

Perhaps he was still developing his investigative instincts, but it struck Dan as just a bit insincere. He wished that Jilly could have been here as well, to compare notes on this.

"You're not the only owner, is that correct?"

"That's right. There are two others."

"And who are they?"

"Lowell and Tony Michaels."

The names meant nothing to Dan. "Either one of them present tonight?"

"No, they're usually here during the day taking care of matters at hand. They're sometimes here in the evenings but in general I'm the presence when the club is in full swing."

"So the best time to speak with them would be during the afternoon?"

"You could likely catch one of them around most days, yes. But it's not guaranteed. The head manager, Sergio, is more likely to be on the premises."

He threw out the loaded question, not really expecting a truthful answer. Were there ever, to her knowledge, any underworld-related figures connected to or in attendance at the club? She expressed the expected shock at the very question. Of course not. She seemed just a bit less forthcoming thereafter. He inwardly chastised himself for even asking—or at least for not waiting until the very end to ask.

Dan explored a few more avenues with her, none of which seemed overly promising.

Finally there was a pause in the conversation and Selena looked up expectantly and said, "If there isn't anything else, I really should get back."

Dan replied that he thought he had covered everything for the moment and stood up. He remembered to leave her a card and fumbled in his pocket for one, handing it to her as she also rose from her seat. She gave him another smile, this time more reserved, and a handshake and escorted him out into the blare of the club.

On the street, returning to his car, Dan considered the options.

Ricky Wright was an unimpressive man apparently desperate to impress. He urgently wanted to be part of whatever was going on. Clearly he had a big ego, a big mouth, and bad judgment. He could have given the word on the cash in the club to someone who followed through on the robbery—or maybe he was just suspected of it.

Either way there could have been a similar fatal result. Had there been a payback?

Neil Cassara, the entertainment big shot whom Ricky was harassing, was another avenue to explore. Maybe Ricky continued to overstep his boundaries outside the club. Two possibilities occurred to Dan: one, the guy's connected and somehow Ricky pushed him way too far; alternatively, Ricky blabbed something in an effort to impress him. If the guy's connected maybe someone else overheard the conversation.

Too many possibilities were opening up. Dan Lee needed to sit down with Jilly and sort it all out.

* * * *

"So what've we got?" Dan asked, flopping into his chair.

Jilly leaned across his cluttered desk and sighed wearily. It had been a long day trying to hit as many objectives as they could, and finally they had reunited here in the squad room to compare notes.

They were hardly the only ones overburdened at the moment. Despite the late hour, detectives, clericals, and uniformed personnel bustled back and forth around the squad room, everyone looking distracted, on their own mission, oblivious to everything else.

"Not a blessed lot, Dan, and then again maybe way too much. Tell me about your day first."

"Well, like you suspected, Ricky Wright might be a can of worms. He seems to have indiscriminately opened his mouth a lot. He might have been involved in a club robbery, and there might have been some phantom owners of that club who didn't like it."

"That sounds like a lot of ifs," Jilly sighed. "And he still might have divulged something about Marina to someone who told someone else. We still can't even be sure which one of them was the intended victim. I tried to trace down any possible connection there today without any luck.

"And I spent another couple hours around Parker and San Mateo in search of our friend Mary X. Not a blessed soul seems to know her."

"Not much on Tia either," Dan said. "She's a mystery woman as well. No family to speak of. Nobody seems to know where she worked, anything like that. Her husband seems to have disappeared too. I've been chasing ghosts all day."

"Lovely," muttered Jilly. "Lucky us."

A shadow fell across the papers smeared all over Dan's desk and someone cleared his throat. Dan looked up. Jilly looked over her shoulder.

Frank Vandegraf, hands in pockets, stood there looking tired and pensive as always.

"I think we should talk," he said quietly.

9.

"So Tia Miyakawa was stabbed to death by her husband Rudy," Dan was saying, looking at the scribbled note cards they had spread around his desk, "after he found out she was cheating on him with this car salesman guy."

"But first, I'm thinking, Rudy killed Al Land," Frank added. "That one's a bit of a puzzle. Rudy was financially strapped, and it's conceivable someone made him an irresistible offer to take out Al.

"But now I'm more inclined to believe it was a case of mistaken identity. Rudy doesn't strike me as the assassin type. The car salesman's vehicle was parked right in front of the bar. Both guys were wearing leather jackets. Maybe all Rudy saw was Tia getting into Lowell's SUV, only got a glimpse of the guy, and followed them. Walks into the bar, sees a guy about the same build as Lowell, there are two drinks on the table and his companion is in, er, the jane, and he figures he's got the right guy. So he just shoots him and runs. What I *don't* understand is why he would reach in and take Al's Glock."

"And why didn't he wait for Tia to come out of the restroom, if he thought it was Tia, and plug her too," said Jilly.

"Probably scared. He couldn't have been thinking too straight. Sounds like he was pretty ripped and through the wringer."

"So he takes off and Land's wife chases him," Dan added.

"Apparently takes a potshot at him, too," Frank said. "But I got her gun and it hadn't been fired."

"So she's got two guns," Jilly said.

"Perhaps," said Frank, remembering his failure to follow up on that in *Saint Expedito* when he suddenly had to move on. "There's another possibility as well. I'll need to discuss that with Anita at the first possible opportunity."

"Apparently at some point Rudy catches sight of Lowell and Tia in the SUV and realizes he's made a big mistake," Jilly continued.

"There's a bullet hole in the passenger side door of Lowell's car," Frank said. "Maybe something like this happened: Lowell drops Tia off at the quickie mart where she picks up some items she decides she needs for the rest of their hot night to come. Rudy pulls up and takes a shot at him, Lowell panics and drives off. Rudy gets out of the car and comes after Tia, just coming out of the store. She sees him and runs."

"Rudy uses a knife instead of his gun?" Dan asked.

"Maybe he's left it in the car, not thinking. Or maybe…"

Frank was pensive for a long moment, working it out. He remembered the gun and the box of shells. "Maybe he needed to reload and there wasn't time."

"Two bullets in Land, one in Lowell's car," Dan said. "Five shots in the .38 if it's fully loaded. What about the rest?"

"Let's wait. We'll come back to that," Frank said. "I bet the blood on the knife in Rudy's truck and on the hoodie matches Tia's."

"Whenever we get those results back," Dan said resignedly.

"He takes her wallet and some other stuff, maybe to make it look like a robbery, maybe to make it harder to identify her, whatever. Maybe he just grabs it reflexively. We know he's not thinking too straight at this point. Anyway, he gets back in the truck, strips off his bloody jacket, and takes off to find Lowell. Lowell is still his primary objective."

"And he finds him in that scuzzy parking lot," Jilly said grimly, pushing the cards around very gently, as if they were actual human lives she was manipulating. "And if he'd needed to reload, he must have done so, since then he takes Lowell out."

"Lowell was in the process of calling Tia on his cell phone when Rudy found him," Frank said. "He had her on his speed dial and had started the call. He might have stopped in the lot to calm down, take stock and contact her, then figure out what to do next."

"*If* this is what happened," Jilly added, "at this point Lowell would have no idea what had happened to Tia. Maybe he wouldn't have quite put it all together in his head yet? He might not have realized it was Rudy coming after him. He might not even have known what Rudy actually looked like!"

"A lot of *if*'s," Dan said with a shake of his head. "I don't know."

"When the ballistics and the DNA come back I gotta believe it all matches up," Frank muttered, rubbing a hand over his mouth.

"So then what happened to Rudy?" Dan asked. "Just randomly hit, or was someone taking him out?"

"Another person is involved in all this?" Jilly asked.

"Accidental hit-and-run seems a remarkable coincidence," Frank admitted. "And if he had the Glock, I still haven't found it anywhere."

Jilly picked up the thread as Frank's voice tailed off. "So maybe there's some connection with this D'Yquem guy…or one of Al's numerous other fervent admirers?"

"I can't dismiss it just yet," Frank allowed.

"Well, anyway," said Dan, "at least one of our DBs—excuse me, one of our victims—is looking good. If only we could catch a break on the others."

Frank looked at him thoughtfully. "Tell me about them," he said. "I have a feeling there's a lot more to Thursday night's story."

* * * *

"That vermin is dead, you say?" Cassandra Washington said without a drop of remorse, feigned or otherwise. "Cannot say as I am sorry."

"He was under investigation for allegedly threatening you," Frank said, watching her as he spoke. They were sitting at a remote table in a coffee shop. She was a slight wispy woman, perhaps forty, unsmiling, dressed in a collar-up trench coat, beret and sunglasses. It was clear to Frank how frightened she was…trying to stay incognito.

"*Allegedly*, my foot," she spat. "The louse was calling me in the middle of the night telling me bad things were going to happen if we didn't retract our suit against DKM. The guy thinks he's some kind of spy commando or something. Remember that guy who worked for Nixon who lived in a tough-guy dream world? That was what Al Land was like. What a jerk. How did he die?"

"Shot at close range." Frank kept his eye on her. There was a short silence. She sipped her latte from the cardboard cup and nodded as if it made sense.

"I was so happy when the indictments came down on him. I figured maybe we'd all be safe now."

"Did the threats stop?"

"Who knows for how long, but yes, they did. You're thinking one of us involved in the lawsuits shot him?"

Frank shrugged. "Just looking at everything."

"This guy was a real piece of work, Detective. I've no doubt he consorted with a lot of scary people and I'm sure he mouthed off at a lot of them. But he was a bully at heart and that means he was a coward. The kind of people he and D'Yquem's thugs liked to threaten were people like me, whom he thought he could put a scare into and wouldn't fight back."

Frank waited a while before answering. "Maybe somebody finally decided they'd had enough and weren't going to take it anymore."

Her turn to shrug. "Maybe. I was happy to let the law step in. We were all in way over our heads. We shouldn't have ever made any deals with D'Yquem to begin with. What did we know? Lambs to slaughter."

"This was a very high-profile lawsuit."

"Sure."

"Anybody, maybe under the radar?"

"I don't get you, Detective."

"I mean, somebody Al messed with who didn't stand to be protected by the lawsuit or the indictment? Somebody a little more—"

"Criminal?" Cassandra finished, pinching the corners of her mouth. "In this particular case, I can't think of anybody like that. But as I said— he slept with dogs. He must have gotten a lot of fleas."

* * * *

As distasteful as it was to Dan, another conversation with Marlon Morrison seemed the easiest way to at least get started, and so there they sat in the squad room with cups of coffee.

"You said you thought there might be some shadow owners behind Selena, right? These Michaels brothers, maybe they're just beards or fronts?"

"It's conceivable," Morrison yawned, showing little to no interest in the subject. "But don't try to read too much into that. Sometimes it's just a matter of someone wanting to stay out of the spotlight. Maybe they don't want to be publicly associated with the enterprise. Or maybe they're someone, who for whatever reason, would have trouble obtaining a license for the joint. I doubt the place is mobbed up—not in a major way."

"How about a guy named Neil Cassara? He owns something called Tech-Now Entertainment?"

"Oh sure, everybody knows him. Major player. Music, films, gaming, all sorts of stuff. You don't read the papers? I guess a young guy like you is more an internet type, but still. Watch TV?"

"Not a lot of any of those," Dan admitted. "So tell me about this guy Cassara."

"He's like what you'd call a mogul. All sorts of deals, works out of Hollywood and New York and other places. He's got homes all over, jets around, but he grew up here and keeps a big old mansion up in the hills."

"Any chance this guy is connected?"

Morrison made a raspberry sound. "Back to the mobbed up stuff again. I'm telling you, forget that angle, Lee."

"Okay, but if he's a mogul, like you say, he's not exactly a choir boy, right? If a guy sufficiently ticked him off, isn't it possible someone close to him might have taken it upon themselves to remedy the situation?"

Morrison raised his hands in exasperation. "Something you're going to learn here, Detective, is that the simplest answer is more often the right one. You're looking for conspiracies."

And you, Dan thought as he stood up, are used to looking for the easiest way out. He headed across the room for the computer.

* * * *

As expected, neither of the Michaels brothers was present at Selena when Dan showed up. The place was empty except for a small crew of bartenders, waiters, and other employees, busily setting up for the evening.

He was directed back to the small office at the top of the stairs once again, where he found Sergio, the lead manager. He was a husky nervous sort, not the sociable type. He looked put out by Dan's intrusion but once he saw the badge and ID, he set aside his papers and sat down to talk.

Dan opened with a few routine questions about the earlier robbery and some inquiries about Ricky Wright. Sergio said that he had indeed been the manager confronted by the gunmen and forced to take them upstairs to the office. He claimed he didn't know Ricky.

"How long have you been with this club?"

"I've been employed here almost five years now. I've been lead manager for the past two or so."

"What can you tell me about the Michaels brothers, the co-owners?"

Sergio shrugged. "What's there to tell?"

"Well, I'm not familiar with them. Did they start this place?"

"Yeah, they were the original proprietors. Then they brought Selena in. She was a local celeb, they knew she'd be a great draw, so they offered her a share and named the club after her. It was a brilliant move. The rest is history."

"So where did they get their money from? Starting a place like this has to be expensive."

More shrugs. "I dunno, I think they're like investment brokers or something of the sort, something in the financial world. They were interested in running this as a sideline."

Dan flipped through the notes he had made prior to coming to the club. He spoke while perusing them.

"They don't seem to spend much time here. Not all that much interested in running it, apparently."

"Tony's usually here a couple days a week. Lowell is on the move a lot, with his financial business. I do most of the grunt work."

"Any chance there are any, what you might call silent partners, involved in the ownership here?"

"What do you mean? There's Tony, there's Lowell, there's Selena."

"No," Dan said, looking up. "There's someone else. The original investment in the startup was pretty substantial. The return is pretty substantial as well. I have a feeling if the numbers were looked into closely, the Michaels brothers' accounts wouldn't add up. You've got two guys supposedly really interested in a place that they never come to. Come on, Sergio." He winked. "You can tell me."

"I don't know what you're talking about," Sergio said, staring at Dan blankly. "Everything is on the up and up here, Detective. What you see is what you got."

* * * *

"So what's up, Officer Pardo?" They were standing in the same parking lot once again, this time with the light of day still dying in the sky.

Frank's hours of chasing down whistle-blowers had not been fruitful. He was hoping for something—anything, to make his day.

The officer had her notebook out and was flipping through pages diligently.

"Thank you for coming out here, Detective. I think I might have something for you on that bludgeoning. As I told you the other day, there are a group of guys who hang out in this lot fairly regularly, maybe buy some motor oil in the Ready Rite for their cars and change it out here in the lot, brown-bag a beer, things like that. Big gearheads, really into their cars, almost always exclusively young men. I came by earlier today to talk to them."

"You're not going to tell me somebody gave up Sonny Foster's killer, I assume," Frank said.

"No sir. Nobody saw anything, nobody knows anything. None of them were even here the other night, even though they were, if you follow me. What we *did* notice was what *wasn't* there."

"Come again, Officer?"

"There's one kid who hasn't been around the last couple of days. He's almost always out here, day in and day out. And all of a sudden nobody's seen him and nobody knows anything about him."

"Who is this kid?"

"Luther Newcombe. They call him Newk. He's like eighteen, nineteen years old. Drives a green tricked-out old Mustang."

"Hmm…"

"And as you know, Detective, there was green paint from the collision where Rudy Caliente was hit."

"Yes, Officer Pardo, I recall." Frank rubbed the back of his neck and looked around. "Got any other info on this Newk guy?"

"Had his driver's license run." There was a slip of paper stuck into her notebook that she handed him.

"Officer," Frank said, taking the paper, "Someday when you make detective, remind me to come congratulate you and say I saw it coming. Thank you."

For the moment she couldn't stay entirely decorous and smiled and blushed despite herself.

10.

The Newcombe address was a small house in an older working-class neighborhood. Nobody answered the doorbell and there didn't seem to be anybody at home. There were no cars parked out front, green Mustang or otherwise. There was a small windowless garage adjacent to the house, locked up tight.

He knocked on neighbors' doors and had no better luck, though he did detect a slight flutter of curtains in one window. He decided to try back later—or perhaps send some uniforms over to pick the kid up.

* * * *

"Yeah, I've known Rudy for a long time. We went to high school together. Went fishing together a lot. Rudy loved to fish especially." Tommy Nathanson was a tall, youthfully good-looking, African-American guy. "This is terrible what happened to him. Any idea who hit him?"

"Working on it," Frank said.

They were sitting together in the break room of the copy shop where Tommy worked, two half-full styrofoam cups of dreadful coffee in front of them.

"Rudy had some problems lately, didn't he?" he added.

Tommy shook his head sadly. "Yeah. You know, he's one of the nicest guys you could hope to meet, just a really good guy, but when he gets to drinking like he did…..man, everything just went down the drain for him."

"I hear he got demoted at his job."

"Uh-huh. He had money hassles, and he was starting to worry about his wife. He thought she was seeing some other guy."

"Tell me about that."

"Not much to tell. He figured she was seeing this guy with more money than him, a nicer car, that kind of stuff. He really cared for her. He used to say how lucky he was he had found her. It was eating him up."

"So he was spending a lot of time in the bar, maybe doing other things?"

Tommy nodded. "To be honest, he was getting pretty messed up. I was worried about the guy. Tried to get him to go fishing with me, maybe get away from all this, but he just kept getting deeper into his funk, you know what I mean?"

"Did he say if he planned to do anything?"

"Yeah, he was talking about running this guy down—I mean, finding him, that's all—and having it out with him."

"Did you see him the day he got killed?"

"Oh yeah. We were in Worthy's, over on Main. He got sent home from his job. Instead he stopped there and had a few." Tommy smiled a little sheepishly. "Well, and there I was too. I had to head to work myself, but I told him he should go home and sleep it off. He looked pretty terrible. He told me he was going to do that, go home. I made him promise. Guess he didn't do that."

Frank rubbed the back of his neck. "Is there any chance Rudy would have been looking to make some money on the side, maybe doing something less than legal?"

"You mean like dealing or something?"

"I was thinking more like hurting someone."

"Aw, no way, Detective. No way. Rudy wasn't a violent guy. We went hunting a coupla times and even though he liked to hunt, he wasn't even any good at that. Hated to hurt animals. He was pretty gentle. He just couldn't have hurt someone. There's no way he could have put someone into pain for money."

"Rudy shot two people," Frank said. "And he stabbed his wife. They're all dead."

Tommy gazed back at Frank, stunned, taking all this in. "There's no way."

"There is, I'm afraid. It's true."

"This had to have been a, what do you call it, a crime of passion. There's no way Rudy Caliente was a cold-blooded killer."

"Have you ever heard of a guy named Al Land?"

"Nope. Who is he?"

"One of the people Rudy killed. Land had a lot of enemies but seems to have been a stranger to Rudy. You don't think someone would have hired Rudy to take him out, and then turned around and killed Rudy?"

"Detective, you are describing someone totally unlike Rudy. No way." He sat thinking for a long time before speaking again. "Rudy was pretty turned around over Tia. Was this Land guy her boyfriend?"

"No, that would seem to be the other guy he killed. Land didn't seem to have any connection to Rudy's situation."

"It's a stretch, a real stretch, but…I could see how Rudy might have killed Tia and her boyfriend if things just sorta got outa hand, just sorta happened. He was that much into her. This other guy—I got no idea. It makes no sense that Rudy would kill for hire. It's just not him. No freaking way."

* * * *

Frank had been sitting at his desk for a long time, mulling it all over for still another long time.

He wanted it to be the simple explanation—that Rudy had shot Al Land out of mistaken identity. But he had to be sure. Too many people had it in for Land. And someone could have gone to the trouble to tie up the loose ends and take out Rudy. It made things way too complicated. He had to cover the doubt. Maybe he was going to have to go back to those lovely folks at DKM again. He definitely was going to have to talk with Anita again.

And there was still the matter, which had almost slipped his mind, of sending someone over to look for Luther Newcombe.

The phone on his desk rang.

"Detective, this is Mallory, down at the desk. There's somebody here needs to talk to you."

Luther Newcombe was tall for his age. In an earlier time someone might have described him as a long drink of water. He could have been any kind of a martini, Frank mused, since he seemed both shaken and stirred.

Sitting on either side of him in the interview room across the table were Luther's stern, prematurely graying father and his slightly-built mother, her eyes wide and filled with tears.

"I've been doing my term in the Middle East," Lawrence Newcombe was telling Frank. "Only got back a couple of months ago. Couldn't be here for my son but I've got to be here for him now. I told him this was the only thing to do."

"And it's the right thing, Mr. Newcombe," Frank said. "I appreciate that. I know this can't be easy for any of you."

"Took me a couple of days to convince him to come in with me. It was all an accident. Boy didn't mean to hurt no one. You got to realize that."

Frank nodded and looked at Luther.

"Sonny and me got into it," Luther said quietly, hesitantly, not looking up from the table. "He's a lot bigger and tougher'n me and he used to give me a lot of sh…" He glanced at his mother. "…the business, you know? This time I decided to stand up to him and he started punchin' me around. He was twisting my arm behind my back, pushin' me to the ground, and callin' me some things, you know? Personal, insulting things? In front of everybody and everything. All I wanted was for him to stop. I grabbed this bar lyin' near me on the ground and whacked him with it, 'cross the head. He let go of me. I guess I hit him a coupla times. I was pissed off."

"Mind the language in front of your mother," his father interrupted.

"Sorry. I was mad, is what I meant. Guess I hit him pretty hard. I got scared and when he let me go I ran for my car. All I wanted to do was get away from there. I didn't even see the other guy. I hit him, musta run him over, smacked into a couple of other cars in the lot, and just got out of there. It was all kind of a blur in my mind, you know? I wasn't seeing straight. I didn't even know I had killed either one of them until I saw it on the TV."

"He's not a bad boy," Lawrence Newcombe said solemnly, putting his arm around his son's shoulders. "He was scared. He shouldn't have run. Now he needs to do the right thing."

Frank made some notes on the pad in front of him. "Well, he's done the right thing, Mr. Newcombe, and I thank you all for that."

"He's got to take the responsibility for this, Detective, but isn't there something you can do for him?"

"We'll see," Frank said. "I'll do what I can."

"Bad night all around," Luther murmured quietly. "I should never'a gone out at all."

"A lot of people shouldn't have gone out," Frank agreed, "that particular night."

* * * *

"Still looking over that map?" Dan asked.

Frank, bent over the desk perusing an unfolded map of the city, glanced up at him.

"So where's Jilly?"

His desk had been cleared of the usual clutter and completely covered by the spread-out map. Frank had used a red marker to put big spots on the crime scenes of that evening.

As ever, he liked to work the old-fashioned way.

"She's around. What've you got?"

"Bear with me here," he said. "Just a thought."

He began running his finger, street to street, while he talked, bringing his finger down with some emphasis on the various red dots. *Saint Expedito*. Parker and San Mateo. *Las Candilejas*. Webley. The Ready Rite.

Jilly had mysteriously appeared at some point behind Frank's right shoulder. Neither man had noticed until she exclaimed, "Are you kidding me?"

Frank looked over his shoulder at her. "Maybe it's all a stretch, but it fits. And it pretty much covers everything. You got anything better?"

Jilly and Dan looked at one another for a long time, and she started to walk away.

"Where you going?"

"To my phone. I'm sure they haven't gotten to the ballistics tests yet. Better add a couple more."

"Frank," Dan said, carefully inspecting the map, silently replaying the earlier narration as he trailed a finger over the route, "this is screwed up enough to be right."

"I wasn't sure until a little while ago. Now I'm starting to convince myself."

"If the ballistics and the labs all come back right…"

"Whenever that's going to happen," Frank said, grimacing. "Meanwhile, I guess there's one more conversation I've still got to have."

11.

"How was the service, Anita?"

They were sitting on the balcony of the hillside condo Al and Anita had owned for several years. It had a view to the west of the far-off harbor. It was a chilly, overcast day but neither of them seemed to mind.

Anita shrugged. "Okay, I guess. Not too many people. DKM sent a few guys. The minister got a couple things wrong. Guess that's what comes of not being a churchgoer…when you die, there's no clergyman to remember you right."

Frank nodded without comment.

Al wasn't exactly a man with a lot of friends. But he wouldn't have been surprised at a lot of ornate Godfather-like crocodile-tear sendoffs from the people who wished they had done the job instead.

People like Billy Wilde or Duane Scudder.

They talked for a few more minutes about minutiae: the service; Anita's plans for the condo. Finally she put down her coffee cup and looked Frank straight in the eye, right through her tinted glasses.

"So thanks for the condolences and all, but what's really on your mind, Detective?"

Frank looked at her long and hard before saying it outright.

"So do you still have Al's gun, Anita?"

She returned his stare, just as steady.

"That nut job who shot him took it, you know that. So you never found it?"

"Nope. Funny thing about that. Just about everything else in the world was in that guy's car, but no Glock."

More awkward silence accompanying unbroken stares. It was like one of those games kids play to see who blinks first.

Finally Frank continued. "Someone saw you taking a shot at Rudy as he drove away. You didn't fire your own gun—you were nice enough to hand that over to me right away to demonstrate that fact. You shot another gun...Al's. You grabbed it from his shoulder holster when you ran to him."

Anita still said nothing.

"You know, GSR can last a long time, Anita."

"Dubious. And *if* a paraffin test showed that I fired a gun recently? So what? I'm a frigging PI. I go to the firing range two, three times a week."

"Cut the crap, Anita." The staring contest continued.

It was Anita who broke the spell, picking up her coffee cup and sighing before taking a decidedly unladylike swig to empty it.

"I don't have Al's gun, Detective."

"So you disposed of it. That would be a smart move. If, that is, there was some reason to do so."

She didn't say anything.

"So you chased Rudy Caliente. Where did you go?"

"I followed him a couple blocks and lost him."

"Where specifically?"

"I don't know—up Corning a ways, over Lawson or Parker or one of those. He was like a bat out of hell. I finally turned around and went back to the bar."

"You caught up with him, is what I'm thinking. You took a potshot or two at him, didn't you?"

Anita said nothing.

"In a building at San Mateo and Parker, there's a bullet in the wall. I'm guessing it's a nine millimeter. And that the shell casings we found there will look a lot like the one I tracked down on the street in front of *Saint Expedito*."

Anita shook her head, still looking down. "I missed the bastard."

"Come again?"

"Pulled up right next to him at a light and had him in my sights. He had his arm out the window and he wasn't paying attention. I'm a lousy shot. Missed him *twice*. He floored it and that was that. I turned around and came back to the bar."

"Did you really dump the gun?"

She looked up at Frank and didn't reply.

"What were you worried about? Why not just tell me?"

"Tell you what—that I raced through the streets discharging a weapon? A few laws being broken there, Detective? Stuff that could jeopardize my license?"

Frank stood up. She had broken more laws than she might actually realize. Maybe. "Thanks for the coffee, Anita. I think you better call your lawyer."

He hated having to take out the handcuffs. He debated if they were really necessary.

12.

Several separate items had appeared on different pages of the morning newspaper over a few days—for those who still read the actual newspaper.

One story noted in brief that three partially decomposed bodies had been found in a landfill in a small township about a hundred miles to the north. Authorities stated that there were as yet no identifications of the bodies but that fingerprints or dental records should ultimately reveal who they were.

A second item accounted that one Sergio Pacelli, manager of a local bar and dance club, had been reported missing by his wife. Five days previous, he had presumably gone to work as usual, but she later discovered that he had apparently packed bags and driven out of town without leaving any notification of his whereabouts. She had found his cell phone left behind in their bedroom. He had not returned nor contacted her since.

A third story concerned an investigation that had been opened into the reported disappearance of Vanessa Wilde, wife of local businessman William Wilde. Members of Vanessa's family had filed statements following inquiries and interviews by Police Detective Frank Vandegraf of the Personal Crimes Unit.

According to a fourth article, several civil cases involving the digital firm Prophet DKM had been settled privately and abruptly. Cases pending against the late Albert Landreaux, a.k.a. Al Land, had been summarily dismissed due to the death of the defendant.

A regular "police blotter" feature noted that various indictments had been returned against three defendants—Gerald Lombard, Randall Joe Harkins Junior, and Amanda Darcy—for transportation of stolen goods across state lines, conspiracy to smuggle, and possession of stolen property, among other charges.

Only a few people actually noticed, much less read, all these items, and fewer made any connection among all of them. One of those few was Detective Jilly Garvey.

* * * *

The events were all still swirling in her head as she and Dan made her way across the squad room to the desk where Frank Vandegraf sat re-familiarizing himself with an older but still active case file.

Jilly tossed a manila folder onto Frank's desk. A few sheets popped out just a bit with the impact.

"Only took a year and a day for ballistics to come back. Thank you kindly, Mister Morgan." She cast a sideways glance at Dan.

Dan pulled and scanned a few sheets. "Oh come on, Jilly, it was only a couple of weeks."

"And?" Frank asked.

"You lucky sonofagun," Dan muttered, shaking his head.

"Sonofagun?" Frank asked. "Jilly, where'd you find this guy?"

Jilly continued. "The .38 slugs that killed Marina Belize and Ricky Wright were from Rudy Caliente's gun. Also the slug in Nick Lowell's car door…Rudy's."

"Lucky sonofagun," Dan repeated, pointing at Frank.

"Too bad we couldn't get Al's Glock. The street lady was killed with a 9 mm and it's gotta be from Anita." Frank scratched his ear. "But Anita's lawyer struck a deal and she's been talking. We might sew this one up yet."

"The part I can't get my head around," Dan said, "is why Rudy shot Marina and her boyfriend."

Frank shook his head. "He was all screwed up, Dan. He had been drinking steadily, he was distraught. His world was coming apart at the seams. He knew that his wife, who was the most important part of his entire world, was seeing some hot-shot flashy guy with more money than him. He couldn't stand to lose her. He saw her get into Nick Lowell's nice ride, nicer than any ride he'd ever have, and he snapped. The rest of the evening, he hardly showed great judgment, would you say?"

"I would not," said Jilly.

"He's driving around, downing beer and vodka, getting angrier and less rational.He sees Nick's car parked in front of *Saint Expedito*, figures they're in the bar. He double-parks in front of the SUV to block it just in case, and goes in. Al Land is a flashy guy about the same size as his guy, sitting at a table with two glasses; Rudy puts two and two together and gets five and plugs him. Anita comes tearing out of the loo, grabs Al's gun and chases after Rudy. She takes a shot as he accelerates away and misses, and decides to pursue him in her own car. Funny thing is, they're only seconds ahead of the valet who's come for Nick's car and sees this scene go down. Anita chases Rudy down the street in the Lexus, catches up to him at a stoplight, pulls up to his left, rolls down her power windows, and squeezes off a couple shots at him. We've already established she can't shoot worth shit, she misses him but breaks his right-side window and, not knowing it, plugs the street lady."

"Mary," said Jilly. "We've been calling her Mary. Mary X."

"We still don't know her real name," Dan added. "Nobody's ever come forward. Sad."

Frank considered how he had come to the conclusion that they all had to count equally and hoped that one day someone would come forward looking for her.

Then he resumed the timeline. "Rudy's spooked and takes off and Anita turns back, but now Rudy goes from scared to indignant, and decides he's going after *her*. He starts driving up and down nearby streets. He's so distraught all he can remember is that she's a sort of long-haired blonde in a silver sedan. Only a few blocks away, what does he see but..."

"...blonde Marina Belize in a grey Acura," Jilly said. "A bit of a stretch. With Ricky Wright in the car, too."

"I don't know, maybe he doesn't see Ricky. He figures this is the crazy dame that dared shoot at him so he drives by and takes a couple shots at her from the driver's side. Ricky, at the first sign of danger, brave and gallant soul he is, tries to escape out of the passenger door and gets it in the back."

"At least," Jilly interjected, "now Jane knows the cartel was *not* after Marina and isn't after her. Her new identity is safe and probably has been for some time now. Not enough to make up for losing her sister, I'm afraid—or learning that her father is truly dead."

Dan returned to the timeline. "And even after that, Rudy's night still isn't over. He apparently encounters Nick and Tia again and starts realizing he's made a big *big* mistake."

"Gotta be how it happened," Frank said. "Tia tells Nick she needs to make a stop for, well, necessities for the rest of their romantic night, and he drops her off. Maybe he's going to park. He passes Rudy in the process."

"That's when Rudy empties the last shot out of his .38 and hits the side of Nick's car," Jilly said. "Nick's no hero either and he floors it, heads for the hills."

"Let's give him a break," Dan added. "He's never seen Rudy. Maybe he's got no idea that Rudy is after Tia. Whatever this guy with the gun has in mind, Nick figures he'll just get out of there before Tia can come back out. Maybe he's actually trying to protect Tia, lead Rudy away."

"Gallant soul," sighed Frank with a shake of his head. "Whatever. In any case, Rudy catches sight of Tia coming out of the store. He steps on the brakes. He's emptied his gun and doesn't have time to reload yet. But he's got his fishing-hunting knife in the glove compartment. He grabs it and goes after her."

"We're still waiting on those blood results," Dan said. "What a surprise. But do any of us doubt that Rudy's knife and Tia's wound and blood are going to be a match?"

"Now Rudy's really in a panic," Jilly jumped in, getting into the story. "Not that up to now he's been a picture of clarity, mind you. He grabs her wallet and cell phone, maybe to make it look like a robbery, maybe just to take something of hers, whatever. He beats it out of there before he can be ID'd. Luckily for him he's in a neighborhood where nobody cares, certainly not the slacker store clerk. It's a wonder that some anonymous citizen would run in to call in the body. Anyway, Rudy knows he has to track down Nick. He reloads his gun, maybe finishes off the rest of his booze, and trawls around the neighborhood, searching. He doesn't have far to go."

Frank reclaimed the narrative. "Nick has pulled into the Ready Rite parking lot, which is maybe the first place he feels safe to stop. He's getting out of his car and frantically trying to call Tia. There's a brawl breaking out in the lot. Maybe that's what gets Rudy's attention. He pulls into the lot, sees Nick, recognizes him, grabs his gun, gets out of the car and walks up and plugs him at close range while he's distracted trying to call Tia."

"Meanwhile Luther Newcombe has just unintentionally killed Sonny Foster and is terrified in his own right," Jilly said. "In his hysteria to get away he jumps in his car, guns it, and…"

"Bang," said Dan, smacking a fist into a palm. "He ties the whole package up for us."

"Question is," asked Jilly, "did his taking out Rudy make it easier in the end—or harder?"

"It just seemed too pat and easy for me from the git-go," said Frank. "It was like something that would happen in a book or a TV show, not in real life. Those other guys—Wilde, Scudder, the DKM bunch—weren't quite right to me but somehow they seemed more logical. I wasn't ready to write Rudy's death off as an accident. Guy kills a perfect stranger with lots of enemies and then gets taken out in a weird hit-and-run? If Luther's family hadn't made him come forward when they did, I'd still be spinning my wheels on that one."

"Hard-luck guy, Rudy Caliente," mused Dan. "Bad day all around for him."

"Yeah," agreed Jilly. "Hard luck. He wasn't a bad guy, it would seem. Nobody even thought he was capable of violence. The Rudy that acted out that night—he was like an alien. He spun out and snapped. Talk about looking down into an abyss. Before he could come back, he took them all down with him. It could have all gone down differently. Too bad. Way too bad."

That seemed to be a sobering thought for them all. It ceased to be an intellectual puzzle they had unraveled and became the real-life catastrophe that had destroyed so many lives.

Dan broke the silence. "Bad luck seemed to come in eights this time."

"*Achtmusik*," muttered Frank.

"Please," Dan said. "Do *not* start that one again."

"For once," Jilly muttered, "I totally agree with my partner there. Maybe it's time for me to change my ring tone."

A momentary attempt at awkward laughter quickly subsided and they collectively grew silent. The squad room around them continued to buzz with activity. The trio had cleared their most recent load but there was no respite in sight for any of them.

Frank sat glumly in silence for a few beats before observing, "And I assume you got the word from the captain this morning, that we are officially no longer authorized for overtime? Oh…and he congratulated me on clearing the murders, pending corroboration by the hard evidence. I assume he's told you the same."

Dan nodded. "Yeah, we got the same speech."

"Did he also 'encourage' you to apply the same magnificent effort to clearing your other cases?" Frank made a theatrical flourish at the stacked folders on his desk while twisting his face a bit.

"Thanks for saving my daughter from drowning," Jilly recited, quoting the punchline to an all-too-familiar joke. "Now, where's her hat?"

"Par for the course," said Frank. He looked at his watch, as if to say, the hell with it. "Lunch? Free of guilt?"

Dan nodded. "Are you treating, Mr. Know-it-all?"

"You mean, out of the magnificent bonus I will be earning for my crackerjack detection and deduction skills? Sure, why not." He said it without a smile as he rose from his desk and reached for his sport coat on the chair back. "Reubens sound good?"

"If it's the place I'm thinking," Jilly sighed, "they have decent salads, so sure."

"Not like you need to watch your weight," Frank said as he turned away from his desk.

"That may be the sweetest thing you ever said to me, Vandegraf. I just happen to like salads."

They filed out of the squad room, three tired and hungry souls, wearily attempting half-hearted banter but none of them smiling. The rush of exhilaration from the solved cases had been short-lived and was being quickly replaced by the realization of what exactly they had solved.

Jilly couldn't help but reflect on the crazy eight they could now be sure they had cleared. She was no stranger to meaningless crimes but these seemed particularly senseless.

You want to find the bad guys, she mused. You want to speak for the deceased and avenge the wrongs against them. At least that was the idealized version of their job.

There was certainly no shortage of bad ones encountered in this case: drug cartels, crooked investigators, armed robbers, racketeers, street hustlers, ruthless and deceitful businessmen. But in this case, they were all innocent. That was the sad irony. This was an irrational tragedy, set into motion and played out in a few short hours, without any set-in-stone villains.

So much waste, so little closure for so many.

Yes, these things actually could still bother her, and sometimes deeply. The night music hadn't totally become routine yet. Holding on to her humanity had its cost, she thought, but it was a necessary cost.

They were already on the street when her phone started playing Mozart once again. The music wasn't going to stop just yet.

Open and Shut

1.

One year later, Jilly Garvey would still recall that September night vividly.

She and Reggie Martinez walked from the dark of the murky alley into the glare of artificial light, where a small crowd was busily mulling around a trash dumpster. They showed their identification to one of the officers, who nodded them on through, past the yellow tape marking the crime scene.

One of the medical examiners rose from one knee to greet them. He had a droopy scowl that brought to mind a basset hound, complemented by a deadpan monotone voice.

"Detectives. Lovely night."

They had already decided it was Reggie's turn to take lead on this one. He nodded to the ME. "Isn't it always, Mickey. So what have we got here?"

"She was found behind the bin there. Stabbed several times." He gestured to the body splayed out on the ground. Camera flashes went off in rapid succession around them.

"Who found the body?"

Mickey pointed to a slight, frightened-looking young man standing at the other end of the alley. He had a thick unruly mop of hair, and wore a dark shapeless overcoat over a white apron and dark pants. He stood between two uniformed officers.

"Works in a restaurant around the corner," Mickey said. "They dump a lot of stuff in here on Wednesday evenings. Apparently he was dropping stuff into the hopper and saw the body. Called it in on his cell."

"I'll go talk to him," said Jilly, exchanging nods with Reggie.

Crime techs were busily at work all around the area, and she stepped carefully, making sure to avoid the places they were processing. She held up her ID to the uniforms and they nodded and stepped away from the witness, who looked even more frightened now.

"I'm Detective Garvey," she said, trying to sound non-threatening.

"You're the person who found her?"

The guy just nodded, eyeing her carefully.

"Don't worry. You're not in any trouble. I just need to ask you some questions, okay?"

"They already did that," the guy replied in a hoarse voice, nodding his head back and forth to the two uniforms.

"Well, I have to ask some more, okay? What's your name?"

"Bertie," he said uneasily.

"Okay, Bertie. Got a last name? It's okay, really."

Bertie waited a beat before quietly saying, "Grossman."

"Okay, Bertie. So tell me what happened."

"I'm a busboy at Monica's, out on the main street. I was dumping a bunch of food into the dumpster, and I saw something back there—behind it." He pointed with a quivering finger. "I could see the blood. I could see her face. Her eyes were wide open!"

"Is it normal for you to be out here dumping food?"

"Oh yeah, the restaurant makes us do it a couple times a week. Kind of a waste, a lot of it is still good—we could be giving it to poor folks or something, you know? In no time there'll be homeless people back here 'cause the word is out that we do that."

"Okay, I get it, Bertie. So you saw her and what'd you do?"

"I kinda…freaked out for a minute, you know? Never seen somebody dead, like that."

"Uh huh, so then what'd you do?"

"I was going to run back to the restaurant but then I decided to call 911 from right here."

"Did you go back to the restaurant after that?"

"Yeah. I told the manager what had happened. I was totally freaked out, you know? She told me, calm down and go back out and wait for the cops. I couldn't bring myself to come back here, so I waited out there." He pointed to the mouth of the alleyway.

"Did anybody else from the restaurant come back here?"

"No, I think Lavonne, she's the manager, kept it to herself."

"Smart lady," Jilly said. "Didn't want to start a fuss."

She asked a few more questions about the restaurant and the manager, and got contact information for Bertie. She tried again to reassure him he was okay, and thanked him for his help.

Then she returned to Reggie, who was talking with another of the uniforms and busily jotting in his notebook. They were standing over the body. The MEs moved aside to let her have a look. She walked around it, looking carefully, crouching to inspect all the details at closer range.

The woman was on her back, arms and legs spread, elbows bent. A pair of stylish tinted eyeglasses lay at an odd tilt on her face. An expensive looking long coat splayed open; underneath, she wore a beige dress with numerous red blotches that had spread from her wounds.

"Whatcha think, Red?" Reggie asked, still writing furiously. Red was his pet nickname for his partner, referring to the natural color of her hair. "Reg and Red," they were called at the station.

"Several stab wounds. Looks like they were delivered hard and fast. Angry assailant?"

"Very possibly."

"Nice clothes. Coat's cashmere. Dress looks like real silk. Expensive jewelry. Nails carefully done, good haircut. Designer eyewear. She's hardly low rent."

Reggie smiled, rather grimly. "The advantages of having a female partner. You don't miss a trick."

"Do we have ID?"

Reggie shook his head. "Negative. No bag, no wallet, no keys, nothing. No phone either. Might have been a robbery."

"Or made to look like one," Jilly mused. Her eyes caught the glistening bracelet on the woman's left wrist. She pulled out a pen and gingerly lifted a tiny dangling golden disc that hung from it.

"If it was a robbery, they missed some of her jewelry," Reggie observed. "Maybe in a hurry? Or…maybe something else."

She liked working with Reggie. They were usually on a similar wavelength.

"Her initials are on this, LHS."

Reggie asked for a flashlight from the nearest uniform and bent over to look at it, shining the beam onto it.

"So they are, Red. So they are."

"Maybe the bag's been dumped somewhere close," Jilly suggested, continuing to sweep her eyes over the body.

"They're out checking already. Anything else on her that might help ID her?"

She pulled a pair of disposable gloves out of her own pocket and donned them, then carefully checked the pockets of the woman's coat. All she found was a stub of green cardboard with a number printed on it.

"Parking ticket?" she guessed, holding it up for Reggie. He nodded and motioned over one of the officers, who peered at it and said, "There's a lot on the next block, might be from there."

Jilly stood up and nodded to the waiting techs, who returned with their cameras and their equipment. She reached back into her pocket and pulled out one of the small evidence bags she always carried on a call. She carefully deposited the paper into it and sealed it, waving it at Reggie. "We should check this out, don'tcha think?"

"All yours. I'll give you a call if anything comes up."

The parking lot was about a block away; it was a 24-hour lot, so there was still an attendant on duty. Jilly showed him her badge and ID and then the stub. He nodded that it was indeed one of their tickets, grabbed a key, and waved for her to follow him.

The car was a silver late model Mercedes. He handed her the key and was about to leave.

"Wait, wait a minute," she said, halting him in his tracks. "Do you remember who brought this car in?"

The guy was dark, with bushy eyebrows and mustache, and deep thoughtful eyes shrouded under a broad-peaked baseball cap. He seemed to literally chew on the question for a long minute. Then he said, "It was a lady. Nicely dressed, very polite. Smiled at me and said 'thank you.'"

"Do you remember what she looked like?"

"Dark hair. Nice smile." He thought a bit and then shrugged. "That's about all. Oh wait, she had glasses, I think. Yeah. I remember, they were kinda smoky tinted, I thought that was funny for nighttime."

"What time did she come in? Don't you punch in the time?"

"Sure," he said. "Be right back." He turned and strode off towards the attendant shack. Jilly hit the button on the key and heard a low beep and a click as the doors to the Mercedes opened. She opened the passenger door and peeked into the vehicle. It still had that new car smell, leather with an undertone of banana oil.

Another stroke of luck, the glove compartment was not locked. Inside she found a copy of the registration and an insurance card. The name on both was Laura Hart Spilwell.

LHS, she thought. She noted the address.

The attendant came jogging back to her with a card in his hand. He showed it to her. She had entered the lot at 9:13 P.M. Jilly told him she was going to need to take the card; they'd notify his boss in the morning. The guy seemed unfazed, just nodded and looked at her expectantly, thick eyebrows raised under his cap.

"One last question. She didn't say anything about how long she was going to be, anything else like that?"

"Nope, that was it." He kept his eyebrows raised in anticipation.

Jilly held up a hand in the usual "thanks" gesture and told him she didn't need anything else from him, and that the car would be processed and should be left untouched. In a flash he was gone.

Must be something good on his TV in the shack, she mused.

A quick search of the vehicle didn't turn up anything else of interest. She checked the trunk and found nothing but the usual spare and jack.

She locked it up and phoned Reggie to fill him in. He said a crew of techs would be over shortly to process the car. She waited about fifteen minutes until they arrived, making some more calls in the meantime, and then headed back to the alley.

* * * *

They compared notes quickly. The techs were efficiently finishing up and there would be more news tomorrow.

"Checked out the restaurant," Reggie told her. "Monica's. Nice little bistro. Upscale crowd. Popular, even on a Wednesday. The manager corroborated the kid's story. Kinda liked her." He smiled.

"I'm sure your wife would like her too."

"Actually she kinda resembled my wife. Same kind of scary smart. Same kind of devil in her eyes."

His smile got bigger. Jilly knew he was giving her the rib.

"She put a lid on it so nobody would leave the restaurant, huh?"

"Like I said, Red, scary smart. How many people would have that presence of mind? Everybody in there is just dining and talking like nothing happened. I got all Lavonne's information so we can go back and talk to her later."

"I'm sure you did," smirked Jilly. He shrugged innocently. Then she gave him the complete story from the parking lot.

"Laura Hart Spilwell," Reggie said thoughtfully. "I know that name."

"I ran the name and address while I was waiting for the techs," Jilly said. "Her husband is Dane Spilwell. *Doctor* Dane Spilwell."

"I've heard of him. Big mucky-muck surgeon."

"*Plastic* surgeon, to be exact. To the rich and famous."

Reggie shook his head. "I guess we better go talk to him."

They both reflexively looked at their watches. It was very late, but bad news never waited until morning.

* * * *

Even groggy from sleep and in a bathrobe, Dane Spilwell somehow looked distinguished, confident and in control. He had a full head of fashionably-styled silvery hair over a high forehead and piercing eyes.

He didn't peer through the security peephole of the door of his apartment; but of course the doorman had notified him that they were on the way up. He asked in a clear voice who was there, and then pulled the door open.

Reggie and Jilly were ready with their badges and ID's on display and he cast a wary eye upon them.

"This can't be good," he said, glancing at his expensive wristwatch

(Jilly wondered, did he sleep in it or had he put it on when he came to answer the door?). "Is there a problem, officers?"

"Doctor Spilwell, may we come in?" asked Reggie.

"Oh my God. Is it Laura? She's not home yet. Has something happened to her?"

Jilly noted what seemed to be sincere alarm in those striking eyes. For just a fleeting moment he seemed to lose that confident control. Then the coolness returned.

"Please, may we come in?"

Spilwell stepped aside.

It was a penthouse apartment in a very high-end section of the city, no surprise there. The living room was huge, furnished sparely and tastefully in beige and onyx, with a deep area rug over a hardwood floor. He motioned them to a comfortable sofa and sat down in a large soft seat across a glass table from them, looking anxious and expectant.

This never got any easier. Reggie took the lead and broke the news of finding Laura's body, then offering his condolences.

Jilly thought Spilwell handled the news surprisingly well. Taking a while for it to set in? Shock? A devastated man trying to remain stoic? Or was it something else?

He stared down at his hands, muttered "Oh my God," and then after a silence began asking simple direct questions: what happened to her, where was she, did they know who did it. They answered him as directly as they could.

Dane Spilwell was high-profile, with a reputation for his patrician bearing and icy detached demeanor. Was this the real man, Jilly wondered, or just a carefully-cultivated persona? She had to admit she didn't run in social circles like his and had a certain antipathy towards this kind of high-born coolness.

Reggie's phone sounded. He excused himself and went into the corner to answer it while Jilly continued to question Spilwell, marveling at the lack of emotion in his answers. Now she had her notebook out, making notes as they talked.

"Do you know where your wife was going tonight?"

"She had her usual book group, I believe. They meet Wednesdays, rotating hosts."

"Where was she going tonight exactly?"

"I think it would have been the home of Maura St. Ashby." He mentioned an address in an expensive residential neighborhood to the north. Not the urban environment where Laura had been found.

"We'll need the names of the other members of that group, if you have them."

Spilwell waved a hand absent-mindedly, looked sideways at nothing in particular. He seemed almost bored by this line of questioning. "Of course. I think I can provide you with all of them."

"It's awfully late. Was it unusual for her not to be home by now, or did she tend to make a late night of it?"

He glanced at his watch again. "Sometimes they would go out for drinks or just, you know, a girls' night out kind of thing, but no, by now she would usually have been home. I would have perhaps been concerned and called her, but I had fallen asleep until just now."

"So you were home tonight?"

"Yes. Things have been exceedingly hectic at my office and the hospital of late. I made a point of coming home around eight."

"Was Mrs. Spilwell still here or had she left already?"

"No, she had gone already."

"Did she tend to leave a note for you or anything when she left, maybe send you a text, just to say goodbye, see you later?"

Spilwell sighed as if trying to make sense to a fool, or perhaps just a lower class peon. "No, we didn't tend to leave each other little love notes, Detective, or anything like that. We kept each other apprised of our schedules regularly and we both knew what the other would be doing on any given day."

Jilly said nothing but the expression "piece of work" came to mind as she kept her head down and jotted a few more notes. Then she raised her head again as Reggie returned and rejoined her on the couch.

"So you went to sleep, you said; around what time would that be?"

"Let me see. I was tired tonight. As I said, I had an exhausting week. I had a brandy, read a bit, probably fell asleep sometime around, oh, I'd say ten."

"And you were asleep until we awoke you now?"

Spilwell nodded. "But why are we talking about me? Aren't there any avenues of inquiry you'd like to explore about what happened to Laura?"

"Absolutely, sir," Reggie replied, working his way back into the questioning. "Can you think of any reason she would have been in that neighborhood tonight? That's nowhere near the destination you mentioned."

"I have no idea."

"There are a lot of restaurants nearby. You said sometimes the group turned it into a girls' night out. Perhaps something like that?"

He thought about that. "I know Monica's is near there somewhere. We would go there on rare occasions. She liked that it was small and intimate and had a surprisingly good wine list. Otherwise, no, I can't think of much of a reason for her to have been there."

Reggie and Jilly exchanged a quick look. Just a coincidence that Monica's had come up again. Maybe.

Reggie took the plunge. "Doctor, this is a difficult question, forgive me, but you must understand we have to consider every possibility. Could your wife have been…"

"…Meeting someone else? I very much doubt it, Detective. You're suggesting her book group outings were just a convenient cover for a, a tryst of some kind?"

Spilwell had reacted reflexively to the question, almost indignantly. There was a long tense moment of silence in the large living room.

Reggie had tacitly left Jilly the opening to be the understanding one while he took the blunt, tactless role. They knew each other well. This might come in handy later.

She interjected, "I'm sorry, we do have to ask. Perhaps it would be better if we were to come back sometime later, maybe tomorrow, and ask you further questions?"

"That might be a good idea, yes," Spilwell agreed. They exchanged contacts and a few formal pleasantries. Then Spilwell's door was shutting behind them as they made their way back to the elevator.

Reggie brought Jilly up to speed on his call. "They already found her bag. Jammed into a trash can a block away. No phone. There was a wallet and money and credit cards still in it."

"Convenient, don't you think?"

Reggie nodded almost imperceptibly. "You're thinking what I'm thinking, then?"

"Made to look like a robbery. Conveniently drop the bag nearby, where it'll be found."

"Hope a vagrant picks through it, maybe gets caught with a card or some personal article from it?"

"Let's go see what the doorman has to say."

In the wood-paneled elevator, Reggie's phone buzzed once again. He answered it and spoke for a moment. He nodded, said, "Thank you, officer," and hit the "End Call" button.

"You're not going to believe this," he said as the elevator smoothly stopped and the door quietly slid open onto the lobby.

"So, tell me, already."

"One of the uniforms is still out there. He just found a knife."

"What? You mean the murder weapon?"

"Well, he can't be sure yet, but would you bet against it?"

"Where was it?"

"He was looking into storm grates, sewers, things like that. He saw a glint of light and pulled up a grate and brought it out. It's a knife. With blood on it. Not even three blocks away."

"It was just lying in there, like it was just dropped?"

"He said he had to crawl down and in to retrieve it. It was like it had been thrown through the grate by someone hoping it wouldn't be seen until it got flushed into the sewer."

"Now, that's a rare break."

"Seems that way, Red. Let's hope."

"I don't like the doctor one bit," Jilly said. "Cold as ice."

They stepped out of the elevator onto the plush carpet of the lobby and walked toward the uniformed doorman standing at the entrance, eyeing them with curiosity.

* * * *

One year later, Kerry Moran would still recall that September night vividly.

"They tell me," Kerry said to Mark as he held her hand across the table, "that this place is the scene for more marriage proposals than any other restaurant in town."

"Is that a suggestion?" Mark smiled back.

"You think we're ready for that?"

Mark laughed. "Well, who knows? Maybe. But this is a pretty cool place. I'll definitely keep it in mind for when the time is right."

It was a small, intimate restaurant, lit by candlelight, three cozy rooms with tables for two, spaced for privacy. They were in the smallest of the rooms, just themselves and two other couples. There was a low murmur of voices, the occasional clink of a wine glass.

Mark lifted his champagne glass and tilted it toward Kerry. "Happy anniversary, my dear."

She picked up her own glass and mirrored his gesture, smiling. "One year. And they said it couldn't be done."

"So, are you lovebirds ready to order?" asked a lean figure in black shirt and pants who suddenly materialized alongside them.

"Need a couple more minutes, Satch," Kerry replied to him, looking down at the menu splayed open in front of her. "We've just been talking about true love and important things like that. A perfect setting for it, don't you think?"

Satch made a face and bent down with a conspiratorial look on his face. He spoke softly, almost in a whisper. "To tell you the truth, there's always a lot of romance going on in here, but it's not always of the 'true' variety, if you catch my drift?"

Kerry matched his whisper as if in collusion. "Satch, I'm shocked.

You mean to tell me there are, what do you call them, trysts and assignations getting underway here?" She opened her eyes wide theatrically. Mark watched with amusement. These two had been friends for a while and shared a flair for the dramatic.

The waiter bent closer, as if explaining a menu item. "I'm not supposed to tell you this, it's highly unprofessional," he said, rolling his eyes to his right and tilting his head ever so slightly. "But that other couple I'm waiting on are *definitely* an item."

Kerry turned her head, subtly she hoped, in the indicated direction. In the low light she could just make out the rather distinguished-looking fellow in the stylish dark grey suit with the full head of silvery hair. His partner had her back turned to them but Kerry could see the spectacular shade of red of her hair, the subdued green of her obviously expensive dress, and the deep green glint of a bracelet and earrings. She said to Satch, "They look like they've been together a long time."

"Don't kid yourself, sister. They've probably been married a long time. But not to each other."

"Satch!" She brought a hand to her mouth, wishing she hadn't said that quite so loud.

"No, really, wait tables long enough and you get to know this kind of stuff. Dressed to the nines—she's got on her best emeralds, and that killer dress? They're shooting all these meaningful looks back and forth? They're just champing at the bit. I'm surprised they're making it through dessert. That's an *affair*."

He punctuated the last word with gleeful malice, straightening back up again.

"Maybe," Mark broke in, "if you wait tables a little longer, you'll get to know how to wait tables, stuff like that?"

"Satch," Kerry said. "You really don't think two married people could have that kind of spark?"

He shrugged. "Cynicism. The mark of the cosmopolitan world-weary. What can I tell you, we waiters are a jaundiced lot. Anyway, did I already mention that our chef's got a great special kale and ginger appetizer tonight..."

After Satch moved away from the table, Kerry tented her hands and rested her chin on top of them, just staring at Mark.

"So how do you know that guy again?" he asked.

"Oh come on, Mark, I've told you about Satch. He and I went to college together."

"Oh yeah, he's the jazz musician. Funny nickname. What would musicians do without waiting jobs?"

"He's pretty good. I bet it won't be long before he can give this up.

And I guess he liked the name Satch better than his real name."

"Uh…which is?"

"Mort. Mort Blessing."

"Mort, as in Mortimer? Seriously?"

"No kidding. I think he was named after his grandfather or someone. Probably will spend years of his life in therapy trying to forgive his parents."

"I'd change my name too. But not to Satch."

"He told me where that came from. Something about bringing his horn to shows and rehearsals in a leather bag, like a satchel. The connection to Louis Armstrong, Satchmo, made it irresistible, I guess. Anyway, he was happy they stopped calling him Mort."

"Here we are on our one year anniversary, my love, discussing satchels and handbags. Let's start over. Lovely place. Lovely night."

Kerry cast another glance at the twosome at the far table. The two looked so captivated with each other. She couldn't see the face of the woman in the beautiful emeralds but the man was distinguished and dreamy-eyed, showing her his full attention as they spoke quietly.

Kerry began fantasizing about the couple, that they enjoyed a perfectly blissful life together. She hoped Satch was wrong about them. She wanted to someday find herself in a long marriage in which she and her husband still looked at each other in that special way.

She had a sudden impulse and smiled mischievously at Mark, pulling out her phone. She made a motion to Satch, who once again descended upon their table.

"Hey Satch, will you do us a favor and take a couple of pictures of us?" She raised an eyebrow at Mark, who nodded in agreement.

"Of course, Madame," Satch replied with a flourish, taking her camera phone.

Kerry rose from her seat and pulled her chair around next to Mark. They struck some appropriate poses of intimate affection, then mugged self-consciously, as if to indicate they really weren't so hopelessly unhip as to be sincere about all this kind of thing. Satch took four or five quick photos. Mark dipped his head to plant a kiss on her temple just as one of the shots flashed.

It was a wonderful moment and all seemed right with the world. She and Mark were in love, everybody smiled and laughed, and even the enraptured couple across the room from them looked to be in their own paradise.

If only, she thought, life could always be so sweet.

2.

"Hey, you're reading that story *again*?" Dan said, interrupting her concentration. She put down the open newspaper and looked across her desk at him. The squad room was full of noise and hustle: voices, phones, vague computer noises. It was a typical morning at the Personal Crimes Unit.

"This brought back a lot," Jilly said.

"I remember the case too. Don't forget I was still a patrolman."

"How could I forget? You're the one who found the knife. Probably how you got your nice new detective badge."

"That paper's five days old now," Dan said, pointing at the open page. "Brings back memories of Reggie. I get it."

Jilly shook her head. "Maybe a little bit. But I'm not going to burden my new partner with tales of my old one. That's like telling your husband about your ex or something." She closed the paper up, folded it and dropped it on top of her IN stack.

Dan Lee, the new guy on the unit, raised his Styrofoam cup of coffee in a peace gesture. "No, no problem, Jilly. Reggie was a righteous cop. One of the good ones."

Jilly was already warming to Dan. He was young, smart, serious, and first generation Chinese-American. His immigrant family was immensely proud of his success and dedication.

"I'm not expecting to replace him," he said. "I couldn't. Nobody could. For the record, I'm really happy they made me your partner."

"Thanks for that," said Jilly. "I'm sorry, Dan, I need to move on."

"At least there's some closure. The guy got convicted. Even that snake-oil salesman of a lawyer, Towers, couldn't spin it any different. Jury didn't even deliberate all that long."

"He'll appeal. We know Towers. He'll definitely appeal."

"Still," Dan mused, taking a sip of the black coffee. "A conviction is a conviction." He paused a beat to swallow. "Was that the last case you and Reg worked on?"

"The last major one."

Detective Frank Vandegraf walked by and laid a hand on Jilly's shoulder, nodding greetings to Dan. He had just returned from four days' vacation and it was his first chance to talk to her since the news had come down.

"Good news," he said quietly. "Reg would be very happy."

Jilly just nodded and patted Frank's hand. He moved on to his own desk and the pile of cases and reports that had amassed in his absence.

"So what's up today?" Dan asked, draining the cup and looking around for a waste basket.

"The usual pain in the neck stuff," muttered Jilly. "That aggravated assault case is getting stale, maybe we need to re-canvass..."

The phone on her desk rang.

"Garvey," she spoke into it briskly.

"This is Mallory, down at the desk. There's someone here to see you, Detective Garvey."

Mallory, an old school adjutant if ever there was one, muffled the receiver with his hand and asked a question of the visitor. "She says her name is Kerry Moran," he added. "...and she wants to talk to the detective who worked the Spilwell case."

"Really," was all Jilly could bring herself to say.

"That would be you, correct?"

"Uh, yes. It would."

"So, can I send her up?"

"I guess so," Jilly sighed. She hung up the receiver, pulled the five-day old newspaper back out from the pile and opened it up once again. She couldn't help it.

The headline screamed out in large-point type.

SPILWELL GUILTY.

In smaller type beneath but still screaming:

TO BE SENTENCED TUESDAY

She scanned several of the sentences, skipping here and there across the page. She had read this many times by now but it still had the impact of a first read.

> An extensive trial that has rocked the city finally concluded today, almost exactly one year to the day after the shocking murder of socialite Laura Hart Spilwell, when a jury of seven women and five men found her husband, Dr. Dane Spilwell, guilty of first-degree murder after less than six hours of deliberation...
>
> Spilwell, 58, a noted plastic surgeon and community figure, shook his head in disbelief as the jury foreman read the verdict...
>
> Spilwell's lawyer, Norland Towers, called the verdict a miscarriage of justice. He maintained his client's innocence and said there would be an appeal of the verdict...

"What's going on?" asked Dan.

"I'm not quite sure," Jilly said. She looked up to see a young woman being directed in her general direction. She figured it would be a good idea to meet her part way and rose to head her off. She laid the newspaper down and stood up. "I'll be right back."

An earnest young woman at that, Jilly figured: intelligent hazel eyes, shoulder-length brown hair styled in a no-nonsense haircut, decidedly non-flashy skirt and sweater. Kerry Moran shook Jilly's hand firmly, introduced herself and asked for a few minutes of her time. Jilly saw no reason to commandeer an interview room so she steered her to an empty desk and pulled over an additional rolling chair.

"What can I do for you, Miss Moran?"

The newcomer laid her briefcase on the desk in front of her. "You're the detective who worked on the Spilwell murder case?"

"I was one of them, yes."

"I saw the news that her husband was convicted the other day."

"Yes, he was."

"I think that he might be innocent."

Jilly couldn't help herself. She ran a hand down her face and took a deep breath.

"It must seem strange that I'd come to you, but..."

"It's more than strange," Jilly interrupted. "You're talking to the person who saw all the evidence. In fact I'm the one who *gathered* it. I don't know what it is you think you've got, but, believe me, he did it, Miss Moran."

"Can I just tell you what I've got, *show* you?"

"Miss Moran, why don't you go talk to Dane Spilwell's attorney? He's the one who might be interested in whatever you think you know."

"I tried. Norland Towers, his lawyer. I called, I went to his offices. He won't see me. I spoke to one of his associates but she basically gave me short shrift, blew me off."

Short shrift, thought Jilly, now there's an expression you don't hear much anymore. She had a well-educated cuckoo here at very least. Murder case groupies and aficionados were a common phenomenon but this one was different from the usual array. That was probably why Mallory had let her through.

"I found that puzzling," she continued. "Wouldn't you think they'd want to see anything that would help in an appeal?"

"Miss Moran, not to be rude, but I'm pretty busy right now. I don't think I'm the one you should be talking to about this." Jilly started to get up from the desk.

"I saw Dane Spilwell," Kerry blurted out, her eyes blazing indignantly. "I saw him the night he was supposed to have killed his wife."

"Really. And for a year you never came forward or said anything?"

"I didn't realize it. Not until now."

"Excuse me?"

Kerry reached into the portfolio case and pulled out a large glossy photo-print. She held it out to Jilly, who glanced down at it. In the lower left corner there were two smiling people, one of whom appeared to be

Kerry herself. The man in the photo had bent his head toward her and over his shoulder could be seen another couple seated at a nearby table. The setting seemed to be a dimly-lit restaurant. There was a man facing the camera and a woman with her back to it.

Kerry pulled out a second photo and held it up, This was a blow-up of part of the first and appeared to have been manipulated digitally to sharpen the features. The man in the background was larger, brighter, and clearer.

"I enhanced this as best I could," Kerry said. "Tell me that is not Dane Spilwell."

Jilly looked at the picture and shrugged.

"This was taken at a restaurant called Light in the Tower at nine-fifteen on the night of Wednesday the eighteenth of September of last year. The night that he allegedly killed his wife."

"Miss Moran, this doesn't prove anything."

"I was there and I saw them. I remember him, and when I saw the photos on TV and online, I knew it was him! And look. That wasn't his wife he was with, is it? I saw pictures of the wife, but that is *not* her."

Jilly rolled her eyes and sighed. She hated when the victim was minimized in any way. "'The wife,' as you put it? Her name was Laura. And all you have is this…doctored photo from where, your phone?"

"It's not *doctored*. It's *enhanced*. I uploaded it from my phone, yes, to my computer and sharpened and clarified it. I'm a graphic designer. That's what I do." She had set her jaw and was almost glaring up at Jilly. "I was there. I saw them." She caught herself and paused. "He was having an affair with a woman, who was likely also married. That's why the news stories said he couldn't provide an alibi for where he was that evening. He was protecting her."

"Even if there were any truth to this, which I doubt, what exactly did you expect would come from telling me about it, Miss Moran?"

That gave Kerry pause. "I…don't really know, I'm trying everything I can think of. I just thought, well, you're a detective. Maybe there would be something you could…"

Jill sat back down again, controlling the rising exasperation she felt. She silently counted to seven. She would never have made ten.

"Okay, look, I'm going to take a few more minutes and just explain something to you, and then I really need to get back to *being a detective*." She stared directly at Kerry and spoke rapidly, her hands moving with the energy of her frustration.

"My partner and I were the ones who assembled all the facts. Nobody knew more about what happened that night than we did. Nobody. The night that Laura Spilwell died, nobody saw or heard from Dane Spilwell all evening. Nobody was able to confirm what time he might have left his office. He claimed he was home but even his doorman couldn't corroborate that. But there *was* video from a camera in his building garage showing him coming in late that night. We found the knife that killed Laura. There was a definite match to blood and stab wounds. The knife came from a kitchen set in the Spilwell apartment.

"There was more, much more. There were means, there was motive, there was opportunity. That's how we work, Miss Moran. There's also something called experience. My partner and I have both worked lots of murder cases and there were signs, so *many* signs, that Dane Spilwell was guilty as sin of murdering his wife. On top of that, he was defended in court by Norland Towers, who is one of the most successful criminal defense attorneys in the business—and not even Towers could sway a jury from being overwhelmingly convinced of his guilt."

Jilly handed the photos back to Kerry, who sat frozen, mouth partly open, and looking abashed.

She spoke deliberately, as if to a child, or a simpleton. "Miss Moran, you said you're a designer, that's what you do? I'm a cop. That's what I do. My job is to find the bad guys and make sure they're punished, and I think I'm extremely good at it. That's what I did in this case and there is no doubt in my mind we got the right guy."

Jilly stood up and composed herself. "Thank you for coming in. I'm afraid I can't be of any help and my advice is to forget about this, because you're on a misguided mission. Leave this to the professionals. Dane Spilwell is guilty."

She nodded and turned to walk away, leaving Kerry sitting at the desk holding the prints.

Dan looked up from his desk as Jilly approached. "So what was that all about?"

"Waste of time," muttered Jilly. "Total waste of time. So what do you think about doubling back on some of those leads on the assault?"

3.

The Personal Crimes Unit was always, it seemed, ablaze with activity. The city generously dropped new serious crime into their laps on a regular basis. Years earlier, the unit had been called Special Crimes and before that had gone by the prosaic but accurate Robbery-Homicide.

At some point the Department had decided Personal Crimes bore more gravitas. The unit still dealt with basically the same types of crime, almost entirely felonies: homicides, severe assaults, robberies. Simultaneously, the unit that handled burglaries and similar non-violent crimes had gained the moniker Property Crimes and was currently housed in a similar squad room one flight up from Personal Crimes.

Jilly, in her years in the unit, had never noticed any great difference in anything except the name.

She arrived at her desk early and dropped the newspaper on her desk. The headline read SPILWELL SENTENCED TO LIFE. She looked at the two telephone message slips greeting her. Both were from Kerry Moran.

Now what? She shook her head and pressed her temples. Wasn't it too early to be getting a headache?

She hadn't even sat down before her desk phone was buzzing.

"Garvey."

"Detective Garvey? It's Kerry Moran."

Jilly took a deep breath. "Yes, Miss Moran, what's up?"

"I've had threats made against me is what!"

"Excuse me?"

"I said I've been threatened, Detective, and it has to do with my involvement in the Dane Spilwell case!"

Another deep breath. "You are *not* 'involved' in the case, Miss Moran. Now tell me just how you've been threatened?"

"I got the call late last night." Kerry sounded distraught and a bit addled. "A man telling me to 'lay off.'"

"Lay off?"

"Lay off trying to convince people that Dane Spilwell is innocent!"

"I've told you, you shouldn't be doing that anyway. Who was the person who called you?"

"I don't know, I have no idea. He didn't identify himself, just told me I should stop, and then he hung up."

"That hardly sounds like a threatening call."

"At two in the morning?"

"Kerry, you need to drop this whole thing. What's the matter with you?"

"Detective, I'm sure Spilwell's innocent. I need to find someone who will believe me."

A third deep sigh was the last that Jilly was going to allow herself. She had to end this conversation—and this problem, before she either hyperventilated or exploded.

"All right, look, where are you right now? Are you far from me?"

"No, I'm about eight or nine blocks away in a coffee house. The JavaBean, on Henley?"

"Okay, I want you to wait for me, I'm going to come over and we are going to have a *short* talk, okay?"

"Really? Sure! I'll wait for you!"

Jilly dropped the phone down, shaking her head. Dan had just arrived, in time to catch the tail end of the conversation.

"What was *that* all about?"

"It's that stupid little Moran girl again. I'm going to go try to explain reality to her in person."

"She's still on the Spilwell kick?"

"And she's making a nuisance of herself in the process. I hate it when people want to go all Nancy Drew on us."

"I'm surprised you're taking the time to go see her."

"I need to lay this out for her in the strongest possible terms. Or else one of these days we're going to be bringing her in."

"Have fun," smiled Dan. "I'll catch us up on some of our reports in the meantime."

"Appreciate that," muttered Jilly as she grabbed her bag and jacket and prepared to head back out of the squad room.

* * * *

Jilly had grabbed a double Americano and now sat down across from Kerry, who looked as if she hadn't slept much recently. She was pale, shaking, and looking around furtively.

"Thank you for coming," she said.

"I'm not going to be here long. I'm just going to explain a few things to you and hope to drive some sense into your head. What have you been doing since you came to the station anyway?"

"Like I said, I've been trying to find someone who will listen to me!"

"Kerry, I've told you there is no question he's guilty! None at all! Why are you so sure he's innocent, getting yourself all worked up over this nonsense?"

Kerry's eyes got big and watery all of a sudden as she stared at Jilly, reminding her of more than one soap opera actress. "If you had been there, you would have understood. He was totally taken with her, the woman with the emeralds and the red hair—kind of like yours, in fact, except it just sparkled and glowed, like fire! It was spectacular!"

Thanks a lot, thought Jilly, catching herself unconsciously raising a hand to her own short ruddy hair.

"The way he was looking at her—he wasn't leaving her that evening! And it was definitely the same man in the photos I saw from the trial!"

This was making no sense to Jilly whatsoever.

"I guess…" Kerry looked down, shook her head and made a strange smile. "I guess I need to still believe in real love."

"Let me get this straight. You think you saw Dane Spilwell having dinner with another woman, not his wife. You're saying he was cheating on his wife Laura that evening."

"Yes, that's what I'm saying."

"And you want to believe that he was cheating because…you desperately want to believe in true love?"

"Exactly!" Kerry said excitedly. She stared earnestly. "People cheat, yes. People make mistakes. They find themselves with the wrong people. I'm not saying that any of that is right, hurting others, betraying their trust. But isn't it possible to decide that the person you truly love is somebody else, not the person you're with?"

"Oh my God, Kerry, How old *are* you anyway? Sixteen?"

"I'm twenty-four," Kerry replied defensively. "What difference does that make?"

"You do realize, don't you, how totally ridiculous your argument sounds? Especially to a cop like me?"

Kerry shrugged.

Jilly tried to find another line of communication. She reached over and touched Kerry's hand and stared into her eyes. "Why is this so important to you? Do you know Dane Spilwell?"

"No."

"Did you know his wife? Anybody in his family?"

"Oh, no."

"Then what?"

Kerry waited a minute, as if trying to gather her thoughts, dropping her gaze down at her hands. "Last year, when I was at that restaurant and saw that couple? I had a boyfriend and we were in love. I had a great job. The world was just wonderful."

She looked up at Jilly. "Right now? I've got nobody, no job, nothing. I suppose I really need to believe that what I saw in that room last year was real. That that man loved that woman so much that he wouldn't have left her for anything that night. That he would ultimately sacrifice himself for her. He never gave anybody an alibi for his time that night, did he?"

Jilly shook her head. "No."

"That's because he didn't want to jeopardize the woman he loved. I bet she's married too. He's protecting her."

Jilly wanted to say, Dane Spilwell is a slimebag, a selfish, arrogant lowlife covered in the trappings of the high life. He's no knight in shining armor. But she decided it wasn't worth it.

"Kerry, who else have you talked to about this?"

"Besides Norland Towers? Or rather his associate, Ms. Grymes? Well…nobody at the *Blade-Courier* would talk to me. I left email messages with three different reporters there. Her brother would have no part of it…"

"Wait a minute. Laura Spilwell's brother?"

"Yeah. Ryan Hart."

"How did you find him?"

"Actually, *he* found me," Kerry said. "He called and asked me to meet him in the park. He said that this was dragging up terrible things for the family, that he appreciated my efforts but they would actually cause more harm than good. He said I shouldn't try to reach him again, or any of the family—not ever. He also said I didn't realize the harm I was causing. He just kept saying to trust him, I didn't understand. The whole meeting lasted maybe five or ten minutes.

"He was right," Kerry added. "I *don't* understand. I know it could mean a bit of a scandal, but if it cleared his brother-in-law, wouldn't he want to find the real killer?"

"Did he give you a number, tell you how to reach him?"

"Oh, no, he said he never wanted to hear from me ever again."

Now Jilly *was* interested. "Who else have you spoken with about this?"

"Well, I tried to reach Satch, my waiter friend from the restaurant, but he's quit since then. We used to be good friends but we haven't talked in a while now." She took a deep breath. "And then I tried Mark."

"Mark?"

"Mark Zanello. He…was with me that night. But he won't answer my calls."

Another pause. It seemed as if Kerry was going to cry. "Can't blame him for that."

She sniffed a little and changed the subject. "And then there was Clea Solana."

"Clea Solana? You actually tried to talk to *her*? In heaven's name, *why*?"

"You know her then."

"Not personally, no. But Kerry…" Jilly shook her head in utter frustration at this dingbat sitting in front of her. "Kerry, you can't just go around stalking people like that, just because they're famous! You're lucky you haven't been slapped with a restraining order, or even arrested!"

Clea Solana, the wife of a world famous film director, was a filmmaker herself, as well as a patroness of the arts. They were both highly prominent in high society in many major cities throughout the world. She and her husband maintained a residence in this very city, among many other international locales.

"Not stalking, I just wanted to talk to her. You know her history with Dane Spilwell, don't you?"

"Yes, of course I do."

It was a bizarre, sad story told in gossipy whispers. Clea Solana had pursued cosmetic surgery for years in search of beautification. Dane Spilwell had been her most recent plastic surgeon and something had gone tragically wrong. At the end of the operation, Clea, rather than being transformed into Beauty personified, had been turned into something more closely resembling a Beast.

In spite of her disfigurement, she had continued to carry on her high-profile international business, in the spotlight and the society columns. Everybody in her circle acted as if there were nothing whatsoever unusual about her appearance. It was a new retelling of the Emperor's New Clothes.

The super-rich could lead very different lives indeed, even bend the very reality around them, it would seem.

"Kerry, are you insane? *Why* would you try to talk to her? Do you have any idea…"

"She just seemed a likely suspect, that's all. He destroyed her appearance—and her life—in a way."

"So you were going to, what? Confront her? Accuse her? You stupid girl! Do you realize what could have happened?"

"I said I was doing a feature on her for a magazine. I used the name of my former employer, the design magazine I once worked for. I proposed a fluff interview, hoping to come up with some clues—if I could catch her with her guard down. But I couldn't get anywhere near her. I was turned down cold at the lowest levels."

"You honestly thought Clea Solana could have killed Laura Spilwell?"

"She was in town that week, I checked. She was here for an art opening. As you would say, she had motive. She hated the Spilwells, wouldn't you? She had opportunity. I figured it was as good a shot as I had."

Kerry pulled a familiar photo out of her bag and dropped it on the table. She stabbed it with a finger.

"This man I saw, he was Dane Spilwell. And he did not kill his wife."

"Kerry, one question that I keep wondering about? Why did you wait until now to bring all this up? Your photo is a year old. The case was all over the news. You had to know about this then. And you didn't come forward, you did nothing."

"That's just it," Kerry said. "I never made the connection until now! This has been a…well, a pretty stressful year for me. I was distracted. My mind was elsewhere. Then I was going through old photos on my phone, finally getting rid of them. It was a, a kind of anniversary this week. Good memories turned bad. That's not worth going into right now. But I saw that picture and it brought up a whole chain of memories… you know how something can do that? I had the TV on and the news was showing Dane Spilwell's picture. It was just a coincidence. And all of a sudden it made sense."

She stabbed the photo once again with her finger. "It was him. I'm positive."

Jilly took the photo and looked at it. "You need to promise me you will stop trying to do police work *now*."

"Are you going to take me seriously and look into this?"

"No, but I will look into this alleged threat you received last night."

"*Alleged*!" Kerry almost yelled.

"I'm not saying I don't believe someone called you last night. I'm just saying there might be dubious grounds for characterizing it legally as a threat. So tell me exactly what this person said to you."

"Well, he woke me up. As I said, it was like around two in the morning. He asked if he was speaking to Kerry and I said yes. Then he said, 'You're going to make a lot of trouble for yourself, you need to lay off this thing you've taken on for yourself.' I asked him what thing he was talking about and he said, 'You know what I'm talking about. Give up on it right now.' I asked who he was but he just hung up. That was it."

"What did his voice sound like?"

"Low, gruff, kind of whispering hoarsely. I didn't recognize it, it was nobody I had ever spoken with. Or maybe he was disguising his voice."

"This was on a land line?"

"No, I don't have one, only my mobile." A common situation: more people, especially younger ones, were dropping their land lines in favor of cells as rates increased.

"And you've been giving out your number in your travels, I assume?"

"Yeah. Maybe not such a great idea, but…"

"All right, does your phone record incoming calls?"

"Yes, of course," Kerry said, punching up the record and showing the screen to Jilly.

"I'd like you to take a screen shot of that and message it to me, okay?" She gave Kerry her number and had her send it right then. "And don't delete those records. I'll see if I can run anything down from this number. I may need your official okay that I could do all this, just in case. Oh by the way…could I see your record of the call you received from Laura's brother?"

"Sure," said Kerry, now punching that up and turning the screen to

Jilly.

"Send me that one too, would you?" Jilly said, writing as she spoke. "And keep it?"

"Of course."

"I can't promise anything, but I will look into it for you."

"This time, do you want to keep this?" Kerry asked, handing her the photo. "I've got plenty of copies."

"Yeah, why not," Jilly said, not really quite sure why except that it might pacify Kerry a little bit.

She stood up, signaling the meeting was over. "Now listen to me. I'm serious. You need to tell me you are *not* going to play detective anymore with this stuff. You're going to drop it completely and let me look into the matter for you. I don't believe you are in any real danger, but I *do* think you could still get yourself in a world of trouble. So do I have your word?"

Kerry, looking abashed, nodded and said, "Okay. I promise. I won't do anything more about this until I hear from you."

"Not ever!" Jilly replied sternly. "I want you to say it!"

"Agreed."

"I have to run, Kerry. I'll call you about anything that comes up from these phone calls." She grabbed her bag and tossed her empty cup into the trash as she headed for the door.

On the street the ringtone of her phone erupted in her pocket, a snippet of music by Stravinsky she had just added. It was Dan.

"Hey, partner, I'm on my way back."

"Actually, I need you to meet me," Dan said. "We got a body." He gave her an address.

"On my way," she breathed, realizing just how exhausting her short conversation with that crazy girl had been.

* * * *

"Kinda looks like nobody expected us to find him for a long time," the female officer said. "After he was shot, someone stuck him back in that building."

They stood on the stoop of a broken down brick edifice that had obviously been abandoned for some time. Its windows were boarded up. The wooden front door, paint peeling and hinges rusting, was jammed partially open.

The medical examiner's van pulled up, and the officer led Dan into the building. They were careful not to touch the door and to watch where they walked, picking their way over the dusty debris on the floor.

It had been a residential building some years ago, and they entered into a hallway leading to a large room, likely designed to be a parlor. There was some light coming through the cracks in the window boards but it did not penetrate to the next room back, possibly once a bedroom.

A second officer stood there, directing a flashlight down onto the ground, dust particles flitting chaotically in the beam. They worked their way through the dark until they could see what was captured in the shaft of light.

A man, not a very old one, lay on his back, eyes wide open in a death stare at the ceiling. Blood had pooled beneath his head. The odor was already unpleasant.

The MEs slammed the doors to the van and headed up the stoop with their equipment. Dan yelled out for them to show caution; the Scientific Investigation Division techs hadn't yet arrived.

"Maybe a gang killing," the female officer said. "Maybe an initiation. But it's kind of odd. Two bullets in the head, from first look."

"Doesn't look like a gangbanger," Dan reflected, crouching down to get a better look at the body in the flashlight's beam. "Not with those clothes. This looks more like an urban hipster."

The officer, whose nametag read KOVETSKY, shrugged. "Trying to buy drugs, maybe?"

"Right neighborhood for it," said Dan, not looking up. He had already snapped on a pair of latex gloves and was very gingerly lifting the dead man's jacket, looking for identification or anything else that might suggest who he was.

"Just wrong place, wrong time maybe," she offered.

"Look at his fingernails," Dan muttered, lifting a hand slightly. "Clipped carefully. The hands look soft, and they're reasonably clean."

Definitely not a gang member. Likely not a junkie. A young professional looking for pot or coke or…?

"Who found him?" Dan asked.

"Homeless couple snuck in here early this morning. They forced the door. Well, they won't admit to it, but it sure looks like they did."

"And they called it in?"

"Yeah, how about that," said Officer Kovetsky. "They've got a cell phone!"

"Where are they?"

"Those two sitting on the stoop a couple doors down. I bought them a couple cups of coffee and asked them to hang around."

"Nice of you," Dan nodded.

"I know 'em, they're regulars in this neighborhood. I didn't want them to bolt. I told them they were in no trouble. I'd say they trust me. I honestly can't see them having anything to do with this."

"Good thinking. Maybe they saw something. It's worth a try."

The medical examiners filled the room and some lights came on as they set up their portable illumination. The room somehow looked even more drab and dreary in the sun-bright arc lighting. There was more noise outside as additional vehicles arrived and multiple feet tramped up the steps. SID techs were now on the scene.

Along with somebody else, Dan was happy to note.

"Hey partner," came Jilly's voice as she stepped into the room. "What've we got here?"

"Come check it out, Jilly."

"Officer Kovetsky, how are you doing?" Kovetsky nodded back at her.

Dan began filling Jilly in on what he had already learned as he continued to search the body. He found something jammed deep into the man's pants pocket and delicately maneuvered it out. It proved to be a couple of folded-up envelopes.

"Doesn't seem to be a wallet or ID," Dan said. "This is all that was in his pocket." He unfolded them and held them up in the light.

"This one's just junk mail…this one's an electric bill. Maybe he had grabbed his mail leaving his home."

Dan read the name off the front of the bill. "Mark…Zanello, looks like? 4356 West Brophy, Apartment 314. He's pretty far away from home."

"Wait a minute," Jilly said abruptly. "His name is Mark Zanello?"

"I'd guess it's his name, yeah. In any case that's the name on the…"

Jilly tried to say it under her breath, but "Holy shit" came out clearly audible. Dan looked up with a start.

"That's unlike you," he said dryly.

"Can I see that?"

By now she was standing directly behind him. Dan passed it up to her. The ranking ME cleared his throat to indicate they were waiting to get to the body. Dan stood up and they both stepped back.

"I can't believe this," Jilly was saying, staring at the envelope. "This could be that crazy girl's boyfriend."

"Come again?"

"She said she's been trying to reach him for several days and he never answered or returned her calls," Jilly said, slightly dazed, struggling to make sense of this.

"This would certainly be a good excuse," Dan replied.

Jilly noted that Dan was rapidly developing a sense of humor, and a dark one at that.

"How long would you say he's been here?" she asked the coroner's man.

"I'll be able to give you a better answer in a little while," he grunted, "but judging from what I'm seeing here, maybe four or five days."

"This is an insane coincidence," she said. She took out her phone and snapped several photos of the body, especially the face, trying to get an angle that avoided the worst of the gaping head wounds. "And that's what it has to be."

"Maybe we should give them some room to work," said Dan, and Jilly nodded.

They moved back to the parlor, now arc-lit. The entire ground floor looked about the same: broken down, covered in dust and debris. Nothing seemed to have disturbed the pristine disorderliness except for what looked like drag marks on the floor. It seemed evident that someone had dragged the body through the hall and parlor, dumped it in the bedroom and left.

"How do you get upstairs?" Jilly asked, looking up at the ceiling.

"There's a separate stairway, has its own door outside. If somebody came in here they might not have had occasion to go up there. We can look and see if that door lock's forced as well."

Jilly paced around for another minute or two. "This looks like a dead end in here. Might as well leave it for the techs to check out." She headed for the front again. Dan was a step ahead of her.

Kovetsky walked them to the couple sitting on a stoop a few doors away. The man was tall, weathered, and had a thick dark beard. His female companion was equally weathered and scowling, puffing away at the remains of a cigarette. Empty coffee cups lay alongside them.

"Thanks for waiting for us, Nate. These detectives got a few questions for you, okay?" The man nodded.

"I'm Detective Garvey, this is Detective Lee. So you found the body in the building?"

"Yeah," Nate answered in a deep raspy voice. "We were looking for someplace to crash, seein' how it's gettin' cold lately. Usually these buildings along here, they're nailed up shut pretty tight. This one had been pried open so we looked inside."

"And you found the body?"

He pointed. "It was back in that room, where you guys saw. It was dark and we kinda stumbled over it. Soon's Nadine saw it, she started freakin' out and we got outa there."

"You weren't too happy to find it neither," Nadine interjected sourly, then returned to her cigarette butt.

"How did you contact the police?" Dan asked.

Nate pulled an old flip phone out of his pocket. "Had this for a while.

I can put minutes on it when I got a couple bucks. Good for an emergency." He showed a gap-toothed grin.

"Do you come across something like this much?"

"No, man, this was the very first time we ever found someone been murdered! Looks like he might been, what, shot?"

"Yes," Jilly replied. "You know any of the gangs around here?"

"Sorta. Roland 29's are around here."

The detectives were familiar with them, homing in around 29th Street only a few blocks away. The name had evolved as a corruption of "Rolling" 29s.

"So, you found the door had been pried open already when you got to it this morning?"

"Yeah, exactly. Had to give it a good shove, but…"

"Any other signs of anybody having gone through the building before you?"

"Hard to tell, it was all messed up in there to begin with."

"Did you go into any of the other rooms?"

"No, when we got back there and saw him, we just turned and got out."

"Did you go in any other places, upstairs, in any of the other buildings?"

"Nope, that was the only one that was open."

The conversation did not get any more fruitful and after a few more questions, they thanked the couple and told them they could leave. Jilly handed Nate one of her cards.

"If you happen to think of anything else you think might be of help, just give me a call, okay? I appreciate it."

Nate cleared his throat.

"Yeah, what?" asked Dan.

"Any chance you might be able to help us out a little?"

Dan and Jilly looked at each other. Dan pulled out his wallet and handed a bill to Nate.

"If you come up with anything else, let us know, okay?" he said as the bill changed hands.

"What do you think, partner?" Jilly asked as they walked away.

"Pretty clear those two had nothing to do with this. Maybe a gang shooting, I don't know. Doesn't feel quite right, but…"

"Agreed," said Jilly. "Can't rule out wrong place, wrong time just yet, but it's weird. I'm thinking body dump from somewhere else."

She still had the photo in her bag that Kerry had handed her earlier. She pulled it out and looked at the young man leaning over in the corner of the blowup. It was hard to be certain, but it could be the same person they had just seen on the floor of the building.

She took her phone out of her pocket with a deep sigh. "I guess we have to go talk to Kerry again."

"I'll meet you there," Dan said. "No way I'm leaving my car in this neighborhood."

* * * *

Kerry answered her phone immediately.

"Kerry, it's Detective Garvey. I really need to talk to you again right away. Have you got some time right now?"

"Detective, time is pretty much all I have right now. I just got home. Come on over." She gave Jilly an address.

Jilly broke the connection and looked at Dan. "I have a feeling this is not going to be a pleasant conversation."

It was not a pleasant conversation. They had gone to Kerry's apartment and sat down around a kitchen table, and Jilly had shown her the photo on her phone, the one that only showed his face, his eyes having been closed. She had told Kerry how they had found him. Kerry had gone into hysterics.

It was now a good five minutes later and she was still sobbing.

"I got him killed, didn't I?" she wailed.

Jilly had put her hand on Kerry's shoulder. She said softly, "We don't know that. This is definitely your boyfriend, Kerry? This is Mark Zanello that you told me about earlier?"

Kerry nodded her head up and down. "He…he *was* my boyfriend. Not anymore."

"I don't think this had anything to do with you. I think it's just a coincidence that we talked about him today. But we're going to look into every possibility on this."

Another minute passed and she seemed to be calming down. Dan pushed the Kleenex box a little closer to her. Finally it seemed the right moment to proceed.

"When was the last time you saw Mark?"

"A few weeks ago. Maybe a couple of months."

"So you two haven't been together in a while?"

Kerry shook her head. "No. No, we….we broke up about six months ago."

"Have you talked in the meanwhile? Maybe on the phone, email, anything like that?"

"No. The last time we spoke was when he came by to pick up some things he had left here."

"We're trying to make sense of where we found him, and what might have happened to him. Can you think of any reason he would have been in that neighborhood?"

"I don't know. He didn't live near there. His apartment was in a kind of sketchy area, that was becoming what you might call gentrified—but nowhere near *that* bad."

"Did he have any friends, perhaps, who lived there?"

Kerry shook her head, looking down. "No, nobody I know of."

"Kerry, did Mark use any kind of drugs?"

"No, never. He drank, sometimes a bit too much, that was about it."

"So there's no chance he was coming to see a supplier, maybe a friend or acquaintance, could that be why he was in that neighborhood?"

"Oh my God no. I can't even imagine that."

Jilly looked at Dan, hoping he'd feel comfortable enough to jump in here. This was now their case, both of them.

"Did Mark have a car?" Dan asked.

"Sure. A Toyota, maybe five years old."

"What does it look like?"

"It's dark green. I think it's a Matrix."

"He was found pretty far away from where you said he lived. Would he have walked over there? Possibly he was passing through the neighborhood to get somewhere else?"

"Mark wasn't much of a walker," Kerry said. "If he was there, he probably drove."

"So his car might be parked nearby. We'll check into that. He didn't have a wallet or identification or almost anything else on his person. No wristwatch, no jewelry, no pocket change, no keys. Would that have been normal for him, to go out without anything?"

"I can't imagine he would do that. Mark was pretty fastidious. Go out without his wallet? No." She paused to think for a moment. "He had an old watch. He didn't like jewelry. He carried his keys in a little leather case."

"He had an electric bill in his pocket. Would he perhaps have been on his way to pay that?"

"No, he usually paid his bills online. He had the bill in his pocket?"

"Yes, does that strike you as unusual?"

"It's just…strange, that's all. Maybe he got it out of his mailbox on the way out of his place?"

Jilly jumped back in again. "Tell me about your recent relationship with Mark, would you?"

Dan took the opportunity to rise and excuse himself, saying he was going to phone in the information about Mark's car and have the uniforms check the neighborhood. But he was more likely hoping Kerry would be more forthright about this if he were absent.

Jilly turned back to Kerry, waiting.

"Like I said, we hadn't been together in months."

"I'm sorry, but it might be important...why did you break up?"

A deep sigh from Kerry, still looking down at her hands on the table. "Cheating."

"He cheated on you?"

"No." Another long pause before she looked up at Jilly. "I cheated on him. And he found out."

Jilly let that play out in silence. She waited.

"I was having an affair with my boss at the magazine."

"Uh-huh?"

"It...it started maybe nine months ago. It just sort of happened. Things got out of hand. I didn't plan for it to go like that. We got more and more involved. I wasn't sure what I wanted to do. Then Mark found out." She made a wry, mirthless smile. "I guess that solved the problem."

"Were you and Mark living together at the time?"

"No, we had our separate apartments, the same ones we still have. *Had*, I should say. But I spent most of my time at his place, just came back here now and then. We had been talking about getting a place together. That was a huge step for him." She brushed a tear away from the corner of her eye. "We had been talking about getting *married*, for God's sake."

"What was the breakup like? Was it...emotional?"

"Surprisingly, no. Not an awful lot. Mark's not an overly demonstrative sort. It's not like he was screaming and throwing things. He keeps things in. It was more like he was hurt—really, really hurt."

The tears began once again. Jilly waited while Kerry wiped her eyes and blew her nose.

"How about you? Were you the demonstrative sort?"

"I was kind of in the wrong place to be yelling or screaming. I was the bad guy. I mostly felt guilty." Kerry seemed then to understand the point of the question. "Are you asking if I might have attacked Mark or something like that?"

"Just trying to get a grasp of what was happening, that's all."

"No, no! Nothing like that! Neither of us was a violent sort! Mark never hit me or anything like that, and I certainly never did anything to him either!"

"Okay. And what about your boss, after all this came out?"

Kerry smirked. "Almost right after that, he broke it off with me. Turns out he's 'happily married.' Things got really uncomfortable at work, and about a week later, he fired me."

And thus, thought Jilly, arose her desperate search to confirm real love could actually exist?

"Does Mark have any relatives in the area?"

"No, his family, what's left of it, is back East, in New York—mostly Brooklyn."

"Where did he work?"

"For Burnt Toast. It's a small advertising and promotional firm. That was how we met. I was doing freelance work for them."

She paused to give Jilly the address of the firm's offices.

"How about friends, anybody he was close to?"

"About the only people I ever knew him to hang out with were Gary and Louie. He knew Louie from New York; they went back a number of years. Mark used to date Gary's sister and the two guys got to be good friends. Aside from that, well, Mark wasn't all that social. He liked to stay in, reading or playing computer games—or watching movies. He has a huge collection of DVDs." She caught herself. "I…I guess I mean he *had*."

"That's a perfectly normal reaction, Kerry. Don't worry about it. Do you know how we can get in contact with Gary and Louie? Do you know their last names?"

"Yeah, Gary…Krasnow, I'm pretty sure is his last name. Louie, his real name is Luigi, his last name is…Ghirardelli. Like the chocolate. It was a joke among us."

Dan returned to the table, tucking his phone in his pocket. "The registration is being run for a plate, and Kovetsky's looking up and down the street for a green Matrix," he told Jilly.

"Kerry, is there any chance that Mark tried to confront your old boss?" Jilly asked. "You said he was very upset over the whole thing."

"I can't see that happening. Mark wasn't like that."

"How about your boss? Would he be capable of hurting Mark if he felt threatened?"

"I wouldn't think so, but, then, I guess I don't really know him like I thought I did, do I?"

"Could you give us his name and the address of the magazine?"

"His name is Kevin Warfield and the magazine's OnTheSpot." She rattled off another address, including a suite number, while Dan jotted it down.

"You don't need to tell him hello for me or anything," Kerry sneered, her eyes burning.

Jilly nodded. She got it.

They asked a few more questions and then wrapped up the conversation, thanking Kerry for her help. As they rose to leave, she asked, "So how can you be so sure that I didn't get Mark killed, asking all those questions about Dane Spilwell?"

"It just doesn't make any sense, Kerry. Don't think that way, okay? But we'll examine every possible angle. We *will* find out who did this to Mark."

She rarely made such a promise, but she felt like she had to say something to the young woman. "In the meantime, I have to stress again, stay away from that whole issue, stay *far* away, understood?"

Kerry nodded vigorously.

"Am I in danger, Detective?"

"I'm thinking not. Someone is trying to discourage you from pursuing this, but, other than the phone call, there have been no express threats to you. Again, I'm inclined to believe that what happened to Mark is not related to the Spilwell case. But I do suggest you keep a low profile and stay away from this whole subject. And I'll be checking in with you regularly to make sure you're all right. Do you understand?"

Kerry nodded again.

"I'm going to be looking into all the people who've contacted you. Now, you're absolutely certain the person who met you in the park identified himself as Laura Spilwell's brother? He said his name is Ryan Hart?"

"That's exactly right. I remember distinctly."

"And you say he phoned and asked you to meet him."

"Yes."

"What day did he call you?"

"Three days ago. Sunday."

"Okay, thanks. Kerry, you'll be all right if you *do nothing* about this whole thing. Don't talk to anyone, and don't try to contact anyone or look into anything. I mean it!"

"I said I won't. I promise!"

"I'll see you back at the station," Jilly said to Dan as they walked back to their cars. "We've got a lot to talk about. We have to figure out how we're going to attack this one."

Dan nodded. "Do you really think the Zanello murder has nothing to do with this whole Dane Spilwell thing she's opened up?"

"I really doubt there's any connection, Dan. But there is one thing that troubles me a little."

"Let me guess. The brother?"

"Yeah. Exactly. Laura Spilwell did not *have* a brother. She was an only child. And her parents are deceased. In fact, there are only a couple of cousins remaining in her family."

"So someone is going to a lot of trouble to get Kerry to stop showing that photo around and asking questions."

"It would seem so. Also, I still can't see a viable connection to the Mark Zanello killing. But there's something else going on there."

"If there *is* a connection—if someone was willing to kill him to hush up whatever it is that Kerry's stumbled into—could that mean that Spilwell might really be innocent?"

"I'm not willing to buy that yet. It flies against all my instincts and experience. But…"

"But?" repeated Dan.

"I've just been thinking," Jilly said, "about something Reggie once said."

"Which was?"

"Well, it wasn't the first time we had run across a faked robbery to cover a murder. Reggie said something like, 'It's a chess game.' "

"A chess game," Dan repeated.

"Yeah. It's like, we see the telltale signs that the robbery is bogus, it's a red herring. We know. We can feel it sometimes. But then he'd talk about the next level of the game. When the killer wants to make it *look like* it's a setup for a fake robbery to attract attention to a third party. A double red herring."

"Wow," said Dan. "I think I'm following."

"The perps figure the cops are smart enough to see through the fake clues and follow through to expose the supposed cover-up, but they *aren't* smart enough to see through the higher deception. It's a setup of a setup. Like out of a spy novel. I can think of only one other time I saw something like that."

"What was it?"

"It was really heavy-handed. There was this girl named Rose. She was maybe in her early twenties, a gang member. She had it in for this other girl, a rival for the attentions of some guy she liked. So she shot her, right on a deserted street corner, and just left her there. Then she left a trail to make it look like a robbery, a clumsy stupid one. She took the other girl's wallet, phone, everything, and left it all in a gutter about a half block away, after taking all the money out of the wallet. But she decided to use the opportunity to settle a second score, with an old boyfriend who had done her wrong. She had gotten hold of something personal of his— I forget what it was now—but she left it in the gutter along with the other stuff. Like he had dropped it while trying to set up the scene."

Dan actually laughed. "Now that takes, I don't know, moxie?"

"Moxie?" Jilly echoed.

"You know, guts. Daring. Audacity."

"Yeah, well…it was a clumsy effort to create the impression of a clumsy effort. Didn't work for more than a few minutes. We were on it like that." She snapped her fingers. "The thing is, these people want to think we're not that bright, but they also think that they *are* all that smart. They're usually not."

"So are you thinking about this in relation to the Spilwell case? Did Reggie ever think there was that extra level going on in that one?"

"No, we both had him good for that one from the start." Jilly sighed in thought. "At least I think we both did."

"So the point here is?…"

"I don't know. Maybe there is no point. It just came to mind, is all."

Dan pulled his car key out of his pocket. "Lots to think about here, isn't there? I'll see you back at the station."

* * * *

Dan sighed as he hung up the phone. He had obtained the license plate number for Mark Zanello's aging green Toyota Matrix and called it over to Officer Kovetsky.

"She's coming up empty," he said. "Doesn't seem that the car is in that neighborhood. In fact, no Matrix of any kind has been spotted there."

"Carjacking maybe?" Jilly replied from her own desk, perusing her computer screen. She had acquired Zanello's phone number and was initiating requests for records of his phone. "Somebody grabbed his car and he put up a fight, so they shot him and dumped the body?"

"Carjacking an old Matrix?" Dan asked. "Kind of a stretch."

Jilly shrugged. "Most cars are boosted for parts these days, and we both know Toyotas are high on the theft lists. They're very popular cars."

"I guess we can't rule it out," Dan agreed. "But it just doesn't feel right."

"My lord, what does feel right about this one?" Jilly muttered. She keyed in a SEND and looked up from her monitor. "So let's figure out our next move."

"I agree with you," Dan said. "Kerry's boss could be a possibility. Mark's a betrayed lover, he goes to confront this Warfield guy, and things escalate."

"Yeah. Mark's two friends might be able to shed some light into his comings and goings, maybe his state of mind. Maybe we should talk to at least one of them first, if we can—before we question Warfield."

Dan nodded.

Jilly heaved a deep sigh as she picked up her phone again. "And I'm afraid we're going to have to look into all the other people Kerry tried to contact this week, just to tie up the loose ends."

"The lawyer, Towers."

"Yeah. And she said she tried to talk to a couple reporters but got no further than leaving an email without any details. Probably not much there. And then there's someone who probably won't talk to me any more than they would to her."

"What kind of reporters?"

"From the *Blade*. She never heard back from them."

"I'm surprised she didn't go tabloid," said Dan. "Lots of people in print and online would have run with anything—if it sounded sensational enough."

"Maybe if she had had more time, she might have. She was trying to find 'respectable' avenues at first. But I'm sure she would have kept going down the line—until I sidelined her."

"You mean when the threats started."

"Or whatever they were."

"Clearly somebody isn't happy with what she was doing."

"Yeah, and whether or not it's connected, I have to look into those as well."

"We," corrected Dan. "*We* have to look into them, Partner. Do I need to remind you?"

Jilly laughed. "I stand corrected. Thanks for that. Are you sure you want to get involved in this one as well?"

"Comes with the territory."

Jilly finished dialing and apparently someone on the other end picked up quickly. She spoke into the receiver quietly, officiously. There was a short exchange, during which she nodded several times, and then she hung up, giving Dan a curious look.

"Now that was strange. Her assistant said that she'd love to meet with me. I've got an appointment tomorrow morning, first thing."

"With whom, exactly?"

"Clea Solana herself!"

4.

More phone calls had established the whereabouts of both Louis Ghirardelli and Gary Krasnow. They contacted both, saying only that they wanted to talk to them about Mark Zanello. Neither seemed aware of the tragic news from earlier in the day. Jilly was hoping that the news media had not gotten hold of the identification yet.

Krasnow was at work and said he would be able to meet with them later, but Ghirardelli was available right then, so Dan and Jilly drove to his apartment. He was heavy-set and friendly, with dark hair and a goatee. He only gave their badges and IDs a passing glance before inviting them in. Stepping through the door, Jilly could immediately tell he was a single guy. He swept a pizza box and some other debris off his sofa and coffee table and invited them to sit down.

"Hope we aren't disturbing anything," said Dan, settling himself cautiously into a mismatched recliner chair.

"Naw, nothing going on right now. I'm freelancing and work is light. So what's up that you want to talk to me about Mark? He's not in any kind of trouble, is he?"

There was a moment's silence. Dan and Jilly looked at one another and Jilly took the initiative.

"Mr. Ghirardelli, something has happened to Mark. He was found murdered this morning."

"What? You're kidding, right? No way!" He looked back and forth at them. "No, come on! Mark?"

"I'm sorry, sir. Yes, it's the truth."

"Holy…" He buried his face in his hands for a long moment. "How… how…?"

"He was shot to death. His body was found in an abandoned building on Pilsen Avenue."

"I don't understand. Why would he be over *there*?"

"That's what we're trying to figure out. We're hoping you might help us. We understand you and he were close friends?"

Ghirardelli nodded. "Oh, yeah. Yeah. We go way back. Back to Brooklyn. We went to high school together!"

"When was the last time you saw or spoke to Mark?"

He seemed to be in shock and it took a few moments for the question to sink in.

"I hadn't seen him in a couple of weeks, I'd say. He'd been busy working. I talked to him on the phone a few days back. Called him at his job. We had planned to meet up at a local club. He said he wasn't sure if he could make it—and he never showed up."

"Do you remember exactly what day that was?"

Ghirardelli said blankly, "Let's see, it would have been…five days ago. Friday."

"And you and he agreed to meet up somewhere?"

"Yeah. Well, sort of. Mark was like that." He looked up at them, refocusing. "He was an 'OBO' kind of guy."

"OBO?"

"As in 'or best offer,' like in the ads for selling stuff? He hated to commit to anything. All the jokes about how guys can't commit, you know? It's like, Mark *really* wouldn't pin himself down, like, to anything. He was always waiting to see if something better would come along and he'd just…I'm babbling, aren't I?"

"It's okay. We're following you. Go on."

Ghirardelli kept shaking his head. "He's really gone? Shit. I can't believe it. I'll never get to talk to him again."

"I'm really sorry. This is hard. But whatever you can tell us might help us find out what happened."

"Of course. Sorry. Where was I?"

"You called and you were going to meet up. Friday."

"Yeah yeah. Told him he needed to stop working so hard, take a night off. He and I were going to go to a local watering hole, the Bucket of Blood."

"Bucket of Blood?" said Dan. "Really?"

"Yeah, well, it's an ironic name. Hipster bar, you know? They have bands, open microphone nights, stuff like that. Craft beers on tap."

"Where is this place?" Jilly asked, notebook on hand.

"Right down the street. Mark doesn't live all that far from here…I mean he *didn't* live…aw damn…"

"It's okay, take your time. What time was he supposed to meet you on Friday?"

"We just kinda left it that he'd show up if he was able, like around seven or eight. I hung out and when he didn't show up, I figured, well, that was Mark."

"Was anybody else with you?"

"I ran into a couple of friends, and we just hung around for a while."

"So it didn't surprise you when he didn't show up? You didn't call him or anything?"

Ghirardelli shook his head. "Nope. That was how Mark rolls. Rolled. As long as I've known him."

"Can you think of anybody who would have wanted to hurt him?"

He ran a hand through his mussy hair. "No, not at all. Mark was…" he stopped and got unfocused again for a moment. "No. There's nobody."

"Was Mark doing any kind of drugs, involved in anything like that?" Dan asked.

"You mean, like, *drugs* drugs? No, no. He drank. Definitely drank. Maybe a bit too much at times. Especially lately."

"No gambling, anything like that?" interjected Jilly. "Anything that might have brought him into contact with a different kind of crowd?"

"No. I mean, he followed sports and stuff, we all do. He may have played in fantasy leagues now and then. I don't think he ever bet, or like that. Once in a while we played poker. He wasn't very good. I can't see him hanging out downtown with the card players or bookies, anything like that."

Dan nodded. "You said especially lately he was drinking more heavily. Would that be because of his breakup with his girlfriend?"

"Oh, yeah. That just crushed him. Totally. You know about that, huh?"

"Why don't you tell us what *you* know about it?" Jilly said quietly, smiling kindly. "It was hard for Mark?"

"The last few months, he was pretty crazy, getting smashed every night. Hanging out with us a lot, crying in his beer, so to speak? Then he suddenly changed, started getting really into his work, working long hours, and fell out of touch with us."

"Excuse me, who's 'us'?"

"Oh, me and our friend Gary, Gary Krasnow. We're like, the three musketeers."

"When did he and his girlfriend break up?"

"Let's see, that would have been—oh, wow, a good six months ago."

"It was traumatic, you're saying?"

"Oh yeah. He found out she was sleeping with her boss. It had been going on for a while. Came as quite a shock to him."

"How did he find out?"

"He *saw* them!" Ghirardelli shook his head and clucked his tongue. "She had been telling him she was working late a lot. She works on this magazine. She's like the art director or designer or something like that. Said there was a chance she might get a big promotion and a nice raise so she wanted to impress the publisher. Mark was kinda excited about it. He figured if they had more money coming in they might finally think about getting married. Do you know what a huge thing that was for Mark, the OBO guy? He actually talked about it, used the M word and the whole thing!"

"But," Dan prompted, "he found out the truth?"

"Oh yeah. *Oh* yeah. Get this: he went out one night with a couple of the guys from his agency, which was strange, since he didn't really hang out with them much. But they had just finished this major campaign thing and they invited him along and he knew she wasn't going to be home until late, so he went. Turns out they went to this sports bar that was *right across the street* from where her boss lived. What are the odds? He saw her out the window. She was coming out of the building with the guy, and they were like all kissy-face and touchy-feely. The guy put her into a cab and went back into the building."

"Ouch," said Dan.

"Exactly. Mark left and hurried home and she was already there. He let her tell him a few lies, and then he let her have it about what he saw. This had been going on for *weeks*, it turns out."

"Couldn't have been too happy about that," Dan said. The way he said it suggested he could relate to Mark's pain. Jilly sat out this part of the conversation, watching fascinated as Dan expertly gained Ghirardelli's confidence.

"Oh, he was destroyed."

"So what did he do? That night, I mean."

"He called me up and asked if he could come over. I figured they had had a fight and she had thrown him out for the evening, so I said sure."

"Did that happen much, her throwing him out, I mean?"

"Nah. Never. Those two, they were like thick, you know?" He crossed his index and middle finger. "Close. Real love birds. But I figured, you know, shit happens."

"So he came over and told you what he'd seen. Louis, right? Can I call you Louis?"

"Sure. Louie is good, that's what they call me. Oh yeah, We got pretty loaded together. He crashed on my couch, This one right here, in fact." He proudly gestured to the sofa on which he and Jilly were sitting. "I had work the next day, but, you know, your bud and all, you gotta be there, Detective."

"You can call me Dan, that's fine. Dan and Jilly. But yeah, for sure. Good thing you were there for him, I'd say. So he stayed with you after that?"

"No, *she* moved out. They both had kept their own places. That old *fear of commitment* thing, again, I guess."

He actually smirked and made quotation marks in the air with paired fingers. The ironic generation, Jilly thought to herself.

"She had been staying at his place," Louie went on. "But by the next day she was gone, back to her own apartment, I guess. She came back a few times, he said, to pick up something of hers or to drop off something of his."

"So that was it, they just broke off contact after that?"

"Yep, just like that."

"So he hung with you guys, the three musketeers, a lot right after that."

"And let me tell you, trying to keep up with him once he started hitting the drinks? A challenge, my friend. A challenge." Louie made a pantomime of tossing back a shot several times, head tipped back.

"Mark must have been really angry at her."

"Yeah, but you have to understand, Mark wasn't like a violent kind of guy. He didn't get in fights. I kinda doubt he ever even hit anybody in anger, like never, as long as I've known him. Once or twice he, like, threw something and broke it. That was about the extent of his anger. He was more...sad. Really, really sad. Like, morose. Depressed."

"He didn't say anything like he wanted to hurt this other guy?"

"Oh, sure, he said some stuff, wouldn't you? For weeks we would toast the bastard, fantasies of things we hoped would befall him, pits of poisoned stakes and such, the smug scumbag. It was all just letting off steam. In real life, I can't imagine Mark actually even considering doing honest harm to the guy."

"Did he ever try to confront the man?"

"No, I don't think so. Mark just decided to write her completely off. It was like she was dead to him. He wouldn't acknowledge her existence, never mentioned her after a while. It was like those Orthodox Jewish guys who ostracize a family member and declare them dead?"

"I've heard of that. In some extreme cases, someone might say the prayers for the dead for them. Real finality. That's a pretty serious resentment."

"Yeah, well, I'm not saying that literally. Mark wasn't Orthodox, he wasn't even Jewish, though being from Brooklyn, we were familiar with that culture. I'm just using that as an example of how serious he was about forgetting she existed."

"So he cut off all communication with her, never tried to contact anyone she knew, not the new boyfriend, nobody?"

Louie shook his head. "Not that I ever knew of. And at that time we were spending a lot of time together, him and me and Gary."

"Do you happen to know the name of the boss, or the name of the place she worked?"

"Oh, let me think, His girlfriend's name was Kerry. I mean, it still is, she's just not his girlfriend anymore. Oh damn, of course she isn't. I'm sorry." He started shaking his head vigorously and grimacing.

"It's all right, you're doing fine."

"Kerry Moran. She works for...it's a hip magazine, they publish a paper edition and they're also online...OnTheSpot. All one word. I used to pick it up on occasion. I guess I felt I had to stop out of loyalty."

"And the guy, her boss?"

"I don't know, I heard Mark mention his name here and there. Kevin something. He used to make comments about '*KEV-innn*.' Or more usually, '*FUCK-inggg KEV-inn*.' Especially when he got sloshed. It would be like a chant. *FUCK-inggg KEV-inn*."

"So you say he was drinking heavily. Did he lose his job?"

"No, his own boss was totally cool about it. He told Mark to take some time off, not to take *too* long but to come back when he felt better. I mean, I'm sure the guy had a limit, but he was cool. They were really supportive of Mark."

"Do you know his boss's name, anything about the agency where he worked?"

"Yeah, it's called Burnt Toast. Young, hip, up and coming. The guy who runs it is named Jamie Farad."

Jilly noted the name in her book. She observed that Dan had made no effort to take notes but was totally concentrating on Louie.

"Louie, I gotta say, Mark sounds like he showed remarkable self-control. I mean, I've been in that kind of a situation, not exactly like that but close enough. And I tell you, I'd have been all over that other guy at some point."

Louie nodded gravely. "It occurred to me, but that's just not Mark, that's just not how he rolled."

"So he finally straightened up and quit drinking and returned to work? How long ago was that?"

"Oh, maybe three months or so now. That's when we stopped seeing him very much."

"His job was there, waiting for him."

"Yeah. In fact I think Jamie gave him a raise or some kind of incentive."

"He felt like he needed to throw himself into his work."

"There you go. He needed the distraction and he must have felt like he owed them for treating him so well." He mimed toggling a light switch. "It was like he flipped a switch on his psyche, you know? Click. Different guy."

"So work became pretty much his whole life for the past few months."

"Yeah, I guess so. If there was anything else going on, he didn't talk to me or Gary about it."

"So you wouldn't have known if, say, he had decided to go look up this other guy, this Kevin, maybe have it out with him."

"I tell you, I sincerely doubt he would have done that. He wanted that stuff behind him."

"Do you know anything about what might have happened with his girlfriend, Kerry?"

Louie shrugged. "No idea. I assume she's still shacked up with *KEV-in*. Maybe she's gonna marry *him*. I don't really care about that bitch." He glanced at Jilly. "Sorry." She raised her hands as if to say, "No foul."

"Is there anything you can do here, to help shed light on this thing for us, Louie? He got killed in a really bad part of town you said he never went to, he didn't associate with drug dealers or gamblers or gangsters, you say he wouldn't have gone looking for a fight with anybody. So…" Dan shook his hands in the air in frustration. "Can you think of *any* reason this happened where it did?"

Louie thought for a long moment, his head slowly shaking. "Only thing I can think of. It's a long shot. But it's absolutely the only thing I can think of."

"Yeah, tell me, I'm desperate here, Louie. Tell us."

"The magazine," he said. "They did articles on gang life, stuff like that."

"Recently?"

"Within the last year or so. They did a few features on the Roland 29s and the Brown Skulls or whatever they're called. Aren't they from down in that area?"

Dan nodded. "More or less."

"Like I said, it's kind of a stretch, but it was while Mark and Kerry were still together, maybe he was down at the offices and met one of those guys when they were being interviewed. It's the only thing I can think of."

Dan and Jilly exchanged a look.

"Let me ask you something else," Jilly interjected. "If Mark had been going to meet you four days ago at the…Bucket of Blood?" She said the name as if it were a tangible object she was trying to avoid touching.

"Yeah?"

"You said it was close to both of you. Would he have driven there, or would he have walked?"

"Mark wasn't much of a walker. I woulda thought he'd drive. It would've been about an eight-block walk from his place. I think he'd still have wanted to drive."

"And where does he usually park his car around his apartment?"

"On the street. There's no parking garage or lot or anything where he is. In fact it's a pain in the neck because there's street-cleaning and you have to move your car two days a week or get a ticket."

There wasn't much more after that. They thanked him, left cards, and moved on.

"Nice job in there," Jilly said as they walked back to her car.

"Not that we got all that much from him," Dan replied.

"Yeah, but you got him to open up. I don't know, he just struck me as kind of a loser. That might have come through. I might not have related to him quite that effectively. It was a help, in any case."

Dan made a wry face. "I guess I relate to losers better than you."

"Oh come on, I didn't…" Jilly stopped as she saw Dan break into a broad smile. He continued to surprise her.

"Actually, this Mark himself strikes me as kind of a loser, you know? At the very least, he was a really private guy. Not too many friends. Kinda passive."

"Played his cards close to the vest, as they used to say," said Jilly. "A definite enigma."

"So I'm thinking the agency is next?" Dan said. "Last people to spend quality time with the deceased."

"Agreed," replied Jilly. "We can talk to Kerry's old boss once we've got a handle on Mark's recent state of mind."

"Save the best for last," Dan said wryly.

5.

Burnt Toast was the kind of young boutique agency that they expected. It occupied a reception area and two large open work spaces in a recently renovated industrial building, with trendy interior decor: exposed pipes and beams, high ceilings, and minimal furnishings. About ten employees, all eager twenty-somethings, occupied plain glass and enamel desks scattered at the peripheries of the expanse. Computer monitors and large wall displays were ubiquitous.

The energy was pervasive, like an anthill: everyone was animated, constantly talking, and moving about. Sound bounced off the walls.

Jamie Farad, the owner, was the sole person with a private office. He came out to greet them with a smile and an extended hand. He looked to be slightly older than his staff, with closely-buzzed hair, a fashionable goatee, black shirt and slacks.

"Detectives," he said. "How may I help you? This is about Mark, I understand?"

""That's right, Mr. Farad, may we talk in your office?"

"Jamie, please," he said, his smile fading as he took in the officers' serious demeanor. "Sure, come right in."

Once they were seated in front of Farad's large glass desk and he settled into his own comfortable chair, he turned to them, truly concerned. "Mark hasn't been in now for a few days. We haven't been able to get hold of him. Is he all right?"

"No, I'm afraid not," Jilly said. "He was killed. His body was found this morning."

"Oh my God," Farad mumbled, looking genuinely shocked. "No."

"I'm sorry we have to be the ones to let you know this way. But we're hoping you might be of some help to us in our investigation."

"Of course," Farad nodded earnestly. "Of course. What happened to him?"

"We're not really sure. He was found in a deserted building on Pilsen Avenue. He had been shot."

"Pilsen? What was he doing over there?"

"We don't know yet."

"That's a sketchy neighborhood, very sketchy. I wouldn't be there any time of day."

"So you can't think of any reason he might have gone there?"

Farad thought, shook his head. "No, none."

"It would seem that you and the people here were the only ones with whom Mark had had any contact in recent days," Jilly said.

"I wouldn't be surprised. Mark was a rather private sort of person. Very intense, very guarded. He'd had some difficult times recently and I think he was throwing himself into his work just to get past them. He certainly was spending a lot of time here in the studios." He paused. "I just can't believe this. This is terrible news. You say he was shot?"

"Yes. Apparently at close range."

"A robbery maybe? Mugging? Carjacking? This could *not* have been someone he knew."

"Nobody you can think of who might have had a grudge against him?" asked Dan.

"No. Absolutely not."

"Did he have any clients from that neck of the woods? Redevelopment agencies, charities, pro bono work?"

"We have a very high-end high-profile kind of clientele," Farad said. "Digital tech, luxury commerce, cutting edge technology. Nobody from the other side of Twentieth Street. I don't mean to sound snobbish, believe me. It's just that's who we work with."

"So when was the last time you saw Mark?"

Farad sat back in his chair and thought. Jilly noted that he was the sort of measured person who tended to think before he spoke. "That would have been the end of last week. Friday. He hasn't been at work all week."

"Did anybody try to go over to see him at home or anything like that?"

"No, we just kept leaving him calls. He never picked up."

"You weren't concerned enough to report him missing?"

"Well, as I said, Mark recently had some personal troubles, so I thought perhaps he had had a relapse, so to speak. I was willing to cut him some slack, give him a few days to sort out whatever he was still going through. If we hadn't heard from in for another week I would have been more concerned. Although…" he hesitated. "…it did bother me that he hadn't tried to get in touch. He had been straight up with me about what was going on from the beginning. It was unlike him to just suddenly not show up. But as I say, I was willing to give him some benefit of the doubt."

Jilly and Dan didn't immediately respond so he continued. "Mark has always been a good guy here. He's a valued worker. Highly valued. He's a big reason a few of our recent campaigns have been so successful. I've been willing to go to the mat for him and I've never regretted it."

"What was his state of mind like the past few weeks?" Jilly asked.

"He seemed to be getting his groove back. He actually was smiling, even telling jokes. He seemed more alert. I think he had given up the drinking."

"I understand you gave him some time off when he first had his personal problems," Jilly said. "You were quite generous and patient with him."

Farad waved a hand. "As I said, I valued Mark very highly here. He had suffered the emotional and psychic equivalent of a ton of bricks dropped upon him out of nowhere…"

"Yes," interrupted Jilly, "the girlfriend. The other man."

Farad nodded. "You have to understand something, Detective. Mark is—I mean *was*, this is so hard to get my head around—he *was* extremely focused, almost as if he had tunnel vision. It was why he was so good at what he did here. But not when it came to his girlfriend, Kerry. She was the only human being who had been able to pierce through that single-mindedness. Oh, Mark was a very likable guy, don't get me wrong, but he was all work. Except where she was concerned. So naturally he took the breakup hard. Insanely hard. I felt my best course of action was to let him go do whatever it was he needed to do, work it out and then when he was ready to come back, he was welcome to do so."

"And how long did that take?"

"I'd say about ten or twelve weeks altogether? To be honest, I was beginning to get a little concerned that perhaps he *wasn't* coming back. Then one day he called and said he was ready. Just like that."

"And you had no contact with him during the time he was away?"

"None. What I heard was that he was deeply depressed. Drinking heavily." He shrugged, continuing to carefully choose his words. "I don't know of any other substances being involved, if that's a concern."

"And when he came back?" Dan asked.

"He was straight as an arrow. Sober. Serious. Focused. And he stayed that way."

"How did he get along with everyone here?" Dan continued. "Any difficulties?"

Farad shook his head, looking almost amused at the thought. "Mark was easy to get along with. He was an odd combination, aloof but friend-ly, rather passive, highly focused on his job, but never difficult, no ego to speak of. He never even had arguments. He had opinions and ideas and we all took them seriously, but he was always willing to work towards a consensus. He was the perfect guy for this kind of work, do you know? A people person of an odd sort, but without too strong or abrasive a personality."

Jilly moved on. "What did he do here?"

"We don't have traditional job descriptions as such. We expect a lot of cross-discipline thinking. Well, except for the really specialized work like the graphics." Farad juggled his hands up and down. "Mark was sort of like what you'd have called an account executive, mixed with a concept man, mixed with a copywriter."

"I see," mumbled Dan, not really seeing.

"And a few other things thrown in as well." Farad laughed. "We all make the coffee and doughnut runs too."

"Did he have a title?" Jilly asked.

"No, on his business card it simply said, "Idea Team." That's what all of our cards generally say."

"I bet yours is a bit more specific," Jilly said.

Farad shrugged. "I've got five separate cards, Detective, depending upon whom I'm meeting. That's the Burnt Toast way. We're very holistic here."

"But getting back to Mark," continued Jilly. "The breakup with his girlfriend. Did he talk about her or about that whole episode much when he came back to work?"

"Not that I'm aware of," Farad said, stroking his goatee with thumb and forefinger. "But I'm often in the office here, by necessity, while the real action is going on out there in the trenches. You'll definitely want to talk to some of the other team members."

"We'd appreciate that, thank you."

"Of course," Farad nodded earnestly. "They're all going to need to know this sad information as well."

They continued the conversation with Farad for a few more minutes before moving on to Mark's coworkers. He led them out of his office into the adjoining workspace and called for everyone's attention.

Not surprisingly, there was general dismay over the news of Mark's death. There were some general remarks made by Dan and Jilly before Farad excused himself, shaking each of their hands and saying, "Please let me know if you need anything else of me while you're here or any time. I hope you find the persons who did this."

Within a few minutes they had ascertained that Mark seemed to have been respected and liked by everyone but had been really close to only three people working in the agency, and Jilly and Dan pulled them aside to have a further conversation.

There were two young men, Pablo and Sam, and a young woman, Janice (which she pronounced "Ja-*neese*"). They were all identically dressed in black tee shirts and skinny jeans. The two men both had carefully stubbly chin hair, and Sam and Janice wore big glasses with heavy black rims.

It quickly became clear that once Mark had returned to work after his breakdown, he been all business, and no longer joined any of his co-workers after closing to socialize. He put in long hours and talked about little else except his own projects. He was friendly and agreeable, they all agreed, but it had become clear that he intended to think of nothing but the job. None of them had seen Mark take a drink since the ill-fated night he had discovered Kerry with her boss: an event, in fact, that had been in the company of Pablo and Sam.

"How did you three happen to become his closest associates here at work?" asked Jilly.

They bobbed heads back and forth at one another before Janice spoke up. "Maybe it was because we all worked together on a few accounts and we all seemed to jibe well. Similar ideas but different. Synergies." The two men nodded vigorously at that.

"So, no arguments, no fights, with anyone here? Everyone played nice together, is that what you're telling us?"

Janice continued, speaking animatedly. "Oh, it gets pretty intense working around here, believe me, there are fights, people blowing off steam. Of course there are. We work long hours in close vicinity to one another, we keep up the energy, we guzzle caffeine and energy drinks all day, we bounce off each other, we get crazy."

She shook her head and her dark ponytail and dangly earrings wagged back and forth, her eyes huge behind the glasses. "But not Mark," she said. "Nobody ever had problems with Mark. I don't ever remember him getting into it with anyone here, not ever. He always backed off, always found a way to be diplomatic and accommodating."

Sam and Pablo first shook their heads and then nodded, both in agreement with her. Jilly was beginning to feel like she was looking at a shelf of bobbleheads wagging up and down and side to side. She shot a sideways glance at Dan, who shot one back at her. Synergy indeed.

Jilly and Dan walked back to their car, still shaking their heads at the encounter with the Idea Team.

"So what we seem to have here," Jilly said to Dan, "is a kind of self-absorbed, passive guy who didn't start fights, kept his feelings to himself, and was redirecting all of his energies into work. Downright ascetic. Hardly the kind of guy who would go out looking for a violent confrontation, if we can believe what we're hearing."

"Those psychology courses really paid off, huh?" Dan replied with a smile. "Of course, there's the possibility that he really *wasn't* redirecting all the anger and resentment and stuff. Maybe he was just bottling it up and one day it exploded."

"Sounds like you took a few of those courses yourself, partner."

"And then maybe everybody's not telling the truth."

"All those sincerely bobbing heads? How can you doubt them?"

Dan rolled his eyes. "And yet somehow it doesn't feel right that one of them is hiding something about Mark."

"Yeah, I'm of a similar mind." Jilly was increasingly finding that she and her new partner apparently had similar instincts. That was all to the good.

"So are you thinking what I'm thinking?"

"Time to go talk to Kerry's boss," Jilly nodded, looking at her watch. "We got a while before we can see Gary Krasnow yet anyway. I have a feeling he's just going to tell us what everybody else has been saying. There doesn't seem to be a break here for us at all."

"The boss," agreed Dan. "He's looking better and better. If that's the right word for it."

A small suite of offices in a fashionably historic building housed OnTheSpot. The magazine was a trendy, oversized, overly expensive slick monthly that was sold in hip coffeehouses and what remained of bookstores and newsstands. The online Internet edition was increasingly becoming the more popular alternative.

They both familiarized themselves further by perusing back copies in the reception area as they waited to speak to publisher Kevin Warfield. Neither of them was all that impressed. It was oriented to an audience in their twenties or early thirties and featured splashy graphics and pithy features on popular culture, fashion, and current events. In some ways it more closely resembled a giveaway tabloid newspaper, the kind one found in newspaper dispensers in most large cities, except that this one had slick shiny covers and cost thirty-five dollars an issue.

Jilly found it all rather shallow, self-conscious and overly clever. She decided the writers were trying to present "think pieces" in the style of more established magazines that she herself had long enjoyed reading, but they lacked the depth to do it effectively. The magazine was, she had to admit, ambitious in its scope. It regularly ran feature articles by currently hot writers and media personalities and series attempting to be "hard hitting" and "socially relevant."

Leafing through a number of back issues only made Jilly feel old beyond her years.

Kevin Warfield greeted them in the reception area, looking very much like a traditional publisher—vest, shirtsleeves, expensive tie. He shook their hands and led them back through a labyrinth of cubicles, filled with the sounds of journalists at work: voices loud and soft, phones buzzing in odd tones, and keyboards and monitors making distinctive keyboard and monitor noises. The workspaces were utilitarian and cluttered. Graphics filled every wall space: photos, posters, and artwork.

Warfield had the corner office overlooking a busy intersection. He motioned them to chairs and sat down behind his desk.

"Detectives, how may I help you?" he said brusquely. He was, perhaps, in his forties, rather ruggedly handsome, well-groomed, and a full head of dark brown hair with just a touch of gray at the temples. He looked as if he worked out and paid attention to his health.

"You had an employee working here until fairly recently, I believe she was your art director, Kerry Moran?" Jilly said.

Her question provoked a deep sigh from Warfield.

"Yes. What is this, has she filed some complaint against me or something of the sort? I expected she might do that but it's been a while now and I thought…"

"No, sir, she hasn't filed a complaint against you—as yet," Dan interrupted. "Not that we're aware, at any rate. Did you know her former boyfriend, Mark Zanello, by any chance?"

Warfield stared at them. "I heard of him, yes. Never met him in person. Couldn't even tell you what he looks like. And this is about what, now?"

Jilly brought up the photo of Mark on her phone and placed it on the desk in front of him. "You've never seen this man, are you positive?"

Warfield looked down at the picture for several seconds, then back up at her. "I've never seen this man before in my life. This looks like he's dead. Is that what you're telling me?"

Jilly took back her phone. "Yes, that is what I'm telling you. You don't know him, you've never encountered him?"

Warfield shook his head, looking a bit surprised. "Absolutely not. What happened? What is this all about?"

"He was found murdered this morning."

"And that's Kerry's boyfriend?"

"He was, up until a few months ago. Mr. Warfield, it's our understanding you had a relationship with Kerry Moran while she was in your employ?"

"Good Lord, you don't think I had anything to do with this?"

Jilly and Dan waited.

"A relationship," Warfield shook his head with a wry smile. "Is that what she told you?"

"We're interested in what you have to tell us, actually," said Dan.

Warfield sat back in his chair and took another deep sigh before answering. "Yes, you could say that. She and I had a *relationship*. We spent some time together."

"You knew she was in a serious relationship with Mark? That they were engaged to be married?"

"She had mentioned that, yes," he said matter-of-factly. "Apparently *that* relationship had some problems. She was very interested in spending time with me, you might say. We would hang out after work, go to lunch, things like that. She liked to talk to me, confide in me. Things just sort of happened."

"You had an affair," Jilly suggested.

Warfield shrugged, raised his hands. "Call it what you will. I think she took it quite a bit more seriously than I did."

"Mr. Warfield, you're married?"

"Yes. Yes, I am."

"Did Kerry know that?"

"I let her know. I was honest with her."

"Were you aware that Mark found out about the two of you?"

"I heard about that, yes."

"Was that before or after you informed her you were married?"

"Look, what is this all about?"

"Were you aware that when Mark discovered you two were having your affair…"

"Whoa, wait a minute. You're using the word 'affair,' not me."

"…When Mark learned about the two of you, he left her? Were you aware of that?"

Warfield nodded. "Sure. She told me."

"And that's when you developed a concern about your own relationship with her and told her you were married?"

"I don't remember the exact sequence of events, Detective. And I'm not sure I like where this is going."

"Kerry was your art director for some time, wasn't she?"

"Yes, more than a year."

"And yet you suddenly decided to fire her?"

"Her work declined. She was distracted. I saw that developing for some time, had addressed that with her on a number of occasions. I documented our discussions as well."

"Up until then, was she a good art director?"

"She started out an excellent designer and art director. Great ideas. Made the whole look of the magazine what it was. I had high hopes for her. I thought she had a great future with us. I considered creating a new executive level post of creative director, branching out into more publications and other ventures. Then everything started going south with her."

It was Jilly's turn to take a deep breath and gather her thoughts before continuing. Dan watched her with interest.

"So, let me see, she enters into an intimate relationship with you—is that term acceptable—which results in the termination of her own long-term relationship with Mark Zanello and apparently a good deal of emotional turmoil for her, immediately after which you inform her you're married, terminate the relationship you two have been pursuing, and then dismiss her from her job shortly thereafter? Would I have this timeline correct, Mr. Warfield?"

He leaned forward, staring at them both earnestly, and spoke quietly but insistently. "Her view of our relationship, as you put it, was clearly different from my own. We had several conversations in which I attempted to clarify that, definitely. She was being unrealistic. If you've spoken with her, perhaps you understand what I'm talking about. Kerry is a lovely girl, very sweet, very intelligent, but with a naïve romantic streak. She's looking for some kind of storybook life that's just never going to happen. I didn't want to hurt her feelings. I only wanted her to be realistic."

"Were you ever aware of how Mark reacted to all of this?" Jilly asked.

"Well, Kerry told me, of course, but I never heard anything from Mark himself. As I said, I never had any contact with him."

Dan had picked up an older copy of the magazine that was sitting on a side table and leafed through it, noting the cover story. "You did a feature on youth gangs of the city a while back?"

Warfield seemed taken aback by this sudden change in subject. "Why, yes. About a year ago. We interviewed a few young men from various cliques and sets."

Dan held up the issue, that featured a stylized photo of a young man in a denim jacket over a dark hoodie, scowling to the side as he walked down an urban street. "Like the Roland 29s?"

"Sure, we did the Roland 29s. And Drew Road. And the Brown Street Skulls. Why?"

"Did you get to meet any of the gang members, I mean you yourself?"

Now Warfield looked truly mystified, shaking his head very slightly. "No, that was a series by one of our reporters. Two, actually, a man and a woman. Great pieces, very sensitive and insightful. I saw them, of course; the editor runs everything by me. We had hopes the series would have social impact in the city. But I wasn't personally involved in any of the stories, no. Why?"

"Just curious," Dan shrugged, putting the magazine back down. "So you don't know anyone who might be a member of the 29s?"

"Of course not." He said it as if Dan had suggested something beyond belief.

So much, Dan thought, for the journalistic social crusader. A slick trendy magazine didn't really lend itself to gritty muckraking, it might get the suit smudged.

"What's your point?" Warfield said. "What's that got to do with what we're talking about?"

Jilly picked up the thread again, finding a new appreciation in how Dan was working with her to keep the witness off balance. "I still want to understand how you viewed this intimate relationship with Kerry. You really didn't find it very serious at all?"

"I liked her very much. As I said, she's a very sweet girl. She's got a wonderful energy for life. She's quirkily attractive, has a vulnerable quality and she's a real charmer. Sure I was taken by her. As I said, things just happened. But she interpreted what had happened the wrong way. And then it began to affect everything in her life."

"So her entire life got upturned in the matter of a few days, maybe," Jilly said. "It pretty much got destroyed, both hers and Mark's. And you just washed your hands of the whole thing?" She opened her eyes wide, gestured with her hands, and having dropped the ball back into his court, just stared at Warfield.

There was a long awkward silence.

"You can see our point of view, can't you," Dan finally interjected, "why we might be a little confused here? You're saying that Mark never tried to contact you, never talked to you? Maybe you can help us out here a little? Maybe he *tried* to contact you, came to the office, and the receptionist wouldn't let him in? Maybe you left word to not allow him in?"

Warfield shook his head, his stare becoming a glare. "I did no such thing. I wouldn't have tried to run or hide from anyone. Kerry never returned; this Mark never approached me. Not here at work, not out of work, nowhere, at no time."

Jilly and Dan kept up their efforts for a while longer but the conversation continued in much the same vein. Warfield continued to insist he had never seen or met Mark Zanello, and that he had had no contact whatsoever with Kerry's world after dismissing her.

Finally Jilly and Dan each handed him a card and suggested that if he were to think of anything that might be of help, to contact them.

As they rose, Warfield asked, "Can you tell me how Mark Zanello died, the circumstances?'"

"He was shot at close range," Dan said straight-faced. "And his body was hidden in a deserted building."

"My lord," Warfield muttered. "How horrible. How bizarre. And you have no clues, no leads?"

"We didn't say that," retorted Jilly.

"Well, I certainly hope you find out who did this to him. Of course." He paused for a beat. "Perhaps the magazine could be of some help. May I have one of our reporters contact you?"

Jilly considered several possible replies but finally just shrugged silently as they turned to leave.

A brief conversation with the receptionist confirmed that she had no recollection of Mark Zanello, or anyone meeting his description, ever coming to the offices or trying to contact Warfield. They left the offices and took the stairs down the two flights to the street level.

Jilly exhaled loudly as they descended. "What a slimebag."

"Yeah," Dan agreed. He looked at Jilly. "Do women really find that kind of guy attractive? I mean, did you?"

"Well, he's rugged, well-built, worldly. Clearly he's got some money—and he's mature—a little bit of a father figure maybe. I could see a certain kind of gal would go for him."

Dan considered that, tilting his head back and forth.

"Totally messed that girl's life up," Jilly continued. "I wanted to ask him how his marriage is doing but I thought that might not be all that appropriate."

"I'd be very surprised if the affair was an isolated incident," Dan agreed. "Quite a few attractive young women working up there."

"You noticed," Jilly smirked. Dan just pursed his lips and said nothing more.

"He takes no responsibility for what he's done," she went on. "Wonder if he's hired any new young ingénue types in the meantime to replace Kerry—in more ways than one. Yeah, he's a real slimebag."

"But," Dan said, "I'm not getting any feelings that he's good for the murder, are you?"

"No," Jilly sighed deeply as they reached the bottom of the stairwell. "No, I'm not either."

Kevin Warfield was guilty, but not of what they wanted him to be.

* * * *

"Long day," Jilly murmured as she pulled out her cell phone one more time. "Let's talk to this Gary Krasnow and get ourselves back to the station. Maybe there'll be some good news."

"Why do I have the feeling," said Dan, "that this guy is going to tell us exactly the same thing that everybody else did about Mark Zanello?"

Dan turned out to be absolutely right.

Krasnow told her he was able to get out of work early and would be glad to meet them at his apartment. He gave her an address and said he'd be there within the half hour.

The conversation was quick and seemed like a rerun of their earlier one with Louis Ghirardelli. Krasnow was also shocked at the news of Mark's death, asked a few questions as to the circumstances, and then asked how he could be of help to their investigation.

He was a pleasant enough fellow, energetic and intelligent. He joked that he was the only one of the "three musketeers" who held down a "normal" job, in an insurance agency.

Some years back he had met Mark when Gary's sister briefly dated him—nothing that ever developed seriously, he said—and while the couple thing had not worked out, he and Mark had become friends. He befriended Mark's boyhood pal Louie as well, and the "three musketeers" had formed.

The portrait he drew of Mark was similar to that of everyone else with whom they had spoken that day: introspective, reticent, and focused to the point of distraction. He told the identical story about the disintegration of Mark's relationship with Kerry, his tailspin into heavy drinking, and his apparent resurrection.

Krasnow had not been in contact with Mark since his return to work with a single-minded vengeance. He could not even begin to account for the hows and whys of Mark's murder. It was as mystifying to him as to everyone else.

* * * *

"There's nothing," Jilly muttered as they drove back to the station. "Unless this guy just stepped into the wrong place at the wrong time and got randomly killed."

"Yeah," said Dan. "Against the odds, but if it turned out to be true, we might never find out what happened."

Random events were a concept they both hated to accept. It did happen on the rare occasion, but all their training and instinct went against it. There was almost always a pattern, a logic to crime. They just had to find it.

"There is one other possible explanation though," Jilly said reluctantly. "That somehow this all really is related to Kerry and the Dane Spilwell case."

* * * *

A large part of every law enforcement officer's day is taken up with the prosaic and mind-deadening pursuit of paper. There are reports to be filled, documentation to establish, every "i" to be dotted and "t" to be crossed in the interest of future prosecutions and court procedures, lest a promising case be scuttled by a technical misstep. Dan and Jilly would be spending time at the squad room filling out their own documentation of their interviews. And the techs who had investigated the crime scene that morning would be busy filling out their paperwork as well. Jilly was happily surprised to find the preliminary reports already on her desk when they returned. She scanned them quickly.

"Two slugs, .38 caliber revolver," she read. "Time of death estimated at five days ago, Friday evening." She flipped a page. "Evidence consistent with his being dragged into the building after being shot. Not much luck with fingerprints, there's too much 'noise' everywhere. No clear footprints on the floor. The homeless couple likely covered up anything that might have remained from the killer."

"What are the odds on our finding the weapon?" asked Dan. "Not great."

"We have to hope for a break on that."

"Let's see what tomorrow brings. So you'll be hobnobbing with the jet set."

"Yeah, that's going to be interesting. Clea Solana herself. I wonder why she's so eager to talk to me."

"I guess you're going to find out."

6.

Clea and Giovanni Solana, when they happened to be in the vicinity, resided in an elite gated community high in the affluent hills to the east of the city. On a day less rainy and cloud-obscured, there would have been a magnificent sweeping view of the coast and the sea to the west. Their home was an elegantly understated villa in an Italian architectural style.

Jilly had to admit feeling self-conscious about meeting with such a high-profile celebrity in a rather intimidating setting. She had quietly scolded herself the entire morning as she drove to the meeting, reminding herself that an effective police officer needed to maintain confidence and control.

She had chosen one of the suits she usually reserved for court appearances, where the proper gravitas needed to be projected. Reggie had liked to kid her about her "power suits," and she would respond by pointing out his own partiality to expensive pinstriped three-piece suits. Soon the "power suit" joke had become a standard with Reg and Red, being bandied back and forth between them regularly.

She smiled at the fond memories of her former partner, distracted from her self-consciousness.

The door was answered by a smiling staffer who obviously had expected her. She was invited into a spacious entry and escorted through several large rooms into a sunken study, furnished with thick carpeting and soft comfortable couches and chairs.

"Ms. Solana will be right with you," smiled the assistant, a dark-haired young woman with a soft Italian accent.

Sure enough, mere moments after she had departed and Jilly had settled into one of the chairs, Clea Solana herself was descending the three steps from the entryway as if she were the Sun Queen herself. She had a long lush mane of hair and wore an expensive silk pantsuit with just a touch of jewelry.

Someone fond of clichés might have said her smile lit up the room.

But what immediately struck Jilly was exactly what she had anticipated with some dread. Surrounded by all the style and beauty her wealth and breeding could afford, her face was still irremediably disfigured. Her lips were swollen and her skin was alternately scarred, creased, and smooth-textured like a plastic doll's.

The effect was bizarre, to say the least.

Jilly had prepared herself for this meeting, having read and heard much of Clea's history. She was an intelligent, talented, and cultured woman from a celebrated international family. But somehow that had never been enough, even after marrying the successful producer-director Giovanni Solana and successfully making her own mark in numerous artistic endeavors. Possibly to overcome some insecurity, she had sought out plastic surgeons all over the world to make herself more beautiful.

Things had somehow gone all wrong.

And chief among those failed surgeons, Jilly reflected, was Dane Spilwell.

All of these facts flew through her mind in a split second and she hoped she had not revealed her hesitation.

She rose from the chair to greet Clea.

"Detective Garvey? I am Clea Solana. How very nice of you to come visit. Welcome!"

Her smile was huge, her manner gracious and inviting, and she acted as if she were indeed the stunning beauty she had tried so hard to become. Somehow she made Jilly relax and feel more comfortable.

So much, Jilly mused to herself, for the police officer taking control of every situation.

"Please, have a seat, let me get us something. Would you prefer coffee, tea?"

"Coffee would be wonderful, thank you," Jilly replied.

She noted that another staffer had already mysteriously materialized alongside Clea and was nodding at her directions. Clea spoke softly and courteously to the young woman and in moments she was gone again.

Clea even sat elegantly, with almost regal bearing. She crossed her legs gracefully and turned her attention to Jilly. Her own voice also bore a lilting northern Italian accent. "I am delighted to have the chance to meet you in person."

"Thank you for inviting me, Ms. Solana. I have to admit, I was surprised to get such a gracious reception when I called."

Clea nodded with a serious frown. "I left word that if you were to try to reach me while I'm still here in your lovely city, you were to be given an immediate appointment. I was told that someone had recently tried to communicate with me about the recent Spilwell trial. Unfortunately the person who took the call didn't handle it well, simply told me it was a woman. I thought it might have been you, and so I made sure our staff was prepared, should you call back."

"That actually wasn't me, but I'm aware of what happened, and it does have some bearing on why I'm here now."

"I followed the trial as carefully as I could. You know, traveling and all, it is not always easy. Laura Spilwell was a dear friend of mine. Her death was a horrible tragedy."

Jilly leaned forward. This was unexpected. Clea Solana had never figured in the trial and she had had no idea that the two women had even met, much less had ever been close.

Clea continued. "I was fascinated by the testimony and the news articles throughout the case about you and your partner—Detective Martinez, I believe?"

"Yes, Reginald Martinez."

"And how is he? I would have loved to meet you both."

"Unfortunately," Jilly said, "Detective Martinez passed away earlier this year."

"Oh no! I had no idea! Please, forgive me!" She seemed genuinely disturbed that she had not known of Reggie's death. "It's the travel, so many things constantly…"

"Perfectly all right, Ms. Solana."

"May I ask, what happened? He was such a handsome man, so… strong, so intelligent, always impeccably dressed. Such a favorable impression he always gave!"

Yeah, that was Reggie.

"Detective Martinez was killed in the line of duty," Jilly said. "He was part of a police action, a raid on a house where two fugitives were in hiding. Gunfire was exchanged. He died in the hospital a day later."

"How horrible! Did he have a family?"

"Yes, a wife and two children. A son and a daughter."

Clea actually rose and walked over to sit next to Jilly and took her hands. "I am so, so sorry. What a terrible loss."

Jilly nodded and smiled, looking down at their entwined hands. "Yes, it was. He was an excellent detective. Great partner. Good friend. And a good man."

"When, if I might ask, did this happen?"

"It was not quite five months ago."

Two young attendants—somehow their personal bearing made it difficult for Jilly to think of them as servants—entered the room and set up a side table with cups and an actual espresso machine, as well as a tray of what looked like small pastries.

The activity created a perfect moment to change the mood of the conversation.

Clea brightened. "I hope good strong espresso is to your liking?"

"That sounds absolutely fantastic," Jilly admitted.

With the serving out of the way, the conversation resumed. Clea sat back but remained in close proximity to Jilly as if they had established some secret intimacy between themselves.

"So now, please, tell me how I may help you?"

"Well, I suppose my main objective was to make sure that the person who tried to contact you hadn't caused any…problems of any sort."

Clea seemed amused. "Not at all. As I said, unfortunately I was never even informed when she tried to talk to me. May I ask what this was all about?"

"It was a young woman with very good intentions but, well, she was interfering with police matters. We were concerned that she might have given the wrong impression that she represented legitimate authorities, that sort of thing."

Clea nodded, thoughtful. "The trial is over. Dane Spilwell was found guilty, was he not?"

"Yes he was."

"I was amazed by everything that happened. It was such a shock to find out that Laura had died, and just how it had occurred. And it was a surprise to learn that her husband had committed the crime."

"A surprise?"

"Oh, I had no doubt he did it. You were clearly extremely competent detectives, I could see, two of the best. If you were confident in the evidence, I was convinced, and very early on in the case."

"It sounds as if you followed the whole thing very carefully, then."

"As closely as I could, given my crazy schedule, mine and Gianni's. We do try to spend some time together despite our demanding businesses. But yes. As I said, Laura was very dear to me."

"Forgive me," Jilly said carefully, "but I was unaware that you and Laura Spilwell had been so close."

"And of course that interests you. I'm glad to tell you about it. You probably know that Dane Spilwell performed surgeries upon me a few years ago."

She stared directly into Jilly's face, as if defying her to stare back. Jilly held the gaze of that oddly misshapen face.

"Detective, when I was younger, I was foolish, I was very, *very* foolish. I grew up in a milieu of beauty and style and appearance and I believed that those were the most important things to life. I was so very unhappy with what I saw when I looked in the mirror. My parents, my family, my various boyfriends and lovers, all tried to reassure me that they found me beautiful, but I could not believe any of them. What I saw was not beautiful. I don't know if you can understand how one can look into the mirror and see only what they shouldn't see."

"Many young women do exactly that," Jilly said.

"Sadly, yes. We can be smart, we can be perceptive, we can be loved and secure, and we still see ourselves as unattractive. We can fear losing those we love and cherish unless we become more attractive. And so, I tried to do that. My family had the resources. I consulted with surgeons around the world. I ignored their advice against many of the things I insisted be done. And well…" Clea raised her eyebrows and extended her hands out. "…when there is considerable money involved, people begin to tell you what you wish to hear, they begin to do inadvisable things because you insist upon them."

Clea raised her head high. "And this is now what I live with. The woman in the mirror is still not what I wish. In many ways, ironically, nothing has really changed in that regard. What *has* changed is that I recognize that the people who love me and care about me, who have stayed with me…they are what make me beautiful. Or ugly."

Jilly simply nodded.

"My last surgeries were with Dane Spilwell," Clea continued. "We came here. That is when we bought this lovely villa, in fact. He is a brilliant surgeon, and he came with excellent credentials and impeccable references from the best people all over the globe. By then I was hoping for someone to perform sheer miracles, to reverse the damage that had already been done. Once again, I refused to listen to his dissenting opinion and pressed him forward."

She smiled wanly. "And here I am. At first it was devastating. It had finally begun to dawn upon me what I was actually doing to myself. I was despondent. That was when Laura showed up at my door."

"Laura Spilwell sought you out?"

"Exactly. She was absolutely charming and lovely. She never said it, but I understood that she had come to support me, to somehow try to make up for what she felt her husband had done to me. She didn't try to make excuses for him or offer silly homilies, she was just…there for me. And we became friends."

"You must have found a way to spend a good deal of time together, then."

"I was amazed to discover that we had much in common. Laura came from an excellent family. She had traveled a lot. She was very familiar with my beloved Tuscany, and she knew of my favorite places in Spain and France. She was a very fashionable woman, and we could talk about so much. I invited her to join me on a few trips as well. Somehow she healed me, Detective Garvey. My bitterness began to vanish and my joy for life began to return. I learned to ignore this strange husk I had acquired and, at the same time, to laugh at those who could only pretend to ignore it."

She laughed a soft enchanting laugh. "Now I feel bad for them, because they cannot see what really matters."

"Ms. Solana, people have said that you are a very remarkable woman. I now see they understated the fact."

"You're most gracious, Detective. Now tell me, has this young inquisitive woman caused you the trouble you feared she might?"

"I don't think so. I think I got to her before she could do any real damage."

"Dane Spilwell is going to jail, is he not?"

"Yes. He was sentenced to life imprisonment at Falcon Island. There will be an appeal but I don't think it will do any good."

"I still do not understand why he would kill Laura. It didn't make sense. I would have thought he was a smarter man than that, more perceptive."

"Murder is seldom an intelligent action, Ms. Solana. But what exactly do you mean about him being more perceptive?"

"Well, for example, did he not realize that Laura knew he was seeing another woman?"

"Maybe you should tell me more about this."

"I was here in your city for the last few weeks she was alive. We got together several times to talk and do things together. She seemed lonely and very unhappy. She had learned that her husband was involved with another woman. I don't mean just a casual indiscretion or anything like that. She was convinced that he was very seriously involved with someone, and that he was going to press her for a divorce."

"Did Laura ever tell you how she had come to that conclusion?"

"Well, wives, girlfriends, they always know, don't they?"

But not boyfriends, thought Jilly. Not Mark Zanello. Aloud she simply said, "I have observed that's often the case, yes."

"Little subtleties we pick up on, don't we? Especially if we are at all perceptive. Laura was a brilliantly perceptive woman. She was possessed of an exquisite sensitivity. She knew."

"But Dane had not approached her about a divorce?"

"Oh no. He was undoubtedly concerned about appearances. And perhaps there was a problem with the woman as well. I would not be surprised if she were also married. But Laura was convinced everything was going to come to a crescendo, so to speak, before very long. And she was resigned to agree to a divorce as well. There would have been no contest on her part."

"So you're saying Dane could have simply, er, eliminated Laura from his life in a much simpler and easier way? Forgive me if that sounds blunt."

Surprisingly, Clea laughed, this time with gusto. "I'm quite relieved! It would seem I don't have to walk as carefully around you as I thought I might! You put it quite succinctly, Detective. It's no laughing matter, of course, but yes, it all seemed quite senseless to me. Could Dane Spilwell have been that obtuse? Could he not have realized his deception was not perfect, that it had..." She reached for the words. "...it had holes like a leaky boat?"

"Laura was on to him," Jilly nodded.

"Precisely. It was clear to her that her husband was infatuated with this other woman, whoever she was. She said there were times he acted like a schoolboy rather than a sophisticated world-famous surgeon."

"Wow," said Jilly. "I have to admit, I had no idea about this."

Clea's eyes widened. "But you're the detective!" She smiled mischievously.

"We never needed to explore this side of things. Everything was cut and dried. It was as clear a case as we ever saw."

"Would any of this information have made a difference to your case?" Clea asked with interest.

"No. Not really. But what does surprise me is that the defense never introduced any of this. Possibly it could have been incriminating, but a sharp attorney could have spun some of this as argument against his motive. The motive was the weakest part of the case. Well, it wasn't weak, really, just less strong. Basically, the prosecution argues motive, means, and opportunity. We had means and opportunity down cold."

Clea nodded. "The murder weapon. The fingerprints. The doctor's lack of an alibi. And so forth."

"Right."

Clea shrugged. "For some reason, the defense refused to consider these things as having advantage. Or perhaps they did not know."

"Didn't know?"

"Dane Spilwell was, what's the expression, playing his cards close to his chest? For whatever reason, he may have felt the time was not yet opportune to publicize his mystery lover, even to his lawyer? Perhaps her own husband did not know? Perhaps she just was not ready to commit to him as he was willing to commit to her? Maybe she wasn't ready to leave her own marriage as of yet?"

"Wow." Jilly suddenly felt like a total *naif*. Here she was, someone considering herself to be a hardened and experienced detective, feeling out of her league with this woman of the world. "Wow"? Had she really just said "Wow" not once but twice?

Clea smiled and waved a hand. "But none of this is of real import now, is it? What's happened has happened." The smile faded. "It's a tragedy. An awful tragedy. A lovely, wonderful woman, full of life and kindness and generosity, was taken from us, and for totally senseless causes. I'm glad that justice will be done to her killer."

There was a rushing sound as one of Clea's assistants operated the espresso machine.

"You must try the biscotti," Clea smiled.

7.

Kovetsky gestured with her thumb at the coffee shop. "He's in there. I better not go in with you. He wouldn't want to be seen with me in public."

She glanced up and down at Dan. "You don't look too 'cop' right now. If you're cool he'll be okay."

She gave him a quick smile, which Dan returned. It was a cold wet morning and the both of them were hunkering down, Kovetsky in her uniform jacket and Dan in his windbreaker.

"Thanks," he said.

"He'll be in his usual dark hoodie. You won't be able to miss him."

"And you say his name is Hojo?"

"Yep. Been a help to me a few times now. I got his sister out of a jam a while back. But it only goes so far."

'Hojo? Really?"

"It's his real name. No kidding, Howard Johnson."

"Are you serious?"

Kovetsky raised her hands and her eyebrows simultaneously. "What can I tell ya, Detective Lee?"

"By the way, Dan is just fine," Dan replied. "Greatly appreciated."

"Anytime, Dan. And you can call me Sandy." She gave him an up-and-down look and a smirk and turned away.

Pearson's was a small old-school coffee shop, not overly full at the moment. It was in a neighborhood that was on the fringes of the Roland 29s turf but considered neutral territory by the local gangs.

Dan saw a young man in a dark hooded sweatshirt and knit cap, sitting alone at the long counter with a plate of eggs in front of him. He ordered a cup of coffee and sat down, leaving a seat between them.

This had to be Hojo. He was in his early teens, but already had the hardened and self-possessed look of someone older. He gave Dan little more than a cursory glance, continuing to simply sit and look straight ahead at nothing in particular, as if lost in scowling thought.

Dan's coffee came quickly. He took a sip and said quietly, "So you must be Hojo." Neither of them looked at the other.

"You the cop? Kovetsky told me you're cool," the boy mumbled, so low he could hardly be heard.

"Got no interest in doing anything to you," Dan said. He pulled out his phone and laid it on the counter, just to look as if he were doing something. "Just trying to find out some information. You heard about the body on Pilsen yesterday?"

"Sure. Everybody heard about that."

"They're saying it was a 29s killing."

Hojo snorted quietly. "Who sayin' that? That's crazy."

"You're saying it's not?"

"Hell, no. No way. That boy, he wasn't no gangster. Not from our territory, not from nobody's. He was like a hipster, you know? Some-one prob'ly killed him somewhere, brought him and stuffed him in that building to get him outa the way."

Out of the mouths of babes, thought Dan.

"Not an initiation, like, some kid earning his bones?"

Hojo shook his head, still looking straight ahead. "That ain't how it's done. And I woulda heard about any, you know, membership drives? Nothin' like that, these past coupla weeks."

"No way a couple of the guys might have gotten into it with him and popped him?"

"Nobody in the 29s would roll that way. That's an insult."

Hojo glanced about a bit apprehensively. He clearly did not want to be caught here taking to Dan. "And if anybody had been popped, proper like, you know, we'd know about it all over. That'd be the point, you know?"

"The hipsters don't come down there to buy?" Dan asked. "They don't get robbed, or get disrespectful and in fights?"

"Oh yeah. Little rich boys out slummin'. Their money's green too. Once in a while they get taken. I don't mean hurt, I mean like what you call *robbed*. But nothing like this ever happened. Nothing like what you're talkin' about *did* happen."

"You're positive?" Dan asked.

He felt like he should be talking dramatically out of the side of his mouth, like in an old detective movie. He kept looking down at his phone screen. "Kovetsky said you'd be straight with me. I'm not looking to get you in trouble. I just need to know what might have gone down."

"Wasn't no 29s," Hojo repeated, scooping up a forkful of eggs and washing it down with a gulp of orange juice. "Look, lemme explain something to you. Two caps in the head, right? Two. In the head. That's how he got it?"

"That's right."

"Around here, that means something specific. Very specific. You understand? Serious reprimand. Something like that happen, it's a message, we all know about it soon enough. Not how you treat a white boy that turned the wrong street."

"Got you," Dan said.

"Somebody from *outside* the neighborhood done this. Guaranteed. Take it to your bank next time you go." He looked about furtively once again. "Not comfortable talking much more here and now, okay?"

"Got it," Dan said, gulping down his cup and standing up. "Appreciate the help."

"You can grab my breakfast if you wanta be appreciative," the boy said, still eating and looking straight ahead, sliding his check a short distance down the counter with two fingers. Despite his youth, Dan could see he already looked hard and even haggard.

"No problem," Dan muttered and picked up the boy's check as well as his own, walking to the cash register.

* * * *

"So was he of any help?" Kovetsky said on the other end of the line.

"They sure grow up fast in the 29s, don't they? He's like, fifteen?" Dan was on a corner, in front of his car, concentrating to hear on his phone over the street noise.

"He's practically an elder statesman. We see nine-, ten-year-olds on the corners all the time. A lot of them have gone cold and dead behind the eyes by their mid-teens. Hojo's still got a spark."

"He says it's nothing the 29s would have done. Not their style. And you say I can believe him?"

"As far as it goes, yeah. I tend to agree. I've been thinking about that. Two bullets to the head. When I see that—and it's not all that often—it's usually a statement of policy. Hojo thinks it's a dump from outside the neighborhood, right?"

"Right."

"I think you can believe him."

"Would he have told me if it *was* something the 29s had done?"

"Can you tell me what he said specifically?"

Dan related the gist of the conversation.

"My read? If he knew of something and didn't want to get too involved, he would have approached it differently. Would have clammed up totally. The way he was telling you was as important as what he was saying, how I look at it."

"Okay, Thanks again, Sandy."

"Dan and Sandy it is, then," she said. "You need to come down here more often, Dan, get a better feel for this part of town. Totally job-related, you understand."

"I'll keep the invite in mind."

Moments later, Dan's phone buzzed. His Lieutenant, Hank Castillo.

"Detective Lee? You might want to get back here. We've got a present waiting for you and Garvey."

"What do you mean, Lieutenant?"

"They got your Toyota. Picked up a guy driving around in it. The officers are bringing him over now. Better inform Garvey as well."

"I'm on it." He rang off and began to dial Jilly.

* * * *

"Stokely James Richardson," Jilly read off the rap sheet she held. "A.k.a. Skeeter, a.k.a Skeets. Nothing really horrible on here, you know? This is kind of surprising to me, what we have going on here now."

Stokely was a tall, thin and bony man possibly in his late thirties, with a scraggly soul patch on his chin and blonde dreadlocks that looked as if they were last washed in the previous millennium. He sat in a plain gray metal chair at a plain gray metal table in the interview room, scratching himself and rocking back and forth slightly. He didn't seem to be focusing on anything very well at the moment.

Dan sat across from him, but Jilly was still standing.

"So help us out here, would you, Stokely?" she continued. "How did you happen to be in that car that doesn't belong to you this morning?"

Stokely shrugged, staring more or less straight ahead. "Found it. I was gonna return it."

"Return it. How nice of you. You're just a regular citizen, Stokely. And I suppose you were going to return the phone as well?" She held up a plastic bag containing a smart phone.

"Man I don't know nothin' about that."

"And here it was on the seat right next to you. Funny thing, there are four calls on it that seem to have been made in the past few hours, and how much do you want to bet when we track those numbers down, they'll belong to people who know you? Want to take that bet?"

He shook his head vaguely. He didn't seem to be quite all there.

"The officers who pulled you over got you on possession as well. Possession of what appear to be marijuana and possibly crystal methamphetamine."

"Man, those were, like, already in the car, I had nothin' to do with any of that."

"Hmm. Do tell. But here's what *really* makes me wonder, Stokely." Jilly held up another plastic bag, this one containing a black wallet and a watch. "These were under the seat, where you probably stowed them for safe-keeping until you could *return* them, right?"

He looked up at the wallet with a start. Finally something seemed to register. "Huh? I don't know nothin' about no wallet. I never saw that!"

Jilly let the bag dangle back and forth as she held the top with two fingers. "So we're not going to find your fingerprints anywhere on this, right?"

"No, no way! I never even saw them, I sure as hell didn't touch them! What is that?"

"Well, it's a wallet, of course. And a watch, see? They belonged to a man named Mark Zanello. You didn't happen to know him, did you?"

"Never heard of him! I don't know no Marks at all!"

"Mark showed up dead yesterday, Stokely."

"What! I don't know nothin' about that!"

"So," interjected Dan, "how did you happen to be driving in his car? If you don't know him, you're not going to tell me a perfect stranger lent you his car and then went and got himself killed."

"And," Jilly added, "you're going to tell us you know nothing about the blood in the trunk, which we think is going to turn out to be Mark Zanello's?"

Stokely shook his head as if to try to clear the obvious confusion.

Jilly and Dan had no doubt he had been dipping into his bags of goodies before the officers had pulled him over.

"Okay, look, I boosted the car, okay? Yeah, sure. It was just sitting there. Doors and windows open. Keys in the ignition! But I really was gonna return it, okay? I mean, I figured I'd just borrow it for a while. That's a lousy neighborhood, you know? Who knows, someone might'a broke into it or stolen stuff out of it?"

His sad grin exposed multiple missing teeth and a few that hadn't seen dental care since long before his last shampoo. "I was, you know, doin' the guy a favor, you wanta look at it like that!"

"And where," sighed Dan patiently, "did you find this car that you so gallantly rescued from the vandals and thieves?"

Stokely thought hard. It was work to which he was clearly unaccustomed. Dan thought he might soon smell his head burning.

"It was onna street, over around 33rd. Somewhere over there."

Dan had an image of Stokely wandering down streets, furtively trying car doors as he walked, until he found one that was open.

"And you just happened to notice this one?"

"There was a ticket on the windshield, made me take a closer look."

"When? When did you take it, I mean?"

"Aw, sometime yesterday, I guess. Just before dark."

And you've been driving around in it ever since?"

"Naw, I parked it near my place last night, locked it up good, crashed out."

"Looks like you made a little shopping trip this morning to fill your cart."

Stokely shrugged.

So here's the thing we have to get back to, Stokely. The guy who owned the car, the phone, the wallet, all of which were in your possession? He's dead!"

"I got nothin' to do with that."

A light seemed to go on somewhere in his brain. He looked up suddenly and said, "I think I'm gonna need a lawyer."

"Magic words," muttered Jilly, sweeping up the items she had brought into the room. "We're done here, partner."

"Too bad," said Dan as he rose, picking up his own notes. "We might have been able to help you out here, Stokely. Copping an attorney, that sure makes us think you might be guilty of something really serious this time."

Stokely shook his head, crossed his arms. He looked frightened. "I didn't do nothin' and I got nothin' more to say."

"Okay, okay. I'm assuming you'll be wanting a public defender?"

Norland Towers was not going to be available for this one. Jilly felt fairly confident about that.

They shut the door on Stokely awaiting his defender.

"33rd Street isn't all *that* far away from the building on Pilsen," Dan observed. "It's a bit of a walk, but conceivably Mark might have parked there and walked over."

"You're thinking Stokely's tale is true?" Jilly asked.

"Maybe yes, maybe no. His jacket is all drug and burglary stuff, a stolen car or two. Nothing violent. No armed robbery, no assault, no possession of a firearm, no carjacking, nothing like that."

"Doesn't mean he couldn't have done it, maybe if something went bad."

"You're right. But I don't know. This guy is a burn brain."

"Meth heads commit murders," Jilly observed. "Stupid ones too."

"No gun," Dan continued. "Nothing in the car, anyway, nothing on him."

"Even burn brains can think straight enough to dispose of a murder weapon. Wouldn't be the first time for either of us."

"Yeah. But then there's this." Dan leafed through the papers he had in his hand and held one out. "The parking warrants on the car. Most of them are from the opposite side parking on street cleaning days around Mark's apartment. He apparently just ignored several of them."

Jilly looked the list over and nodded.

"Then there's this one. Not gone to warrants yet. In fact it's only a few days old. Look at the address."

"Vega near 33rd Street," Jilly read.

"I think this doofus might just be telling us the truth."

* * * *

"So what've you got there?" Dan asked, eyeing the cardboard evidence box on Jilly's desk. She had unsealed it and was extracting various items, laying them out in front of her.

"Got this from the evidence room. They hadn't sent it over to Records yet. Lucky break there. It's the Spilwell case."

"Looking for the link," Dan said.

"Yeah." Jilly drew that word out like a long, resigned sigh. "It's sure looking like there's something there."

"But you're not convinced Spilwell is innocent?"

"I don't *want* to believe that, Dan. It was open and shut clear."

"Cop heart versus cop brain," Dan nodded. "We have to follow the evidence."

"Yeah. Pull up a chair, help me muddle through this."

Jilly walked him through the steps of their investigation and the evidence. She started by describing the discovery of the body and the first conversation she and Reggie had with Dane Spilwell.

"He had a story about being in all night. But there was camera footage in the building's garage of him coming in and parking in his space around midnight. He couldn't adequately explain that."

She leafed through the loose-leaf binder that contained all her reports. "Laura was stabbed by a fairly ordinary carving knife, the same one that you found shoved down the storm drain not far away. It turned out to be part of a set of knives in the Spilwell kitchen. They were in a butcher-block case and that one was conspicuously missing. He had no explanation of why it was missing and said it had been misplaced for several days. It was easy enough to match the murder weapon specifically to the set. And of course it had a print of his on it."

"Was it ever explained how Laura ended up in that alley?" Dan asked. "She was expected at her book club, right? That was a couple of miles away in another part of town."

"We never found her phone but got her phone records," Jilly said, leafing through to the relevant page. "The last call she received was at eight twenty-five P.M. The number turned out to be a public phone."

"Public phone? There's still such a thing?"

"Yeah. Pay phone at a convenience store. A Ready-Rite on Webley. No working security cameras anywhere around."

"She made a call out after that, right?"

"Yes, to the St. Ashby residence. She told her friend she'd be late for the book club, that she had to make another stop."

"You reasoned that Spilwell hadn't come home, that he called her from there and lured her somewhere. Convinced her to take a detour, maybe to meet him at that restaurant she liked, Monica's."

"Exactly. It all fit together. The Ready-Rite was pretty much directly between Spilwell's office and the alleyway. It would have been an easy and efficient route. He would have known she would park in that lot, maybe even told her to park there. And he laid in wait."

"And then set it up so it would look like a robbery-mugging gone bad. That's all plausible. But the knife, that seems all wrong. If he went to that much trouble to make it look anonymous, why use a weapon that was so identifiable?"

"We went over that. Best explanation, it was what he could find. Maybe despite the apparent careful planning, he had thrown it all together at the last minute. There were certain other indications of that. Anyway, we figured he thought he could toss the knife far enough down the drain that it wouldn't be found. Maybe he hoped for it to be washed away." Jilly shrugged. "It was perhaps the most tenuous part of our case, but for us it fit. We were afraid Towers would hit it hard, but for some reason he didn't."

"That," Dan nodded, "and the motive angle was weak."

"When the evidence is that solid," Jilly replied, "you can work around the motive."

"And again, Towers didn't hit that as hard as he could, did he?"

"No. He did bring it up. But, in retrospect, he could have hammered at us with it. Instead, he pulled his punches. Not very noticeably, but still…"

"Sure seems pretty solid," Dan mused. "Open and shut."

"But something about this case seems to be riling up somebody. What exactly, and why, I haven't got a clue."

Jilly peered at the sheets in the binder in front of her. "I need to go over this stuff one more time."

"We," said Dan, holding out a hand. "We're a 'we,' partner. Fresh pair of eyes. Can't hurt. Hand me over something."

8.

The offices of the prestigious firm of Towers and Bridges were located on the top floor of a tall downtown building. As they rode the wood-paneled elevator up, Dan remarked to Jilly, "Appropriate, don't you think: Towers and Bridges, way up here in the sky?"

"Norland Towers and Harrington Bridges. Couple of prep-school Ivy Leaguers. Reggie used to make a joke that nobody working here was allowed to have an actual first name."

Norland Towers was not one of her favorite people, nor was he looked upon with much favor by any of her colleagues. He was celebrated in some quarters for his uncanny success at acquittals in high profile trials, generally on behalf of clients who could afford his spectacular charges or who promised a further measure of celebrity.

Jilly was a firm believer in the judicial principle of presumption of innocence, but when she was the one who had done the hard work of gathering and analyzing the evidence and evolving an understanding of what it all indicated, it was difficult to see some of Towers' victories as anything but a triumph of manipulation over the truth.

Towers himself was smug and arrogant, not a man she would have liked even if he happened to be on her side in the courtroom. She had never really gotten to know him, nor did she really want to.

On the phone Jilly had been told that Towers would be in court today but that they would be able to speak with his assistant, Cynthia Grymes.

She only kept them waiting around fifteen minutes.

Dan remarked it was the most sumptuous waiting area in which they had ever had to cool their heels. Grymes finally arrived and ushered them back to a conference room, where they sat in dark leather chairs around a table of polished dark wood.

Grymes herself was buttoned-up, serious and self-possessed, and Jilly had the feeling that if she ever smiled, her face might actually crack. She sat straight up, now and then adjusting her stylish glasses but otherwise remaining almost stock still. She asked how she might be of assistance to them.

"It's our understanding that several days ago a young woman named Kerry Moran came to these offices to present to Mr. Towers evidence she felt might indicate Dane Spilwell's innocence."

"Oh yes. I remember. Last Friday. I was the one who spoke to her. Mr. Towers was out of town. She had a flash drive that she asked me to give to Mr. Towers. You know, a plug-in storage device for a computer?"

"Yes, we're familiar with them. And she explained why she felt the information she had was relevant to the case?"

"Yes, somewhat. She had some kind of a story about a photograph and having encountered the person in the picture on the night of the murder. She was scattered in her delivery. But she was clearly very earnest in believing the photograph would be exculpatory."

"And you didn't think so, Ms. Grymes?"

"Well, I have to say, she wasn't very compelling to my mind. She was passionate, but she did not persuade. But it wasn't my call, after all. I told her I would make sure that Mr. Towers got the flash drive, and asked for her contact information—which she told me was also on the flash drive which contained the whole story."

"And you passed the flash drive on to Mr. Towers and told him what she had said?"

"Oh, of course."

"When was that?"

"When he returned to the office, on Monday morning."

"Is there any chance he might have seen the photograph or the files on the drive before then?" Dan interjected.

"It's doubtful, since he was out of town. He told me he returned to the city late Sunday night. The flash drive was marked for his attention, along with other matters, before I left the office on Friday night. Had he returned early enough, he certainly could have seen it. But when I spoke with him first thing Monday morning, to fill him in on office affairs, it seemed obvious that was the first he had heard of it."

"And when you told him about it, what was his reaction?"

"He said he'd look into it. Perhaps an hour later he called me in and told me that Ms. Moran's photograph was inconclusive. There was no way to be sure the person in the picture was Dane Spilwell, and the enhancements that had been applied actually made it appear to be an attempt to alter an image.

"He also said that even if it could be argued that it was Dane Spilwell in the photograph, it could conceivably do more harm than good for many reasons. It suggested that he was having an extramarital affair at the time his wife was murdered, which would only add motive, while doing absolutely nothing to establish a credible alibi. He said the ongoing appeal could be seriously jeopardized if the photograph came to light and I should ignore it."

"Did he tell you to contact Kerry Moran and tell her that?"

"No, he said that from what I had told him about her, she seemed to be a bit of a 'loose cannon.' That was the precise term he used. He said we should ignore her, have nothing to do with her, and that I should inform our receptionists to not let her speak to anyone if she should return."

"That's rather curious, don't you think?" Jilly asked.

Grymes adjusted her glasses while staring at Jilly, never changing her glacial lack of expression.

"Not really. This office gets its share of…shall we call them *unhelpful* individuals? Many of them are well-intentioned but, well, a bit divorced from reality. We've learned that any kind of attention is taken as encouragement, and that we're better off ignoring them."

"Until they go away," said Dan.

Grymes leveled her iceberg stare at him. "Yes, Detective. We're extremely busy here and don't need irrelevant distractions."

"I'm sure you are," Jilly smiled. "Busy, that is. Do you still have the flash drive that Kerry Moran gave you?"

"No, Mr. Towers had it and said he was going to securely dispose of it. He didn't want the slightest possibility of it falling into anyone else's hands."

"Do you know if Mr. Towers would have discussed this matter with anyone else in the office? Would he have considered, perhaps, that this was a situation that needed to be further addressed?"

"Not to my knowledge. I'm his administrative aide and just about everything goes through me. He did not ask me to pursue it with anybody."

"And he didn't seem concerned that she might have taken her photograph and story elsewhere, to other people?"

"He didn't seem at all concerned about that, no. He dismissed her as a crank."

"And has he ever brought the subject up again since?"

"No, never. Clearly we consider it a dead matter."

Grymes actually made an almost imperceptible twitch, as if she were growing impatient.

Jilly and Dan glanced at each other. This one had run its course. They both rose from the table.

"Thank you for your help, Ms. Grymes, we appreciate it."

Cynthia Grymes led them down a carpeted corridor toward the reception area. There were nicely-framed photographs and graphics along the walls.

As they walked, she looked back at Jilly. "If I might ask what importance this all might have?"

"Just a routine inquiry," Jilly smiled back. She paused at a photograph. "This is Mr. Towers, isn't it?"

Grymes stopped and looked at the picture. "Yes, that was last year at the Legal Society formal banquet, when he received their Outstanding Professionalism Award."

"That's his wife next to him on the dais then?"

"Yes, that's Mavis Towers."

"I don't believe I've ever seen her before, in person or even a photograph."

"Mrs. Towers does tend to avoid the limelight. She's a very private person, very seldom photographed."

Jilly continued to stare. Dan stepped over and looked as well.

"She's quite lovely."

"Yes, Mrs. Towers is stunningly beautiful, isn't she?"

"Is her hair really that color in real life? She was most fortunate to be born with such a beautiful hair color. We're both redheads but I can hardly say my hair color is anything like hers."

"If anything, in person it's even more striking."

Grymes was clearly uncomfortable with the small talk and wanted them to move on and leave her to her agenda, but Jilly persisted.

"And it goes so well with that shade of green of her dress. I bet she wears that color quite a bit. And those emeralds. Is she partial to emeralds?"

"I really couldn't tell you," Grymes smiled almost painfully. "I'm sorry, but I really have pressing matters, if there's nothing else…"

"Of course." Jilly kept smiling as she turned away from the photo on the wall. "We can find our way out, so please don't let us keep you. And thank you for your help."

They were in the elevator before either of them said another word.

"That son of a bitch," Jilly muttered. "It's *her*. It's his wife. And he knew. He *knew*!"

Then she fell silent again until they were in the car and Dan was pulling away from the curb.

Dan could hear Jilly cussing under her breath as he drove. "He beats us all the time," she said. "But this time he didn't. He didn't *want* to. His old friend, Dane Spilwell. He scuttled the case, let him hang out to dry. He must have. He'll blow the appeal as well."

"That's something that would take a lot of finesse," Dan observed. "And it's a pretty outrageous idea, you have to admit."

Jilly sat thoughtfully for a long moment. "Now that I've got the idea in my head, I can kind of see it, Dan. Subtle things. Certain things he didn't push as hard as he could have. Certain things he let drop. The man's a master in the courtroom."

"So you're thinking, Spilwell was fooling around with Towers' wife, Towers knew, but Spilwell did *not* know he knew? So Towers got back at him by sabotaging his defense?"

"Pretty wild, huh? Yeah. That is *exactly* what I am thinking."

"Let's suppose for a moment you're right. It's a stretch, I'm not sure I can get my own head around this one, but let's just suppose. What does this mean, that Spilwell is really innocent?"

Jilly sighed. "I don't know. Not necessarily. It could be argued he wanted her out of the way. But then, Clea told me Laura would have given him the divorce. I just don't know."

"Is there some way this could relate to Mark Zanello? I mean, let's suppose Spilwell is being railroaded by his attorney, whether he's guilty or not. Suddenly Kerry's photo shows up, and her story about her and Mark in the restaurant. This could throw a huge monkey wrench into the works, couldn't it?"

"Someone threatens Kerry—or at least attempts to shut her up. Mark gets eliminated. Wait a minute."

She dug into her nag for her notebook and flipped through it. "There's one other witness that she mentioned, and what happened to him? The restaurant. A Light in the Tower. The waiter. She called him Satch."

She grabbed her phone. A couple of calls later she had reached the manager of A Light in the Tower and was asking about a waiter who worked there named Satch.

"You must mean Mort Blessing. Everybody calls him Satch."

"Mort? Okay, if you say so. I understand he recently quit, is that right?"

"Yes, rather suddenly in fact. He's a musician and he got some kind of unexpected offer of a regular gig. In Chicago, I think he said."

"He just up and quit, no notice?"

"He felt really bad about it. He's worked here for a while and we all like him. He's one of our most popular servers. But he said the offer came out of the blue, it was an enormous opportunity to play with some major band and he couldn't afford to turn it down. They needed him to leave that night. So I wished him well and reluctantly let him go. Well, maybe it wasn't all that willingly, but what could I do? I mean, after all, he's a musician first and a waiter second, isn't that always the case?"

"And you don't remember who the offer was from or any other details?"

"I'm sorry, no. Honestly, I was more focused on the fact I was losing a waiter I needed badly. But he was incredibly excited. He said he couldn't believe his luck. This was a once in a lifetime chance."

"Did he leave a forwarding address, someplace to send his last paycheck, anything like that?"

"No, I agreed to settle up his paycheck right then. We've got a good history. And he said he'd contact me when he had a regular address there. Chicago, I'm pretty sure."

"What day was that?"

"Let's see. It was Sunday. He was leaving on a red-eye flight."

Jilly thanked the manager and hung up, dropping the phone back into her bag.

"By another strange coincidence, the other witness has left town. Chicago, the manager thinks. An unbelievable job offer."

Dan shook his head. "I'm not a fan of coincidence. This sounds really hinky."

"'Hinky'?" said Jilly. "Did you really just say that? Are you trying to talk like cops on TV now, Dan? 'Hinky'? Really? Have you ever actually heard anybody say that?"

She laughed in spite of herself.

Dan shrugged, and Jilly could swear he reddened slightly. "Just seemed appropriate. Okay, note to self. Avoid 'hinky' from here on out."

"Anyway, for the record I agree with you: this is not coincidence. And now I'm wondering if Kerry might really be in some kind of possible danger."

The tones of Stravinsky cried out. She looked at the caller name on her screen. Speak of the devil.

"Yes, Kerry, what's up?"

"Detective Garvey, I just got another call from Laura's brother. He said it's urgent I meet him right away."

"What did he say exactly?"

"Just that it was vitally important and how soon could I meet him in the same park where he meet me last time. He sounded really anxious."

"What did you tell him?"

"I said I had to clear a couple things—that's a laugh—and that I'd call him right back. Then I called you. Thank God I got through."

"All right, listen, Kerry. We're coming by to get you. Do not—do not under any circumstance—go to meet him alone. Do you understand? How far away from the park are you?"

"Oh, five or ten minutes, it's close."

"All right, call him back. Tell him you can meet him in—" she glanced at her watch and did quick calculations. "Tell him a half hour. No, forty minutes. Tell him whatever you need to. Make it clear you're serious about meeting him but there's no way you can be there until forty minutes from now. Got it?"

"Sure."

"And call me back afterwards to let me know if he agreed or not. Got that?"

"Got it." She rang off.

Jilly turned to Dan, already dialing her phone again.

"Something's up. Laura's so-called 'brother' got back in contact with Kerry and wants to see her right away."

She put a call into Lieutenant Castillo. When his aide answered she rapidly laid out the situation. She waited while Castillo himself came on, described the situation in greater detail, and requested a backup unit.

She emphasized they were now *en route* to meet Kerry Moran, and stressed that having a low profile might be crucial, so as not to scare away the person meeting the young woman.

Dan accelerated the car through traffic towards Kerry's apartment. "You're thinking she really could be in danger," he said.

"A guy deliberately misrepresenting himself in order to meet with her? And I'm starting to think he's probably the same guy who called to scare her later that night. Now, for some reason, he's decided he needs to come back and try something else? We can't take the chance."

Kerry called back shortly to say that "Ryan" had agreed to meet her in forty-five minutes at the same bench where they had met before.

"Okay, Kerry. We'll be in front of your apartment house in about ten minutes. Don't come out to wait for us, just in case anybody is looking for you. We've got an unmarked car. I'll call you on your phone when we're here. Just wait for us in the lobby, but stay out of sight from the street. Okay?"

* * * *

Sunset Park was its formal name but most people in the city simply referred to it as the Park. It was a green area covering about four city blocks, with one entrance road on each of two sides.

Two uniformed officers had shown up to join them. Jilly directed them to enter from the far side and approach the bench where Kerry had agreed to meet her caller, but to stay back out of sight. She and Dan would do the same thing from this side. It was three minutes to the agreed meeting time and Jilly told Kerry to start walking in.

"We'll be a little behind you. You and the guy, hopefully, won't be able to see us, but we'll never let you out of our sight," she told Kerry, who was beginning to look quite apprehensive.

"Do you think I'm in some danger here?" Kerry asked. "Should I be worried?"

"No, I don't think so," Jilly replied, hoping she sounded more sure of that than she actually felt. "You said he didn't seem threatening. And there are people all around right now; it's very public. But we need to talk to him. We don't want to scare him away. So we'll let you approach him first. Then we'll take over. You ready?"

Kerry nodded but she looked less than confident.

"It's going to be okay, Kerry. Go on now."

Kerry turned and strode down a paved pathway that led over a small rise to a set of benches. It was chilly and overcast, and that had discouraged many visitors from coming here today. But there were still a few stragglers scattered about: children and dogs playing, a couple of people sitting on the benches, reading or talking.

Dan moved off across the grass to position himself on another side of the bench that Kerry had described as her rendezvous point. Jilly stopped at the top of the short rise and watched.

There was a man sitting on a far bench, arms crossed, moving his head back and forth. He looked, from this distance at least, to be perhaps in his fifties. He saw Kerry approaching and waved.

Jilly pulled out a walkie-talkie and thumbed the button to talk to Dan and the uniforms. "That looks like him. She's approaching the bench now. Everybody hold steady."

The man rose to greet her, they shook hands, and they sat down. He began to speak animatedly to her. Jilly couldn't hear what was being said but it was clearly being conveyed with a sense of urgency.

"All right, let's close in, slowly. Don't spook him."

Jilly had taken about four steps toward them when the man's head shot up. He looked around and saw Dan coming down the grassy hill from the other direction. He bolted out of the seat and grabbed Kerry's arm, yelling something at her. She wrenched her arm back in alarm and recoiled from him. He looked around and saw Jilly also coming. He sprinted off at an angle away from them both.

Jilly barked at Dan and then yelled into the walkie-talkie, "He's moving!"

Dan instantly changed his course and broke into a run across the grass at a path to intercept him. The man turned away, angling in towards Jilly, who was also now running. She had unholstered her sidearm and had it in her hand as she moved.

"Police!" she shouted. "Stop!"

The man saw the gun in her hand and froze. He skidded to a halt in the grass, struggling to keep his balance, and threw his hands up. It was almost comical.

Dan reached him first. The uniforms suddenly appeared as well. In another few moments, the four police officers had surrounded the man.

He was unarmed and suddenly indignant.

"What's going on here?" he demanded. "Why are you chasing me? What's with the *guns*?"

"We just wanted to talk with you," Dan said officiously, "but you suddenly ran from us. That tends to make us suspicious."

"How was I supposed to know you were the police?" he sputtered. "For all I knew, you were someone meaning me and the young lady some harm!"

"You were expecting someone like that?" Jilly asked.

"As a matter of fact, possibly, yes!"

"All right, let's go talk about this, any objection?"

"Am I under arrest?"

"Not yet," said Dan.

"We're asking you to come voluntarily with us," Jilly said.

He looked back and forth at them, and at Kerry, who was now carefully approaching the gathering.

"All right," he said.

* * * *

The station interview rooms tended to the sterile side: functional but not overly comfortable, painted in muted beiges and grays, with hard backed chairs and simple heavy tables.

They had sent Kerry home with the uniforms and driven the man back with them. He had voluntarily shown them identification, a state Private Investigator's license in the name Earl Ryan and a driver's license with the same name.

Now he sat across the table from them, all three of them holding Styrofoam cups of rather dreadful coffee.

"I wasn't trying to threaten the girl," he was insisting. "I was trying to help her."

"You told her your name was Ryan Hart. You said you were the brother of Laura Hart Spilwell."

He nodded. "Yes. Yes, I did that."

"You also approached her earlier," Dan added. "Told her the same thing."

"You deliberately misrepresented your identity to her," Jilly continued. "Want to tell us why?"

"I had a feeling she was wary of strangers. I needed to get her to meet me, so I could warn her."

"Warn her of what, exactly?"

"I thought that what she was doing was going to get her in trouble."

"What do you mean?" Jilly asked. "What was she doing?"

"She was opening up a can of worms she knew nothing about." He stared at them, arms crossed.

"How did you find out about her and all this?" Dan asked. "Maybe we should start at the beginning?"

Ryan shrugged. "I was contacted by an attorney that I do occasional work for. He asked me to look into her story."

"And this attorney was…?"

He hesitated.

"If this is all on the level, surely you can tell us who it was?"

"There's a possible issue of client privilege here," he said, thinking it over.

"And there's a possible issue of us arresting you on various charges of endangering Miss Moran," said Jilly pointedly. "And endangering your license."

Ryan nodded and pursed his lips. "Norland Towers."

"When did he contact you and what did he say?"

"He called me Saturday and asked me to check her out."

"Saturday? You're sure of that?"

"Positive. Saturday morning. He said he wanted to meet me at my office. He said it was urgent for me to look into it. He said she was endangering one of his cases with irresponsible assertions, and that I needed to find out who she had been talking with and try to dissuade her from continuing. We spent a while talking and I got all the information."

"So you contacted Kerry Moran after that?"

"I called her the next day. I decided my wisest move was to approach her as 'Ryan Hart.' The impression I got was that she was a bit of a space cadet and could be spooked easily. That's what Mr. Towers was also concerned about. He stressed we needed to be diplomatic, to finesse her."

"So it was your idea to pretend to be a relative of the deceased."

"Yeah. I called her up, put on a grieving sibling act, and asked her to meet me."

"How did you get her phone number?"

"She left her contact information with Mr. Towers. It was easy to reach her."

"So you met with her, told her the family was concerned about dredging up whatever she had found, and asked her to stop?"

"I practically begged her to stop. It was an Academy Award performance. I'm pretty good at that kind of play-acting."

He actually smiled heartily.

"And she told you, what, that she wouldn't try to talk to anyone else about her theories?"

"Well, no." The smile faded. "She said she'd have to think about it. I could kind of tell she wasn't going to cooperate. I reiterated that she was potentially causing more harm than good to the entire family, and that I was speaking for all of them. I laid it on heavy, the whole guilt trip. She seemed like she'd be most receptive to that."

"You apparently weren't aware that Laura Spilwell had no brother, in fact almost no family to speak of."

Ryan shrugged. "It didn't matter. I didn't figure she was the sharpest tool in the shed, if you know what I mean. All I needed was to get her to back off. I just made the story up on the fly."

"But that didn't seem to work. By any chance did you try to contact her again right after that?"

A deep sigh. Ryan looked down at his folded arms. "Uh, yes. Yes, I did. I called her back Tuesday evening under another persona and tried a different approach."

"What you mean is, you called her in the middle of the night and anonymously threatened her."

"I said nothing that could be legally construed as threatening," he said sharply. "I didn't identify myself, but all I said was that she was intruding into areas that she didn't understand and she should stay out. It was not a threat, it was a warning."

Jilly and Dan just stared at him. It was so quiet that they could hear the click of the minute hand on the old-fashioned wall clock.

"Maybe not the smartest way to play it, agreed," Ryan finally admitted. "But I was right in trying to head her off. What happened after that proves me out. That's why I came back again as Ryan Hart."

"What do you mean?"

"Mr. Towers had a point. Somebody found out about what she was doing and may have had more severe methods of dealing with it. I heard about her boyfriend being found dead in that old building."

"How did you know about the connection?"

"The gal had put *everything* in the stuff she left for Towers! Her whole story. She named the names and the places and the times. It was a damned book, rambling on and on! He had me review it. I remembered the name, Mark Zanello. Then, when the news came out about his body being found, I figured it *had* to have something to do with this. She's a nut but I thought she was a sweet kid. I had to talk her out of pursuing this any further. That was all I was trying to do, meeting up with her today. I swear it."

"After your first two contacts with Kerry, did you contact Towers to tell him about your activity and her reaction?"

"I told him about the brother act. Not about the night call. In hindsight, I decided that might be embarrassing. He seemed okay with my meeting with her and her reaction. He said okay, we'd just wait and see what would happen and I was done for now."

"So you didn't happen to try to contact any of the other people she named?" Dan asked.

"No, all he asked me to do was to talk to her. I guess he had a point. What she was doing really *was* dangerous."

"Your two calls on Sunday and Tuesday came from different phones," Jilly said.

"Yeah. I have several prepaid burners. Just buy 'em, and put minutes on 'em. Pretty anonymous. They come in handy."

"Yeah, I bet they do," Jilly muttered.

"Hey, I haven't done anything wrong! I resent the implications! I'm on the up and up, and my clients are legitimate! I was just trying to help the girl! And my client as well!"

The remainder of the interview was fruitless. They left him in the interview room and headed down the hallway.

"Think we can hold him on anything?" Dan asked.

"We could come up with something. But why bother?"

"So you buy his story?"

"The only part that makes me wonder, is why Towers would employ a guy that thick."

"Think he'll call Towers when we let him go?"

Jilly shook her head. "I'm hoping he's too scared to talk to him now, that he realizes Towers will be angry at him for screwing up."

"So Towers was back in town by Saturday, despite what he told his aide."

"If he ever left at all." Jilly stared at Dan. "Sounds kind of *hinky*, doesn't it, partner?"

Dan winced good-naturedly. "Indeed it does. So I guess that's going to be our word after all, huh?"

"In any case, I think Mr. Towers bears further scrutiny, wouldn't you say?"

Back in the squad room, Dan noted that he had new messages on his computer. He sat down and tapped them up.

"Got the records from Mark Zanello's phone," he said, scrolling through a list. Jilly peered at the screen over his shoulder.

After a short time he asked, "He was killed Friday night, right? Around eight?"

"More or less."

"He made no calls out for two or three hours before that. But....he received a call around seven fifteen." Dan moved the computer's cursor over the number. "Doesn't match any other incoming calls listed here."

He opened a new window and tapped in instructions. Quickly he was into the department's reverse directory that listed according to telephone number.

"A pay phone. Do you believe it!" Dan said. "2435 Webley. Weren't we just talking about that street a while ago?"

"Yeah. The Ready-Rite where the last call was made to Laura Spilwell."

"Just for the hell of it..." Dan said, opening another browser window and typing further. "The Ready-Rite is at 2435." He turned and looked over his shoulder at an amazed Jilly. "Our victim's last phone call came from the same place as Laura Spilwell's last call."

Jilly's brain went into overdrive. There was no longer any way to deny a connection between the murders.

Dan perused the web page for the store number of the Ready-Rite, then picked up his phone and dialed. He spoke briefly, ending with, "hold on to it. We'll be right over," and hung up.

Jilly was still silent, lost in thought.

"We might have caught a break," Dan said. "Something new has happened since the Spilwell case."

"What do you mean, Dan?"

"I mean that there's now a security camera outside the Ready-Rite. A *working* one." He rose from his desk. "The manager's pulling last Friday's footage for us."

* * * *

"I've only been the manager here for a few weeks now, and one of my first priorities was to install a working security camera system."

The manager's name was Arjuna Patel and his store's ambience was already quite different from the way Jilly remembered it from a year ago. It was better illuminated, cleaner, more orderly, and the two people behind the counter looked as if they actually were concerned about doing their jobs rather than just waiting for their shifts to end.

Patel was pointing with obvious pride to the security camera poised in a dark alcove over the doorway. They were standing just outside the store. The public telephone was several steps away, on a metal pedestal, weather-beaten plastic surrounding it top and sides.

"There have been several incidents in this store over the past months," Patel said. "Even a shooting. The previous management cared nothing for making it safer or more efficient. I set up several cameras inside and out. I want to upgrade this store, bring customers back. Perhaps even save a few jobs, including my own."

Jilly was examining the camera. "Someone using the phone over there might not even notice that camera's up there. It's silent and it's in a dark spot."

"It's got a clear shot of the phone too," Dan noted. "Do many people use that phone?"

Patel shook his head. "Not really. I'm surprised the company hasn't asked to have it removed. Or that the phone company hasn't done so on its own. This neighborhood tends to be overlooked in general."

He shrugged resignedly.

"So you have the tapes from last week?"

"Not tape. Everything is on digital file. You're lucky you called when you did. I keep the video files for about two weeks and if there is nothing noteworthy, I erase them."

"So if we could see the videos from last Friday?" Jilly asked.

"Of course," Patel said with a smile, motioning them inside. He had a small office in the back—really not much more than a storeroom with a cluttered desk. He picked up a flash drive and handed it to them.

"This is a copy I made of everything from Friday evening, from about noon to midnight. Everything is time coded as well."

"Could we just give it a quick look on your equipment?"

"Certainly," Patel said, walking to a desk computer. The monitor was currently showing a montage of images from his four security cameras in real time. He popped the drive into a slot and tapped a few keys, and the image changed.

"Can we jump ahead to…" Jilly turned to Dan. "What time was the call?"

"Seven thirteen in the evening. Maybe we could start just a couple minutes ahead of that?"

Patel clicked on a mouse, moving a cursor onscreen. The image fast-forwarded and the time signature in the upper right corner sped more rapidly. He stopped the forward motion at 19:11 and stepped back. Dan and Jilly moved in closer. The digital image showed the parking lot off the street directly in front of the entrance. The pay phone was on the far right. A few people walked in and out of the store. The front bumper of a car appeared as it pulled into a parking spot. Another bumper receded from the picture as the car backed out of its spot.

"The times don't agree," Jilly said impatiently. The time signature had just changed to 19:14.

"There!" Dan said, pointing. "There's our guy."

A figure, a man, had entered the picture from the far right and was looking back and forth as he picked up the receiver on the phone. Possibly because he did not want to call attention to himself, he was not acting furtively or going to any effort to hide himself. Even in the relatively low resolution of the camera footage, his face was clear for several seconds as he spoke into the receiver and then hung it up.

"Oh my God," Jilly muttered. She swallowed hard.

"Is that who I think it is?" Dan asked.

Jilly nodded. "Yes. Yes, it is."

* * * *

"There's no way this could be a coincidence," Dan said as he drove.

"I'm afraid not," said Jilly, still stewing in her thoughts. "We have to handle this carefully. We're only going to get one shot. We could blow this."

"Agreed."

"What we've got going for us is that he's been so sure things would go his way. He expected the body to remain undiscovered for a much longer time. He either figured there was still no security camera at the Ready-Rite or that the footage would be recorded over even if we could get that far. He's been wrong on a number of things but he thinks he's smart enough that things haven't gone *too* wrong."

"As someone once told me," Dan said, "they think we're not that bright, but that they are. And almost always, they're not."

"Smart person who said that," Jilly said wryly. She had her phone out and called Kerry. Kerry answered after several rings. Apparently the shock of everything had finally hit her. Her voice was thick and morose.

"How are you holding up?"

"Not great, Detective. Today really scared me. I've really screwed up."

"I'm sorry to bother you but I have a question, it might be important."

"Shoot. Nobody here but me. I've got nothing but time."

"You left a flash drive for Norland Towers, right?"

"Yes, one of those thumb-drive thingies."

"Can you tell me exactly what was on that drive?"

She spoke slowly. "I put together a little presentation, in a PDF format. Kind of like things we did at the magazine now and then. There was a high and a low resolution copy of my enhanced photo, and an accompanying text describing the circumstances in detail and why I felt they were important. I had a feeling I might not get to talk to Mr. Towers myself and explain things so I wanted it all laid out for him."

"And Ms. Grymes did not look at anything?"

"No, she just took it and said when Mr. Towers got back she would make sure he saw it."

"In that text, did you mention any of the other people at the restaurant that night? Mark or your friend the waiter, Satch?"

"Yes, I described the whole situation carefully. I knew this could be valuable exculpatory evidence." She had some trouble articulating those last two words. "Well…I *thought* it was going to be. I guess it wasn't."

"Kerry, was there contact information for you or anybody else in that text?"

"Uh-huh. My phone number and email address. I put Mark's phone number on there and the number to reach Satch at the restaurant." Kerry paused for a long moment then her voice grew more animated. "You're saying that Mark's death *was* connected to what I did? Did I get him *killed?*"

"Take it easy, Kerry. No, I'm not saying anything like that. We're just looking into the threats you reported to us and I'm getting some further information. What I think you should do is get some rest. I'll talk to you in the next couple of days and maybe I'll have some news for you. In the meantime, just stay low and take care of yourself." She considered the way Kerry's voice sounded. "Umm…have you eaten tonight?"

"Crackers," Kerry slurred. "And some cheese."

"Sounds like you've been washing it down with something too. Maybe you better go easy, okay?"

"Just trying to get through this," Kerry said softly.

Jilly could hear she was starting to cry. She attempted a few more supportive statements and then rang off. There was nothing more she could do. Kerry was in a downward spiral for the moment.

"Want to hear how I think we should handle this?" asked Dan as he took a corner.

"Go for it," said Jilly.

"If Spilwell is protecting Mavis, he thinks the affair is still a secret… maybe if he decided that his silence was actually putting her in danger…"

"If he opens up, it might change everything."

"I think it's worth a shot. We have to play a couple of the players. And if our scenario is right, we'll need to fill in a lot of the blanks. So here's what I propose…"

Jilly listened in wonder. It was close to what she had been considering, but, she had to admit, with some improvements. Her new partner might just work out.

"We've got a lot to do over this weekend," she said. "I'll push Castillo for some overtime. Let's hope it pans out."

9.

Saturday morning, Jilly made the drive to the Island.

Falcon Island would sound like a lovely place to anyone unaware that it was the site of one of the state's most formidable maximum security prisons. There was little else on the small island, in fact, but rocky tree-lined cliffs that were home to the isle's namesake bird. Anyone clever enough to escape the prison itself would have to contend with a tortuous descent to the coast and then deal with the ferocious rip tides to try to get to the mainland. It was a facility that had seen few breakouts in its history.

This was the new home of Dr. Dane Spilwell.

"Well, Detective," Spilwell said as he was led by a guard into the sparse meeting room. "I'd like to tell you it's a pleasure to see you again, but you'll understand if I don't."

He did not smile. He looked haggard and much older than he had in court. The guard sat him down across the table from Jilly and stepped back. He silently glared at her.

"Totally understood, Doctor," said Jilly, reaching into the briefcase she had already laid on the table. She held up a large blowup of a photograph and showed it to him. "Is this you in this photo?"

Spilwell looked at it impassively and said nothing.

"Certainly looks like you. Do you by any chance remember the occasion on which this was taken?"

He said nothing, just looked at the picture.

"Suppose I were to tell you this was taken the night that your wife died?"

Still nothing in reply. Spilwell could have been a statue of a seated man in an orange jumpsuit.

"I assume you recognize the woman in the photo with you, her back to the camera? I think you know who she is. I'm told she's got beautiful flaming red hair in real life, and she's partial to emeralds. Real ones, no doubt. A very classy woman, isn't she?"

Spilwell turned his eyes to glare at Jilly once again.

"Have you spoken to your attorney recently, Doctor?"

"Every day," he said slowly.

"The person who gave me this? They took this picture last year. They brought it to your attorney, Norland Towers, last week. They thought it might be valuable exculpatory evidence, maybe even prove your innocence. They thought you might have spent the evening with this woman, the very night the horrible murder of your wife Laura happened. Has he told you about it?"

Spilwell said nothing.

"By that silence, I'm going to assume that he hasn't. Don't you find that rather strange?"

Jilly had to play this carefully. She couldn't come out and just say certain things. She wanted for him to come to his own conclusions.

"Your attorney, he's been a good friend of yours for quite a while, right? If anybody is going to be looking out for your best interests, it's got to be him. You two even hung out together, had dinner in each other's homes, things like that?"

Something seemed to be dawning in Spilwell's eyes. A small light was going on in that darkly smoldering gaze. Somebody close to him, somebody welcome in his city apartment, someone who could have walked out with, say, a kitchen implement one evening.

"When I found out about this, I knew I needed to come right over and talk to you about it. I thought maybe, *maybe*, you really didn't commit this murder after all."

"Of course I didn't do it," he said measuredly, not breaking his gaze. "I've told you that from day one."

Jilly, eyebrows raised, put her hands out in exasperation. "So what I don't understand is, why is your attorney not here behind this? A man who by all rights is willing to go to the mat for you, whatever it takes, especially when your appeal is your very last chance? I'm confused, Doctor, can you help me out here?"

He took the photo from her and stared at it. Finally he put it down on the table and laid his head in hand.

"My God," he murmured, almost too low to hear.

It was the first crack in his cool shell that Jilly had witnessed in over a year. He was catching on. Even a brilliant surgeon can be slow at times, she thought.

"You know, I have to say, I was surprised at how the trial went," she said. "Gotta be honest, our track record against Norland Towers isn't all that great. He's smart. He's brutal. I was really ticked off because I figured he'd have you waltzing without breaking a sweat, and I *really* wanted you for this. I still don't quite get how we nailed a break on this one. The jury didn't do much more than sit down and vote."

She could tell, point made. The glow in his eyes flared briefly.

She looked at the guard and held up the photo. "Can I leave this with him?" she asked. The guard approached and inspected it and handed it back with a nod, saying he would deliver it to Spilwell's cell after their meeting.

"If you did not kill Laura," Jilly said quietly, bending in close to Spilwell, "then for God's sake, where were you? Why haven't you told anybody that?"

Spilwell sighed deeply, looked as if he might break. Then the wall descended around him again. He just stared at her without a further word.

Damn this guy, she thought. He's stone cold. Of course everybody thinks he did it. Of course it was open and shut.

Jilly stood up. "The photo is now yours, Doctor. I'm thinking that maybe you need to do some thinking about this." She carefully placed one of her cards on top of the photo. "In case you want to give me a call. But in any case, you should definitely consult with your attorney when he next contacts you. Maybe he just overlooked telling you about this. Or maybe…it wasn't news to him."

She told the guard she was ready to leave and looked one last time at Spilwell. He simply stared up at her without a trace of an expression. The Ice King to the very end. But there had to be a heart beating underneath that façade. If not, it would never have come to this.

Driving back to the city, Jilly put her phone on speaker and called Dan. "How'd it go, partner?"

"A very productive morning. We're getting there. Things are falling into place. I've been checking on the security cameras along the route and there are quite a few."

"I'll be back soon and we can divvy up the load."

"I think with any luck we'll be ready to go before Monday morning. The pieces are actually fitting."

"Let's hope, partner. Let's hope."

* * * *

They arrived in mid-morning on Monday. As luck would have it, Norland Towers was just coming off the elevator in the lobby of his building as they were entering.

And as luck would have it, his wife Mavis was with him.

She wasn't dressed in green but in stylish black, but Jilly noted her hair was as striking as in the pictures and yes, she was wearing emeralds. Beautiful and confident. Beloved, perhaps desperately, by two powerful men. Towers himself, in an expensive dark suit, seemed taken aback as he saw the two detectives approaching.

"Detective Garvey," he said smoothly. "I was told you were by the offices the other day. I'm afraid you've returned at an inopportune moment. We have an important engagement. Have you met my wife Mavis?"

"I've never had the pleasure." Jilly nodded and smiled briefly at Mavis, then turned her attention back to Towers. "I'm afraid, Mr. Towers, I'm going to have to ask you to come with us. Your engagement is going to have to wait."

Whatever passed for an icy smile disappeared, replaced by an imperious glower. "I beg your pardon?"

"Are you coming with us willingly, sir, or do we need to make this an official arrest? We don't really wish to make a scene or anything."

Towers looked back and forth from Jilly to Dan, who both stood, with serious expressions, blocking his way. He quickly surmised that intimidation was not going to work.

He turned to Mavis. "I don't know what this is, dear, but I'll clear it up quickly. Do you mind going on without me?"

For a moment she seemed taken aback but quickly recovered, smiled graciously, and said, "Of course."

She disappeared through the front door of the building before Towers gave the detectives a supremely nasty look and said quietly, "Whatever this is, you're both going to regret it."

"We'll see about that," Jilly smiled brightly. "This way then?"

* * * *

"Would you like an attorney present for this interview?" Jilly asked. They had deliberately selected the least inviting interview room, resplendent with peeling wall paint and the oldest and hardest chairs in the building. Towers still sat with patrician bearing, as if his ratty metal chair were a throne of a sort. But he was clearly uncomfortable despite himself.

"I *am* an attorney," he growled. "As you well know."

Jilly and Dan were on the opposite side of the slate-gray table from him. Dan was half-sitting on the table, leaning in slightly, and Jilly was standing, going through a large manila folder, pulling out various sheets and scanning them.

"Would you happen to know a man named Mark Zanello?" she asked suddenly.

"The name is not ringing a bell with me, Detective. Who is he?"

"So you didn't make a phone call to him on Friday the eighteenth?"

"I cannot say as I remember having done such a thing."

He was sure they were bluffing. He was sure the evidence didn't exist. He figured they'd check his phone records—if they could get by his legal stonewalling—and find nothing. Smug bastard.

"Were you in town on Friday?"

"Actually, no. I was out of town until late Sunday. I didn't return to my office until Monday morning."

"And may I ask, where were you?"

"I was at a professional seminar, one hundred miles away. Would you like to check on that? I'll be glad to provide you with references."

"Thank you. We'll get to them. Did you fly?"

"Actually, I drove. It's a beautiful drive, down the coast. Santa Cristina, you must know it. A lovely beach resort town, perfect for a getaway seminar."

"You were alone, or did your wife accompany you?"

"No, alas, she had prior commitments and couldn't join me. It would have been quite nice. Although I was insanely busy. You know how those things are."

"Suppose we were to tell you that there is someone who claims to have met with you in their office on that Saturday morning?"

"I'd say they were mistaken. Or lying."

"Mr. Towers, the office you maintain in this city, that's not your only one, is it?"

"No. My partner and I practice in several states. Towers and Bridges has satellite offices in New York, Chicago, and Houston."

Jilly again switched gears.

"Mr. Towers, are you aware that a person named Kerry Moran came to your office with what she believed was evidence that might clear your client Dane Spilwell?"

"Oh yes. I heard about that when I got back. She left some kind of computer file for me. It was nonsense. Just a crank."

"So you looked at what you call the computer file that she left for you?"

"Very peremptorily. Just enough to see it was a waste of my time. I instructed my assistant to make sure the woman didn't get through again."

"Had there been any possibility of it being something exculpatory, of course you would have given it serious consideration, given your client's position, what with you preparing an appeal of his murder conviction and all."

"Of course. What's your point, Detective?"

Dan still had not spoken. He simply sat on the edge of the desk and watched Towers silently. It seemed to be slightly unnerving to Towers.

"So you didn't look at the file until Monday then?"

"That's correct."

"She dropped it off with your assistant on Friday. And you were not in the city after that until late Sunday?"

"That's correct."

Jilly played the first card. She extracted four photographic printouts and laid them, one by one, in front of Towers.

"So you're telling me this could not be you, at a pay phone at a convenience store on Webley Avenue, last Friday evening?" She pointed to the date stamps on the pictures.

Towers looked momentarily flustered but he recovered instantly. "Ridiculous. That is not me. And I don't know that I want to persist in this nonsense any further. Whatever you're suggesting, I don't like it." He started to rise. "Am I free to go?"

"No, Mr. Towers, you are not. Please sit back down."

That was Dan, and he said it abruptly enough that Towers did stop and sit back down in surprise.

"As an attorney," Jilly continued, "you'd likely advise your client to stop talking right about now, so suppose you just listen to what we have to say for a little bit."

She pulled out more sheets and looked them over. "You drive a late model Lexus, silvery-gray—the official name of the color is Opaline Pearl. You have vanity plates, they read MAG IURIS. I'm told that's a shortening of *Magister Iuris,* which is Latin for 'Master of Law.'"

She laid two more printout sheets over one of the others.

"You know, it's an interesting thing, nowadays there are *so many* security cameras everywhere. It's pretty much impossible to go several blocks without showing up on one or another of them. This is a blowup from a security camera on a bank ATM four blocks down Webley from the convenience store. You'll note the automobile parked at the curb there. The plate is visible. That's your car, Mister Towers. You'll note the time stamp on this one as well. We've got you at that phone, Mr. Towers."

She pulled out another sheet. "Now, the interesting thing is that Mark Zanello, whom you say you never met and don't know, received a phone call from that very phone at that very time."

Towers began to say something but thought better of it. He was beginning to act as lawyer and client in one, seeing the situation was much more perilous than he had originally thought.

"Going back to that photograph of you at the phone," Jilly said, fishing one of the photos out and holding it up, "that's a very nice tie you're wearing in that picture. Very distinctive, not just the tie but that stickpin, as well."

She pulled out still another photograph, this one a blowup from a slick magazine. "Suspiciously resembles the tie and pin you wore a couple of months back when you held a press conference during your client Dane Spilwell's trial. Rather sloppy of you. Frankly, I'm disappointed. Now, you say you didn't know Mark Zanello. I assume you have no idea who Mort Blessing is either?"

"No, I do not," Towers spat.

"He's better known to his friends as Satch. He's a waiter. Well, that's what you'd call his day job. He's actually a musician. He just left town this week. He received an irresistible offer to play in Chicago."

Towers said nothing. Jilly looked at Dan. "Seems Detective Lee, here, dug up some fascinating information about that."

"I located Mr. Blessing in Chicago," Dan said. "It turns out he took his cell phone with him and once I obtained that number, it was easy enough to contact him. He told me he had received an offer to front a jazz band with some mind bogglingly high-end gigs. A jazz combo. Television, radio, live concerts. Go figure."

Now it was Dan's turn to dig through his own file and pull out a sheet.

"It was an odd offer. He had to accept it on the spot and leave town that night. It came from a booking agent and promoter named Len Garfield."

Dan looked up and down the paper he held. "Quite a colorful gent, this Len Garfield guy. The Chicago police know him well. A few racketeering charges and some rather serious stuff."

Dan stared directly at Towers. "He spent a little time behind bars, but was acquitted of most of those charges. Perhaps you're familiar with Mr. Garfield, considering you were his attorney on many of those cases?"

"I am not going to listen to any more of this idiocy," Towers said. "If I'm not under arrest, I'm leaving."

Jilly sighed. "Okay. Then I guess that's that."

Towers stood up and straightened his tie. "I'm going to go."

"No, Mr. Towers. We are going to place you under arrest."

She pulled out her Miranda Rights card and began to recite. "You have the right to remain silent..." Dan had the handcuffs at the ready and snapped them on his wrists in front of him. Now, she thought, maybe we get his attention.

Jilly finished the recitation and waited for the answer to "Do you understand each of these rights I have explained to you?" Then she proceeded. "Now then. Do you want to talk, or do you want to keep listening? Please sit back down, Mr. Towers."

He eased back into the chair and coolly eyed them without saying a word.

"Let me tell you what we think happened. We may revise our overview as we fill it in with new evidence, but be assured, we *will* fill it in, with good solid work. My partner and I are good at that. You may or may not have actually driven down the coast, but you were in your office on Friday evening. You found the computer file to which you referred, and were possibly intrigued by whatever note your assistant Ms. Grymes left with it. You didn't just give it a cursory look; you explored it carefully. And it disturbed you. Just why, well, let's come back to that.

"You were more than disturbed. I'd say you were distraught. You saw the need to take action immediately. Perhaps, for whatever reason, you weren't thinking very clearly. In any case, for some reason you decided to start by contacting Mark Zanello. You had his phone number. You called to set up a meeting with him. But you thought it unwise to use your own phone. So you drove to a convenience store that you just *happened* to know had a public phone. Not all that many of those around anymore, are there? You parked three blocks away from the store. A bit of a marginal neighborhood, I'd say. I bet you were concerned about that beautiful Lexus of yours the whole time.

"Mark was on his way out to meet somebody but he must have agreed to see you, so you drove over to his apartment. We know he was there because he grabbed the mail from his box as he left. We're thinking you had him drive you somewhere quiet to talk. There's a nice little 'pocket park' several blocks from Mark's place. Very quiet side street. Almost no traffic. The park has lots of trees, little gardens, a gated fence around it, used by the neighborhood. There's even a little indented drive-up off the street. Very private. It's usually closed up at night but you were able to get in.

"The conversation did not go the way you had hoped. You wanted to convince him to get his girlfriend to shut up about what they had seen. Possibly you were prepared to offer him a lot of money. What you couldn't have known was that she was no longer his girlfriend, and things were exceedingly bitter between them. Mark was experiencing his own demons. I imagine he wasn't very cooperative. He probably got angry. Maybe physical, I don't know. In any case, being the brilliant strategist, you had a Plan B at the ready. You brought a .38 special with you and shot him twice in the side of the head."

Towers said nothing but took on an expression as if this was the silliest tale he had ever heard.

"As it happens," Dan interjected, "someone in the apartment building next to the park called in to the police that she had heard what might have been shots. Coming from the pocket park."

"There must have been blood," Jilly continued. "We've got crews scouring the park now, looking for traces. No doubt you disposed of the gun. We'll do our best to find it, just like you did your best to get him out of the park and into the drive-up on the dark, quiet street. Into his trunk. You drove him somewhere you thought he wouldn't be immediately found, and when he was, it'd look like a gang shooting."

Dan pulled out another sheet. "Abandoned buildings on Pilsen. Interestingly, the former owner of a few of them recently copped a plea on several charges of arson and insurance fraud. He was represented in his pleas by one Stillman Morris, who is an associate partner with...Towers and Bridges. Now what are the odds?"

"Pretty good plan, in fact," Jilly resumed. "You knew nobody was likely to go anywhere near that building for months. Maybe years. What you didn't figure on was a homeless couple ingenious enough to get into the building."

"You helped," Dan added. "You didn't bother to nail the door back up again. You figured if the door lock snapped, it would be good enough. That was a little sloppy, don't you think?"

Jilly shrugged and looked at Dan. "Well, it's not like Mr. Towers hangs out with the kind of people who frequent that neighborhood. How was he to know?"

She turned back to Towers. "I like this next set of moves; these were pretty slick and imaginative. But you are, after all, a criminal lawyer, as you reminded us. You undoubtedly wore gloves throughout all of this, left no fingerprints. You took Mark's valuables—his wallet, watch, and phone. You left the wallet and watch under the seat of his car. You left his phone on the seat where it could be picked up by anybody exploring the car. You drove Mark's car a few blocks away, still in a very sketchy area, and left it open with the keys in it, figuring it would be stolen and all sorts of interesting things could happen to throw us off your trail. The possibilities were endless. We might be sent racing to the four winds before all was done. Nice."

She tilted her head. "You may have been congratulating yourself on handling a bad situation so well, but you must have started to come down from your adrenaline high by now and realized that this was not the way to cover your tracks. You couldn't go around knocking off all the other principals in this little play. It was messy. Your visibility increased, the danger grew with every moment. You had to get more subtle. So you summoned your investigator the next day and had him ply a scheme on Kerry Moran. In the meantime you contacted your friend Len in Chicago and had him tender Satch an offer he couldn't refuse. You got rid of Satch, Mark was not going to be talking to anyone, and you figured Kerry could be motivated to give up. And then, maybe you really *did* drive back down to Santa Cristina on Saturday, where you could make a point of being seen."

"Now the question is," Dan chimed in, "just *why* was all this so crucial to you to silence these people and suppress this when you just told us it was inconsequential and meaningless evidence?"

"Well, he might argue it could actually harm Dr. Spilwell's appeal case," offered Jilly. "After all, Mr. Towers has been a close and valued friend of Dr. Spilwell's for many years now. He no doubt feels terrible since he booted the doctor's case so badly."

"Good point," Dan replied. "I certainly would feel terrible about such a thing. What a remarkable upset."

"A true debacle," Jilly agreed, nodding, lips pursed. "And what with how close the two of them were, spending so much social time together, in each other's homes, with each other's families…"

"Sharing so much," Dan said.

"Perhaps even lending and borrowing back and forth," Jilly said.

She noted Towers' expression was growing darker. She turned back to him. "Perhaps you borrowed one of Dr. Spilwell's kitchen implements, for example, but then you turned around and lost it? Which leads us to another interesting little detail…you know, Mr. Towers, there's someone else who used that very same pay phone at that convenience store a while back. Are you familiar with what I'm talking about?"

Towers said nothing, just glowered darker and darker.

"The very last person to call Laura Spilwell before she died. How about *that* for a coincidence? Laura's friends in her book club said she called to say she'd be delayed. She had been detoured by a call from someone she must have known and trusted, with, perhaps, an invitation to stop at a restaurant she liked for a mysterious impromptu conversation over a drink. That detour took her past the alley where she was stabbed to death. By a killer who then also attempted to fabricate a fiction about a robbery gone bad." Jilly shrugged. "We find this fascinating, don't you?

"So the point of all this," continued Jilly, pulling still another photo out of her folder and dropping it on the table in front of Towers, "is just *why?* Why the desperate and *very* risky attempt at a cover-up? And why the death of Laura Spilwell to begin with?"

The picture on the table was Kerry's shot of Spilwell and the back of the mystery woman in red hair and emeralds.

"You knew," Jilly said. "You knew Dr. Spilwell and your wife were having an affair."

Towers made a noise deep in his throat. "Shut the hell up."

"Not just a fling; a very passionate affair. Spilwell loved her. He was going to divorce his wife. Likely Mavis was going to do the same with you!"

"No!" Towers shouted, jumping up. "No! Never! It would never have come to that!" His eyes glowed with sheer hate at the two of them.

"Spilwell thought you didn't know," Jilly said. "He was never going to let it get out. He cared too much for Mavis. He didn't want to hurt her. He was afraid of what you might do. He never suspected you knew, did he?"

"Stupid fool," Towers muttered. He grew quiet and sat back down.

"How did you find out, anyway? Someone earlier this week told me that they thought women always knew about cheating spouses, but that men tended to not even have a clue. But you knew. You picked up on the subtle clues, didn't you? You might have made a good detective, Mr. Towers. You notice details. You figured it all out. Mavis was cheating on you, and with your good friend Dane Spilwell. That had to really eat at you."

Towers sunk his head deep into his hands, making the cuffs clink, and all of a sudden began to laugh. It grew louder and more bizarre. The silence that abruptly followed was even stranger.

"Oh, what the hell," he suddenly said, lifting his head and sitting back.

"It doesn't matter," he said with a serene smile. "I'll never serve a single day." He just kept staring and smiling at them, a cat who had just consumed not one but several canaries.

"Just what do you mean?" Jilly asked.

"Detective, I was indeed in Santa Cristina that weekend. And yes, there was a conference at which I was registered. But it was a cover. I've been back and forth to Santa Cristina a few times the past couple of weeks, even back and forth this past weekend."

"More privileged duplicity, Mr. Towers? Don't tell me you've been carrying on an affair as well!"

He shook his head in amusement. "You are nowhere near as smart as you think. No, I wish it were something that…pedestrian. There's an excellent clinic in Santa Cristina. The Treadwell Clinic. Perhaps you've heard of it."

"Cancer," said Dan. "You've got cancer."

Towers' eyes bulged open in mocking awe. "Very good, Detective Lee. Would you like to tell me what *kind* of cancer?" There was no reply. "Pancreatic cancer, Detective. A very virulent case. Do you know much about that particular little devil?"

"It's basically a death sentence," Jilly said somberly. "How long, Mr. Towers?"

"A matter of weeks if I'm lucky. I'm told it's very, very fast."

"When did you find out?"

"Less than a fortnight ago. You do know the term 'fortnight'? Pity it's fallen out of use."

"So you've known for under two weeks. Just before the verdict came down."

"That's when the first pain began, yes." There was an awkward silence. "It doesn't really matter. My legal team will keep this hung up for as long as it takes. Then, well…then I won't be around."

"And your wife? Does Mavis know? About the cancer, I mean."

"Of course she knows."

"But not about your murders, I presume. Or that you knew about her and Spilwell."

Towers said nothing.

"You were willing to kill the wife of one of your best friends."

He snorted. "Some friend. Plotting to steal my wife."

"And you would send him to prison for life for something he didn't do."

"In return for something he *did* do, that he'd never be called to account for. A despicable traitor. He got off easily. He deserved far worse. It was diabolically ingenious of me, don't you think?"

"You killed another innocent young man. For what?"

Towers shrugged. His voice had turned low and dark but stayed very calm. It was as if some switch had been turned inside of him; Jilly found it unnerving. "Necessity. What's the expression the government likes to use? Collateral damage? Acceptable losses?"

"And you likely destroyed the life of still another person that you don't even know. She probably feels she might as well be dead."

Jilly bent down, leaning on the table, and stared into his eyes. Nothing but unrepentant coldness and death stared back. "None of this means anything to you, does it?"

Towers shrugged. "You know, you got the story pretty close. Not perfect. A few minor details are off. But better, far better than I would have given you credit for."

"So the only thing that seems to matter to you, Mr Towers, is… what? Winning? Your ego? You're not going to tell me you actually love Mavis. What I'm looking at right now, I don't see much love and tenderness there."

"Shows just what you know Detective." He had a way of making the term "Detective" sound like a contemptuous slur. "In fact Mavis is what

I love above everything and anything else in this world."

"And to have her stolen from you," Dan interjected. "To *lose* her. You'd never allow to happen, right?"

Towers turned his gaze to Dan, narrowing his eyes. "Never. Nobody beats me."

"We beat you in the Spilwell case. But then, you threw that one, didn't you?"

Towers just tilted his head with a tight smile.

Jilly couldn't help herself. "I'd like to know something, Mr. Towers. You made some pretty stupid mistakes here. Here we all thought you were so brilliant and all. Did you want us to catch you, once you knew your days were limited? Or did the news upset you so much that you got sloppy?"

Another deep glare. For a moment he appeared to begin to say something, but thought better of it. He said, with sarcasm, "Perhaps it's the level of pain. Are you familiar with cancer, Detective? There are things that distract even the most single-minded."

* * * *

They sat at a table in the police station cafeteria—it was really little more than a dispensary for coffee and other drinks—neither really wanting to say a word. Jilly stirred her tea and Dan contemplated his cup of coffee. They stayed that way for what seemed a very long time.

"The man's a monster," Jilly finally said quietly, not looking up.

"You told me that Reggie once said that murder was the ultimate act of narcissism, right? He's the ultimate narcissist."

"He's going to beat it too."

"I wouldn't say a death sentence from fast-moving cancer is exactly beating it," Dan observed.

"He'll never serve a day in jail. He was right. He'll keep it knotted up right to the end."

"He can't be happy about what kind of hit his reputation is going to take. Not to mention Mavis will be gone as fast as she can clear out. He may never see her again."

"He'll still find a way to see this as a win," Jilly muttered.

"For once," said Dan, "I'm rooting for the cancer."

10.

To Jilly, it seemed that everything moved at light speed from that point on. Before the end of that Monday, Dane Spilwell had fired Norland Towers and retained another high-powered attorney, who immediately announced that new developments in the case "would exonerate Dr. Spilwell and necessitate an expeditious reversal of his guilty verdict."

Clearly Spilwell had decided that he needed to tell the whole story, and he did, publicly and in shocking detail. It dovetailed with the Police Department's announcement that the Laura Spilwell case had been reopened and that Norland Towers was being charged in her murder as well as in that of Mark Zanello. The various news media sought out Mavis Towers to interview her, but she was ahead of them. She had already left her husband and seemingly dropped off the face of the earth. She would never appear in the public eye again.

Norland Towers' cancer accelerated with a vengeance, almost as if he were goading it to move ever more rapidly. He was hospitalized within another two weeks and placed in hospice shortly thereafter. He would die less than a month after his arrest. He never saw the inside of a jail or prison. It was reported that not a single person, except for medical personnel, had ever been observed at his bedside.

Jilly attempted a few phone calls to Kerry Moran over the following weeks. Her depression had seemed to darken steadily for a while but finally she was beginning to put her life together. One day they agreed to meet briefly in Sunset Park, not far from where Kerry had met Earl Ryan.

Kerry was already on the bench, holding a cup of hot coffee in her hands, staring blankly ahead of her, looking pale and thin. She looked up when Jilly approached. She actually smiled, though it seemed weak and belabored.

"How are things?" Jilly asked.

Kerry shrugged. "Okay, I guess. I haven't been drinking in two whole days now. I'd forgotten what it feels like to not have a hangover."

"You have to move on, Kerry."

"I know. But how? I killed everything around me. I destroyed my relationship with Mark. I destroyed him emotionally, and then I destroyed him for real. And I screwed up my whole life as well."

"You didn't mean for any of that to happen. I know that's not much help. You still made mistakes, and yes, you will have to contend with the consequences of them. Some pretty serious ones. Take it one day at a time."

"You know what's funny?" Kerry said. "I got a call from a big advertising agency. I mean, like a multinational. They said they want to talk to me about a position. I can't be sure, but somehow I think Dr. Spilwell had something to do with that."

"I didn't know whether he'd be grateful to you or not. He damned well should be. But I wasn't sure. Maybe he is behind this. I hope you're going to go talk to them."

"I said I needed a little bit of time to get myself together, but yeah, I think I will."

Jilly nodded. "Good. Don't wait too long."

"Funny, they told me that was how Mark got his spirit back. He stopped his downward plunge and threw himself into his job. Maybe I'll find that works for me, too."

"Be patient. You'll come out of this."

Kerry turned to look at Jilly and her eyes were moist. "You've been so nice to me these past few weeks. By all rights you shouldn't be able to stand me. I've been nothing but trouble for you."

Jilly had to laugh, which surprised Kerry. "Yes, you were. You were the biggest pain in the ass I've had in some time. But I guess I just decided you needed a break."

Her gaze turned faraway as she thought of earlier times. "My old partner, his name was Reggie Martinez. He once told me that most of the people we encountered in our job were lost causes. By the time we got to them, they were beyond any help we had to give them."

"That's pretty cynical," Kerry sniffed.

"But the funny thing was, underneath that tough surface, Reggie wasn't really all that much a cynic. There was more to that thought. He would finish it by saying that it was that much more important that we do what we could to salvage the ones that still had hope."

Jilly started to stand up, putting a hand on Kerry's shoulder. "You're savable. Think of yourself that way."

She still didn't really like this crazy young woman who had caused so much havoc, but she did feel sympathy for her. She hoped before it was all over that she'd find some peace, and maybe even grow up in the process.

Staying in motion, that was the answer, she was convinced.

Just as she had to move on from her memories of Reggie.

Don't look back.

Stravinsky on her phone interrupted her reverie.

"Jilly, it's Dan. We got a new one."

"Tell me where, partner, I'm on my way."

She took the info, said her final goodbye to Kerry and headed out. It was time to change gears and move on.

About the Author

Tony Gleeson, an inveterate fan of jazz and classic mysteries, is a writer, illustrator and graphic designer. He lives with his wife Anne and their cats, Django and Mingus, in Los Angeles, California.